THI
CALL
TH
CAT LADY

BOOKS BY AMY MILLER

Heartaches and Christmas Cakes
Wartime Brides and Wedding Cakes
Telegrams and Teacakes

THEY CALL ME THE CAT LADY

Amy Miller

Bookouture

Published by Bookouture in 2019

An imprint of StoryFire Ltd.

Carmelite House
50 Victoria Embankment
London EC4Y 0DZ

www.bookouture.com

ISBN: 978-1-78681-904-8
eBook ISBN: 978-1-78681-903-1

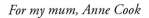

For my mum, Anne Cook

Cats possess more sympathy and feeling than human beings.

Florence Nightingale

Chapter One

The key to Nancy Jones's heart dropped through her letter box at 7.35 a.m., as she carefully shared out cat biscuits into five blue saucers. The key fell to the floor with a clatter, a label tied to it with string addressed to 'Ms Jones, Cat Lady, ref. 38 Evelyn Road, as discussed'. Dressing gown steadfastly knotted, Nancy opened the door a crack, blinking in the sunlight, to see if she could catch the tail of the person who'd delivered it. Nobody was there, but that was no surprise. People didn't hang around her front garden. Cats did. It wasn't on the town's Open Gardens Day programme. Dense and tangled, it was overgrown, with towering holly trees and clumps of thorny brambles like military rolls of barbed wire. Teenagers tossed energy drink cans and Kentucky Fried Chicken wrappers into the long grass. Last winter one person dumped an old mattress and it had taken her two weeks to summon the courage to have it removed.

'People think this place is derelict,' the council collection officer had said, while Nancy shivered in her cardigan, releasing a small nervous laugh.

'What a cheek,' she'd tried to joke, retreating indoors to find a wall to cling to, blushing with shame. But while it was true the garden was a wilderness and the exterior of the house a little run-down, inside was a slightly better story. She'd moved in thirteen years ago, the town of Christchurch in Dorset chosen from between the starched white sheets of a hospital bed in Northampton.

Walking in through the front door of the house had been like stepping into time forgotten; the house being previously lived in by an old couple who hadn't lifted a paintbrush since the 1940s.

Nancy had hastily viewed the rooms, the forest-green walls, jasmine-patterned wallpaper, chessboard floor tiles and floral curtains blurring into a scene from another century. A grey-and-white cat, with a proud fluffy tail, purring as if playing a tiny trumpet, had convinced her to stay.

Close to Christchurch's historic quay, where artists painted at their easels near the bandstand, pleasure boats and swans sailed on the water, Norman castle ruins and the Priory church stood alongside a café selling American-style waffles, it was the noise of the seagulls she liked. Their evening chorus was deafening, like a recorder group blowing into their instruments all at once.

She picked up the key and moved to put it in her handbag; she had to get ready for her job at St Joseph's junior school. Watched by five pairs of cats' eyes, she glanced at her name on the label. *Ms* Jones. Years ago, she had been a Mrs, but there wasn't a shred of physical evidence. The wedding photographer, a friend visiting from Wales who had offered to do the photographs for free, handed her the Kodak film roll after the wedding for developing. She had excitedly put them into the one-hour service at Snappy Snaps, ripping open the packet before leaving the shop. All thirty-six were blank. He had failed to properly close the back of his Pentax camera and light had spoilt the film. She had posted him a bottle of Scotch, and written a note: *The photographs are beautiful, thank you so much!* The marriage certificate was lost, wedding ring buried in a jewellery box and the off-white lace wedding dress donated to Help the Aged. There must be proof on a register somewhere, locked in a vault in Northampton Registration Office, or had it been shredded since? Nancy tried not to think about that time in her life at all, but memories played on a loop in her mind.

'Better get dressed, Ted, if you don't mind,' she said to the now elderly cat who had first welcomed her to the house. With a splendid white ruff reminiscent of an Elizabethan aristocrat, Ted was phenomenally polite. He stayed perfectly still and closed his eyes, as any gentleman would.

Passing the linen cupboard on the landing – stuffed not with linen, but with boxes full of a life she couldn't bring herself to look at – Nancy quickly moved into her bedroom and dressed in a long floral print skirt, a cream top and beige ballet pumps. Glancing at herself in the mirror, she wondered at her reflection. Slim, pale-skinned, with a straight nose, large grey eyes, arched eyebrows and high cheekbones, she had once been quite a beauty. Now, she wore no make-up or jewellery. Nothing to draw attention. Her brown hair, streaked with grey, was pulled back from her face with tortoiseshell hair combs. At fifty-six, she searched for her 26-year-old self in the reflection, but she'd been lost on the way. Thumbed a ride on the back of a Harley-Davidson, perhaps, and roared off into a different future.

After calling goodbye and blowing kisses to each of her five cats, she left for work. 'I'll love you and leave you and come back later,' she said to Elsie, her loyal and devoted second-oldest cat, who followed her down the garden path.

Nancy made her way to St Joseph's, where she worked as a part-time administrator, and took a detour on the way to the address on the label: 38 Evelyn Road. The house was an enormous Georgian property with wrought-iron electric gates that screamed wealth to anyone in the vicinity.

She stood awkwardly, waiting for the gates to open, eyeing a stone statue of a rearing horse by a pond peppered with lily pads. Her shoes crunched on the long gravel drive. A dignified Persian cat, chin raised, was framed in an upstairs window like a portrait of Marie Antoinette. Perfumed wisteria clung to the wall above the glossy black front door and buzzed with fat, rapturous bees. A glint of blue caught Nancy's eye – there was a swimming pool in the back garden!

She looked through the window to get a closer view, astonished to see a woman slumped on the floor in the hallway, tapping her temples with her fingertips, her back against the wall. The woman's chestnut hair obscured her features, but Nancy guessed she was in her twenties. Startled, Nancy stepped back and knocked into a planter. Soil spilled out. She yelped. Correcting the toppled pot, she heard a voice from inside the house.

'Who's there? If that's you, Gerard, I meant what I said,' the woman called. 'It's now or never, and I'm rapidly inching towards never.'

Nancy cleared her throat. 'Oh, hello, it's… um… I'm feeding your cat this weekend I believe, Mrs… Loveday?' she called through the door, biting her bottom lip. 'Your husband – he called into the school and asked if I could cover your long weekend away, so I thought I should come this morn—'

She let her sentence drift. There was an exasperated silence.

'Oh yes,' said the woman. 'But not until tomorrow. Didn't Gerard give you the dates, for heaven's sake?'

The woman's words faded into a strangled sob, which she disguised as a cough. Nancy blushed.

'No dates, just the key. Shall I come tomorrow then?' she called, biting her bottom lip again.

'Yes, tomorrow!' the woman snapped. 'We'll be on the beach in Norfolk by then.'

Nancy's heart capsized. Of course, she heard the word 'Norfolk' often, but it always hit her between the eyes like a flint dagger. She opened her mouth and closed it again. Feeling light-headed, she muttered her mantra: 'This too shall pass, this too shall pass, this too shall—' But it was too late. How easily she was knocked off balance.

Retreating from the house, she walked towards the school, trying to focus on her surroundings. The Citroën garage on the corner. Tapper's Funeral Service, opposite. The neon sign of the Advanced Cosmetic Centre that did laser hair and red-vein removal. The row of terraced houses with pots of red geraniums outside, cars parked nose to tail.

She joined the stream of children walking to school, dressed in yellow T-shirts and black shorts, a thistle in a field of buttercups. With wretched secrets locked in her heart, she gripped the key to another person's life in her clammy hand.

Chapter Two

Bright red blood, the colour of strawberries, oozed from the nose of Alfie Payne, a boy in Year Four. Hovering near the iron railings of St Joseph's school – a Grade II listed building which had been standing since 1890 and audibly groaned with age – Alfie smudged the blood onto a sleeve of his yellow school T-shirt, his unzipped rucksack at his feet. He was skinny as a blade of grass. Head bowed, he battled not to cry. Nancy's heart splintered. Squeezing her fingers around the key, she straightened her shoulders and forced all thoughts of Norfolk, and the unsettling sight of Mrs Loveday slumped on the floor at 38 Evelyn Road, into a dark corner of her brain.

'Nosebleed?' she asked Alfie with a gentle smile, wondering if, in actual fact, he'd been in an altercation. It wouldn't be the first time. 'You might need an ice pack on that.'

Alfie sighed, opened and closed his big blue eyes and gave her an exhausted nod, before spitting a big, bloody globule onto the hopscotch that had been freshly painted on the asphalt. Their eyes met and, despite his obvious distress, he gave her a tiny, rebellious, upside-down smile.

'It's not that bad,' he muttered. 'I just… banged it.'

'Let's find you a wipe so you can get cleaned up,' Nancy said, her heart still pounding, 'and a fresh shirt.'

She took another deep breath to slow her racing pulse. Over in the playing field, the rest of the schoolchildren were star-jumping on the sun-scorched grass, in a wake-and-shake exercise session led by the PE teacher. Music blared from speakers and parents stood on the sidelines laden with bags and gym kits and lunch boxes, some wearing enormous sunglasses like spies. The other office ladies were there too, in their glittery sandals, lanyards swinging, holding their sides as they shook with laughter. Nancy felt a familiar pang. She allowed herself to imagine, for the briefest moment, what it must be like to join in. Heart leaping as you unselfconsciously move to the music, shrieking at the silliness of it all, without a single care in the world.

Scanning the field for possible culprits, she caught sight of the caretaker, George, hammering a nail into the roof of the gazebo. George wore a khaki sun hat, the sort a hiker might wear, and lifted it three inches from his head when he noticed Nancy, as if a brass band was belting out the national anthem. George was something of a hero at St Joseph's. He'd saved a schoolboy from choking to death one lunchtime last April, by hitting him firmly between the shoulder blades and dislodging a cherry tomato from the boy's throat. The tomato had popped out like a champagne cork, to a communal sigh of relief. A reporter from the local radio station had interviewed him.

'Anyone with a pulse would have done the same thing,' George had said to the reporter, batting off the praise, trying to make the extraordinary ordinary. 'Have you finished? I've got work to do.'

He had a weathered complexion and the broad shoulders of a man used to physical labour. Nancy found herself wondering if he had a wife at home to apply sunscreen to the back of his neck or whether he did it himself in the bathroom mirror. The thought made her blush deeply and she stared intently at her skirt. It was coated in cat hair. Ted shed more fur than the others put together – as if he was constantly too hot, like a toddler refusing to wear a coat. She plucked hopelessly at the fluff.

'Come on in, Alfie,' she said, opening the school entrance door.

Nancy had learned not to fuss over Alfie. He was a quiet boy, with unkempt hair and eyes like saucers. He moved around the school with his head bowed, as if trying to take up as little space as possible. He lived on the street that ran parallel to Nancy's, and the bottom of his garden met the bottom of hers, separated by a dilapidated fence which often collapsed in the wind. Nancy knew that Alfie's parents had recently split up and she had seen him in his garden, swinging on a rusty old swing, which creaked eerily as it moved. There was something dejected about Alfie that made her long to scoop him up in her arms like an injured kitten, take him home for a bowl of ice cream, but she couldn't do that, not least because of his timidity. Even a direct question asked in the wrong voice could made him scatter, like clapping at a pigeon.

The school reception was quiet and cool, with teachers ducking in and out of classrooms, preparing for the day ahead, an occasional 'Morning!' bursting forth in a reassuring, sing-song tone. Nancy felt the tension begin to slip from her shoulders and she reached inside her bag for wipes.

'Look at my shoe,' Alfie said, his eyes bulging with enraged tears. 'The sole is falling off.' He lifted his left foot, to demonstrate the flapping sole. He had to drag his feet to keep it on, as if he was wearing skis. 'I wish I was invisible. He emptied my bag and took my crisps.'

'Who did?' Nancy asked, trying and failing not to sound too interested. 'Who took your crisps?'

He stood perfectly still.

'I don't remember,' he said, refusing to look at her. 'Nobody.'

'Was it someone from this school?' she asked gently, passing Alfie a wipe and tissues. 'Sit down for a moment.'

'Not this school,' he said unconvincingly, perching on the edge of a chair in the corridor.

So many things about Alfie seemed to make boys want to pick on him: the wrong hairstyle, no mobile phone, broken shoes. Meaningless things. Nancy wanted to empty the mobile phones and smartwatches out of those boys' rucksacks – whoever they were – and stamp on them until they were crushed into a million pieces. Would that teach them empathy?

'Oh, let me check – I think I might have spare crisps,' Nancy said, suspecting that he had packed only crisps for lunch. The school catchment netted areas from the rich side and the poor side of the town – so the children were an incongruous mix of haves and have-nots. Mr Phillips, the head teacher, was proud of saying the school represented their diverse local community, but Nancy often wondered how the poorer kids felt as they watched their wealthier counterparts eating smoked-salmon bagels and plump, fragrant strawberries for lunch, while they survived on free meals. Not that she begrudged children the right to strawberries. If life had worked out the way it was supposed to have done, any child of hers would have eaten strawberries. Bowls of them. *Fields* of them.

'Have these,' she said, quickly taking a bag of crisps, a cereal bar, an apple and a banana from her own bag and pushing them into his rucksack. It was the least she could do. 'Your nose looks fine now,' she said. 'Do you feel okay?'

He nodded.

'I can clean your shirt if you like,' she said. 'Meantime, let me find you a fresh one. Wait here a moment.'

She let herself into the front office, leaving the door open while Alfie waited on the chair. Placing her bag on her desk, she quickly dug through the lost-property box – mountain-high with abandoned uniform – and pulled out an unnamed yellow shirt. There were black plimsolls in his size in there too, better than the broken shoes he had on.

'These should fit,' she said, watching relief rinse through him.

'Thank you,' Alfie said, suddenly standing as he caught sight of the gold maneki-neko fortune cat on Nancy's desk. The Japanese ceramic figurine with a beckoning hand was supposed to bring the owner good luck. Alfie stepped inside the door to get a better look and pointed at a blurry image of Nancy in a copy of the school newsletter also on her desk. 'Is that a picture of you?' he asked.

Nancy blushed. The newsletter had been Emma's idea. The school secretary, Emma, kept the day-to-day life of the school running smoothly, and while she dealt with the snowstorm of pupils, parents and visitors who needed attention, Nancy worked quietly in the wings. Words fizzed out of Emma like she was a shaken can of Vimto. Her life was a soap opera, but though she never stopped talking, Nancy was grateful for her stream of news. It meant she could wordlessly organise the class registers and allocate the wristbands for school lunch, while Emma chatted on. And on. Last month, on a warm Friday evening, Emma had invited Nancy for a drink at the pub with the other girls, and despite part of her longing to accept, Nancy had instinctively invented an excuse.

'I'm cat-sitting this weekend,' she'd lied. 'Sorry. It's, um, for a neighbour. I can't let them down.'

'Urgh cats,' Frances, personal assistant to the headmaster, who sat alongside Emma and Nancy, had said, dramatically shuddering. 'I've always thought cats are evil. Do you know they steal the breath of a baby while they sleep? I'm one hundred per cent a dog person.'

Nancy had felt her hackles rise. Images played out in her mind. Elsie, her beautiful, loyal tabby cat with deep green eyes and the serious air of the deeply religious, waiting anxiously, velvet white-socked paws neatly together, at the end of the garden path for Nancy's safe return from work. Ted, sitting on the top of wardrobes and cupboards, keeping watch, like a grey-and-white version of the Queen's Guard. Tabitha, plump and orange as marmalade, who slept on the pillow spooning Nancy's head – a living trapper hat. William, dressed in a black-and-white tuxedo, whatever the time of day, straddling his latest kill with muscle-bound shoulders. And finally, sweet Bea, with a patchwork coat of white, brown and black, as if having rolled in paint, always willing to butt heads. They were her everything. They were her *family*.

'That's horrible.' Emma frowned, stretching her lips into a grimace. 'Anyway, perhaps you could take advantage of this, Nancy? Everyone around here already calls you the "cat lady" because you have millions of cats. Not to mention your little friend here.'

Emma pointed a long fingernail at Nancy's Japanese cat figurine, her words repeating in Nancy's head. *Everyone already calls you the cat lady.*

'Five cats,' Nancy muttered, knowing Emma wasn't listening. 'I only have five.'

'Five!' scoffed Frances. 'Good God, even that's insane. How can you stand it? All that fur. I'm terribly allergic. Show me a picture of a cat and I'll sneeze for twenty-four hours straight.'

Frances's eyes dropped to clumps of fur visible on Nancy's skirt. She pulled a nasal decongestant from her bag and squirted it up her nose.

'The very thought makes me shudder,' said Frances, clasping her hands together. 'Give me a black Labrador or a cockapoo any day.'

If I had five children, Nancy thought but didn't say, *you wouldn't bat an eyelid. You'd think I was unremarkable – blessed even.*

'I can whip you up an advert, then if Mr Phillips approves, we can put it in the newsletter, on the board in the staff room, and email the trust staff,' Emma enthused. 'I bet plenty of parents need an animal sitter for when they go on their fancy weekend breaks. It'll be a money-spinner for you and' – she lowered her voice – 'get you out and about a bit more. Never know what it might lead to. I don't like to think of you all alone in that old house of yours. Apparently, my mother was telling me, your house used to be stunning, but the old dear who lived there before you lost her husband then her marbles, and the place went to pot. Shame, isn't it?'

Nancy imagined marbles spilling from the previous inhabitant's head, in the hallway of the ramshackle house. Each marble bouncing off to dark corners and mouse holes and cracks in the floorboards. The cats would go wild for them. That poor old woman. Even on her hands and knees she would never have been able to find those marbles again.

She swallowed, knowing what people thought of her. It was obvious in their overly polite smiles, and the speed with which they checked the time and found they had – *ohmygod* – run out of it. They thought she had lost a few marbles herself. That she was a cat lady who collected cats' whiskers (she did, as to find one and keep it in your purse meant good fortune), allowed all of her cats to sleep on the bed (she did, they were brilliant hot-water bottles) and who loved cats more than humans (debatable). It suited them to pigeonhole her, but even real pigeons don't want to sit in holes. They sit under bridges, perch on ledges, balance on branches. Fly six hundred miles, if they wish, in one single day.

'What do you reckon?' Emma said. 'Might be fun – you can have a poke through people's lives and find out their deepest, darkest secrets, then tell us all the juicy details!'

Emma cracked up laughing. Nancy paled. Emma had a generous heart at the core of her, Nancy knew that. Like an artichoke.

'I'm not sure about that,' Nancy mumbled, but Emma was already designing an advertisement in bubble font.

With the head teacher Mr Phillips's approval, the advert had gone out in the newsletter and had been pinned up in the staff room, alongside staff notices including the sale of a nearly new paddleboard and a polite reminder about contributing to the tea fund. It seemed like everywhere she looked, her services were being advertised.

'Yes, that's me starring in the newsletter,' sighed Nancy, now, in reply to Alfie. As she picked up her rucksack again, the Evelyn Road key slipped out of her fingers. Alfie caught it and read the address label.

'Thirty-eight Evelyn Road,' he said. 'Sounds like it's in the posh end.'

He looked at her questioningly. Nancy's mind went to the sparkling blue swimming pool she'd seen through the window. Mrs Loveday on the floor, pointy shoes at the end of thin legs like a scene from *The Wizard of Oz*. The unexpected mention of Norfolk making Nancy feel she'd been pushed off the top of a slide before she was ready. Her stomach flipped.

'I'm feeding their cat,' said Nancy absent-mindedly. 'They have a swimming pool, would you believe, in the garden? It's so blue I wonder if they might have added some sort of dye to the water.'

'Wouldn't their skin go blue if they did that?' Alfie asked. Nancy laughed and before she could reply, Emma and Frances rushed in, their skin glistening from the exertion of the wake-and-shake session.

'Nancy!' Emma shrieked, steering Alfie out of the way by his shoulders, before taking her seat. 'You know the rules! No children in the front office. What are you doing in here anyway, Alfie?'

'I found Alfie a fresh shirt and some shoes from the lost-property box,' Nancy mumbled. 'He only just stepped inside the door. He also had a nosebleed. I've been looking after him.'

'Log it in the incident book then, will you?' Emma said. 'Go on, Alfie, love, on your way. Bell's about to go.'

Clutching the fresh yellow shirt and plimsolls, Alfie dashed off down the corridor.

'Rush hour!' continued Emma. 'Stand by your phones! We've also got to talk about the school summer fair this morning, God forbid. I'm supposed to be running the barbecue and, what with my wedding coming up, I shouldn't be allowed within ten feet of a hot dog,' she said, patting her soft belly. 'Oh, Nancy, I'd forgotten to invite you to my hen do. God, I'm a daft cow. No cat-sitting for you that night, we're going to have a fun night out.'

Nancy blushed. In the time that she'd worked at the school there had been so many events to excuse herself from, it had been exhausting. Girls' Night, Quiz Night, Clothes Swap Night, Pamper Night, Film Night – Nancy had missed all the Nights.

'I'm going to have a special dress made,' Emma said. 'Costing an arm and a leg of course!'

In a postcard from her past, Nancy suddenly saw herself as a young woman, seated at a sewing machine working on a bridal gown. Shelves of silks and satins and velvets and lace chiffons had lined the walls around her. There were boxes of buttons and bobbins and ribbons and patterns and pins. The eternal hum of her sewing machine. Silent, motionless mannequins, draped in veils. Faceless brides, waiting for their lives to begin.

'The girls have promised me a stripper!' Emma said, interrupting her thoughts. 'Not that I'm interested. My fiancé is definitely and absolutely the love of my life. We're going to get married and grow old together, like you and your husband, Frances. How long have you been together now? Thirty years?'

'Thirty-six,' said Frances, violently stapling some papers together.

'And what about you, Nancy?' Emma asked gently. 'Have you ever been in love?'

Tiny beads of sweat sprung onto Nancy's forehead. Her tongue stuck to the roof of her mouth as she tried to form an answer. The pencils on the desk danced a waltz in front of her eyes.

'You're blushing,' Emma said. 'Come on, out with it. Who's the love of your life, Nancy? I'm dying to know!'

Nancy swallowed. The office ladies loved asking Nancy personal questions; they reminded her of children circling a jellyfish that had washed up on the beach. The more they poked at her with the sharp end of their plastic spades, the more she played dead.

'I've never had much luck…' she started, but her words faded into silence. The phone rang, and Emma's attention was, thankfully, diverted by a case of gastroenteritis in Year Five, then there were parents to help and latecomers to register. Nancy exhaled with relief. She felt Frances's laser-sharp eyes burning into her back – she probably had a great tuft of Ted's fur on her shoulder, or a line of muddy paw prints running down her spine. Sitting at her desk, with a pen in her trembling fingers, she opened the incident book and began to log Alfie's nosebleed, Emma's question ringing in her ears, in sharp, urgent bursts, like the school bell. *Have you ever been in love?*

Chapter Three

Later that evening, Nancy found a large goldfish on her pillow. After a chicken supper for the whole family, she stood in front of the linen cupboard on the upstairs landing, wondering if she would ever have the courage to open the boxes stacked inside. Though she stored sheets and towels in the cupboard, the boxes had remained untouched since she first moved into the house. With a deep, doubtful sigh, she turned away and went into her bedroom, moving her thoughts to her day at St Joseph's. Recalling Emma's question about Nancy's love life, she frowned. It was getting more and more difficult to not talk about her past. It wasn't enough, realised Nancy, for people to know you as the person you were that day, or in that moment. They wanted a curriculum vitae, a backstory, an explanation. Something. *Anything.*

'The thing is,' she said to Ted, who padded across her dressing table, carefully navigating her moisturiser and deodorant, 'when people ask me those sorts of questions, I clam up. Perhaps I should just be honest about it all, but something stops me. Fear, I suppose.'

Ted purred wildly, as if she had just announced a lottery win, knocking a pot of Vaseline to the floor with his tail. Nancy sat down on the edge of her mattress, took off her shoes and wriggled her toes. Elsie, who was hiding under the bed, stuck her head out from underneath and pawed Nancy's feet.

'Hey, leave my toes alone!' Nancy said, patting her knee, encouraging Elsie to jump onto her lap, which she did, kneading Nancy's legs like bread dough.

'Aren't you beautiful?' she said to her, staring into the cat's deep green eyes. Nancy reached for the cat comb and began grooming Elsie, who purred wildly, loving the attention. She was named after Nancy's mother, who had died when Nancy was eight years old, and who also had deep green eyes and a warm, loving nature. Elsie gazed adoringly at Nancy, and pushed her face against Nancy's chest, giving her a slow blink. 'I love you too,' said Nancy, gently combing the cat's ruff. 'Yes, I do.'

Despite the delightful sound of purring, meowing and the occasional clatter of the cat flap, the house was too quiet. It didn't matter how much she chatted to the cats or listened to *Book at Bedtime* or imagined the people she had once loved were there with her. Nancy sighed. Moving position, she saw the bright orange goldfish on the pillow and screamed. She leaped up, quickly covering her mouth to muffle her alarm. Elsie rocketed out of the room.

'What the hell is…?' she choked, before registering that this was probably William's doing. The Al Capone of the carnivorous cat world, he regularly deposited 'gifts' of freshly killed mice, rats, birds and even a rabbit once in Nancy's bedroom – either to remind her who was boss, or in gratitude for her loving care, she wasn't sure which. Though she routinely tried to rescue those poor animals, this fish was definitely dead.

'For heaven's sake, William,' she muttered, 'I know it's your survival instinct, but I do not want dead things on my pillow, thank you!' Using a carrier bag as a glove, she quickly scooped up the fish and tied a knot in the bag. She would have to bury it outside.

She changed the pillow case, throwing the soiled one into the washing basket, disturbing a sleepy Tabitha from a nap, and hurried downstairs to bury the fish. Finding a shovel in the cupboard under the stairs, she went outside and instantly became entangled in a holly bush. Navigating the overgrown bushes and scratching her arms in the process, she reached a spot clear enough for her to dig a shallow fish grave.

Drifting through the air were the sounds of her neighbour, Alan, having a barbecue. Meat sizzling, male and female laughter, music. Slicing the earth with her shovel, she glanced up to see Alan staring at her from over the top of his fence, a mortified expression on his face.

'It's just a dead fish, not a person!' Nancy called out, smiling, lifting a hand to wave, but he quickly ducked. Nancy exhaled noisily.

'Good evening to you too,' she muttered, shovelling the last of the soil over the corpse.

Dusting off her hands, Nancy returned inside. She went into the kitchen, where the fridge was humming and the remains of a bowl of strawberry Angel Delight waited to be washed up, and stared down at the list of chores written on the notepad by the kettle. Words blurred in front of her eyes. *Mend hole in wall, fix chain on downstairs loo, decorate whole house, mend guttering, prune garden – need chainsaw, check roof tiles for slipping, sweep chimney – pigeon nesting?* The list had been made months ago yet she hadn't done a thing.

Her eyes rested on the first 'to do'. *Wash and bleach the net curtains…* so simple, but she never got around to it, and, as a result, the nets were now a shade of grey and were punctured by the claws of the cats who swung on them as if they were climbing ropes in a school gym. The nets made the house look a little shabby around the edges, as did the peeling floral wallpaper, the occasional light bulb without a shade, threadbare carpets, cobwebbed corners and the once-elegant greenhouse in the back garden, grown-over with decades of ivy. She loved her home, but something happened to Nancy at these moments – inertia overwhelmed her. When she made a start on the cobwebs and balls of cat fur, invisible hands grabbed her wrists and her arms turned to lead. Now she sat heavily on a chair at the kitchen table, with Tabitha on her lap, and finished off the Angel Delight, letting Bea have a lick of the near-empty bowl with her surprisingly long, sandpapery tongue.

'Imagine if Frances could see us now,' she said to Bea. 'She'd have a field day, wouldn't she?'

Bea licked her lips, collapsed onto the floor tiles and stretched out her paws into points. She hated it when Nancy was maudlin, but Nancy couldn't help herself tonight. To make matters worse, thoughts of Alfie, Norfolk and the woman at 38 Evelyn Road wouldn't abate. Why had Mrs Loveday been slumped on the floor like that? Should she have offered help? And what of Alfie – did he lie in bed dreading the following school day?

Switching off the kitchen light, she went upstairs to bed, with three of the cats close at heel.

'Look at this mess,' she said to them. Quickly, she shook the duvet, sending cat fur and tiny pieces of grit from muddy paws flying through the air, and then opened the sash window, glass rattling in the battered wooden frame, as wide as it would go. She held aside the curtain.

'Where did William steal that fish from?' she wondered, staring out over Christchurch's roofs and gardens, hoping that it wasn't from the lily pond at 38 Evelyn Road. The evening sky was purple and pink – like a bride had thrown a bouquet of sweet williams into the air. A beautiful pure white, long-haired cat moving along the narrow top of a nearby fence turned to face her – an elegant tightrope walker. Nancy marvelled at its grace. In some cultures, a white cat at your door symbolised good fortune and happiness. 'Come here, white cat,' she whispered, making a squeaky mouse sound with her lips. 'Come here! Come here!'

The cat ignored her, and Nancy became distracted by the open window of her neighbours living opposite; a large multi-generational family congregated around a dining table, in an impenetrable circle. They were all laughing at something. For one paranoid moment, she hoped it wasn't her. A gust of loneliness assailed her.

'Thank goodness I have you all,' she said to Tabitha, who, too hot in her thick ginger coat, had jumped onto the bed and stretched out to her full length in an exclamation-mark position. Ted joined Nancy at the windowsill and she picked him up, hugging his warm, soft grey body close to her chest.

'I'm sorry, Ted,' she said, as a sudden tear dripped onto his fur. 'Thanks for putting up with me.' He remained in her arms and didn't complain. He never did. She was so grateful to him for that. Just like Nancy's father, after whom Ted was named, he listened in gracious silence.

She adored him and all of her cats, named after people she had loved – and lost. It was a relief to voice those names in the privacy of her own home. The cats brought her great comfort, yet didn't she secretly long for a human companion? The self-pitying thought made her blush. She knew damn well why she was alone. She had made it this way. It was easier with cats. Cats didn't ask questions. They didn't need to know the details. They were grateful for her unending love. Understanding of her foibles. They left goldfish on her pillow. A rather splendid gift if you looked at it through a cat's eyes. It was Emma's question that had got under her skin: who's the love of your life, Nancy?

Leaning against the windowsill, with Ted in her arms, her gaze settled on the English Channel in the distance, flat and silver like a sheet of tinfoil. There was always a painter, with a mop of curly salt-and-pepper hair, working at his easel down by the bandstand at the quay. He was there every morning and evening in fine weather, feverishly trying to capture the sunrise or sunset on canvas. She wondered what he did when it rained.

Trying to think of anything other than Emma's question, she failed miserably. In hospital in Northampton, a zen-thinking patient had tried to help Nancy by giving her a lesson in impermanence. The patient, a young woman with an eating disorder, had explained that emotional disturbances and troubling thoughts do not define who we are. Nothing remains forever. The young woman had clutched Nancy's hand and made her close her eyes and repeat after her: this too shall pass. But, no matter how many times she said the words, Nancy knew she would always be defined by her thoughts, memories and emotions because she could never escape them. They had her under lock and key.

As the sun dipped into the sea, the gulls sang their discordant song and the painter packed up his easel for the day, she exhaled and reluctantly followed her thoughts to the man who, despite every damned terrible thing that had happened, she had truly loved.

Chapter Four

When Nancy first spoke to Larry, he was sellotaped to a chair on the pavement outside the *Kettering Evening Post* newspaper building. The bridal boutique Nancy worked in was on the same side of the street and so she had no choice but to walk past him on her return from her lunchtime break in Poppins café. It was a scorching hot summer in 1989 and the oppressive heat had wilted plants and people everywhere. There was no breeze, and the atmosphere felt heavy, as if the sky was a paperweight rendering everything beneath immobile. Most people were wearing very little, but Larry was dressed in suit trousers and a blue shirt which clung to his lightly sweating, whippet-thin body. She admired the contours of his chest, her pulse galloping.

'Are you alright? Do you need help?' she asked him, feeling instantly foolish. In her red mini dress and huge Madonna-inspired green earrings, she suddenly felt too noticeable. A walking traffic light. Registering Larry's eyes on her, she found herself breathing in and correcting her posture.

'Birthday tradition – they're just having a laugh in the office,' he murmured through the tape stuck over his lips. Behind him, laughter erupted from an open window.

'Do me a favour and set my hands free?' mumbled Larry. 'Or they'll leave me here all day to get heatstroke and die!'

She stared at his face. Even with a strip of parcel tape over his mouth she enjoyed his features. His eyebrows were straight, strong and dark brown, like his short wavy hair. His cheeks were slightly sunken as if he was sucking them in, even though he wasn't, and his jawline angular. In between his deep brown eyes, he had two frown lines, like brackets, separating his worries from the rest of his thoughts. His limbs were strong but elegant.

'Bit cruel, isn't it?' she asked, beginning to unwind the tape, which had been wound round and round his torso, legs and arms like an Egyptian mummy. When free, he leaped up from the chair with a bark of laughter and shook his head.

'It's a rite of passage,' he said, offering her his hand to shake. 'When it's your birthday, you get sellotaped to a chair and pushed outside. I'm twenty-seven today so it's my turn. I'm Larry, by the way. Larry Jones. Magnificent to meet you.'

She smiled, taking his hand in hers, enjoying his use of the word magnificent. Twenty-seven. Same age as her. One of his co-workers – a chap with long shaggy blond hair and a moustache – leaned out the window and burst into a verse of 'Happy Birthday'.

'Bugger off, Barney!' Larry swore at the man, who swore back in a friendly sort of way. A sudden clap of thunder rattled across the sky. Larry looked upwards and held out his palms, checking for rain.

'There be a storm brewin',' he said, putting on a growly Cornish accent, unselfconsciously throwing his arm over her shoulders and steering her towards the entrance of the *Post* building. She burst out laughing, his grip releasing firecrackers in her heart. A few big drops of rain splashed onto the pavement.

'Wait here until it passes,' he said, turning to face her. 'What was your name again? I'm sure I've seen you before.'

'Nancy,' she said. 'I'm Nancy. I work next door, as a dressmaker in Bespoke Bridal, so it's possible…'

'Ah yes,' he said. 'If you ever come across a good story in there, a jilted lover, a bride on her tenth husband, a bespoke dress with a "made in China" label, that kind of thing, come and find me, won't you?'

He tapped the side of his nose and grinned. Nancy laughed and blushed, her attention suddenly caught by raised voices coming from the newsroom. Hot and sweaty-looking reporters of differing ages sat around a messy wooden desk strewn with copies of *Who's Who*, dictionaries, piles of newspapers and a disco-dancing daisy. A desk fan rotated, rhythmically lifting the corners of nearby loose papers. Most of the reporters were working on word processors, but there were a couple of typewriters there too. One young male reporter was shouting about something; another was slow-clapping. There was an air of tension in there; excitement. On the wall was a map of Northamptonshire, a list of phone numbers and a poster of a scantily clad woman. Cigarette smoke clung to the ceiling. From upstairs came the smells of a staff canteen: mince and potatoes. Rhubarb crumble and custard.

'You rescued me,' Larry said to Nancy, lightly kissing the back of her hand. 'Thank you. I've got to be in court in an hour but come to the pub later and let me buy you a drink. Two. I'll buy you two drinks. One for saving me and one because it's my birthday.'

'Make it three and it's a date,' said Nancy, startled by her own daring.

'Three it is,' said Larry with a grin. 'I like you already.'

The receptionist wolf-whistled, and Larry rolled his eyes, giving Nancy a conspiratorial look, which brought a red glow to her cheeks.

She had noticed Larry before. In his sports jacket, shirt and tie, she had seen him jumping into an orange Mini, with *Kettering Evening Post* sign-written across the side, where he would deftly roll and light a cigarette, before driving away at speed, usually with that shaggy-haired photographer in the passenger seat.

Having recently ended a stale relationship with her childhood sweetheart, William Green, Larry had become an object of Nancy's fascination. The way he walked, so upright and with such determination, caught her eye. He seemed ready to take on the world in a bare-knuckle fight. She wanted to run after him and grab on to his coat-tails to go along for the ride. 'Wait for me!' she imagined herself yelling.

Instead, in the quiet of the sewing studio at the back of the bridal boutique, she invented romantic scenarios: he would request an interview with the dressmaker who had sewn a particularly impressive wedding gown for a local celebrity. He would be wowed by her stitching talent. Though her boss, Imogen, would want to take the glory, he would insist that he spoke to the person who actually did the sewing. Who? Me?

'The Eagle,' he said now. 'Half seven. That rowdy lot in there will be there too, but don't let that put you off. They're harmless, really. Good fun, usually.'

She agreed, and when the thunder faded and the rain never materialised, she returned to work. All afternoon, making alterations to a customer's wedding dress and veil, her mind was with Larry, unwrapping the tape from his body. Had he felt it too?

Distracted by thoughts of him, she accidentally pricked her finger with a dressmaking pin. 'Ouch!' she exclaimed, as a tiny seed of vermilion blood burst from her skin, soiling the white lace veil.

In the same way that clouds sometimes seem to be made from cotton wool, you could almost slice the smoky air in The Eagle. The pub had continued to trade during a time when many pubs in the neighbourhood were closing down and, as a result, was packed to the rafters. Despite the hot and sultry weather, there wasn't even a single window open, making it difficult to breathe.

By the time Nancy arrived (she had walked past twice before finding the courage to go in), Larry and his friends were on their third pint – the army of glasses on the table before them lay testament. She had fought through the cigarette fog to reach their table, tucked into a corner of the wood-panelled bar. While she slipped off her cotton jacket, revealing a sleeveless dress, aware of several reporters staring at her appreciatively, Larry tapped a lighter on the rim of one glass with a 'ting, ting' and quickly introduced her to his friends.

'My rescuer,' he said, to which she shrugged and felt awkward. 'Meet Nancy.'

One of the reporters whistled and Nancy blushed boiling red.

'You're a quick worker,' muttered the shaggy-haired photographer who had sung 'Happy Birthday' earlier.

'This is Barney,' said Larry. 'His bark is worse than his bite.'

'If I were you, I wouldn't trust anything that man says,' retorted Barney, pointing at Larry. Nancy searched for a spiky answer, but failing, she sipped her half-pint nervously as the group's conversation darted from bad beer to office politics to world events. Whenever she tried to strike up conversation with Larry, Barney interrupted and drowned her out. Eventually, she gave up battling for airtime – it wasn't as if she had anything fascinating to say. She feared that Larry would be totally unimpressed.

'You've all seen that photograph of the Tank Man, the guy who walked out in front of the tanks, holding his shopping bags, right?' Barney said, launching into serious current affairs. 'He was just nineteen years old.'

He was talking about the dreadful Tiananmen Square massacre in Beijing that had happened a couple of weeks earlier, where thousands of student pro-democracy activists were killed by the People's Liberation Army. When she'd read about it in the newspaper, Nancy had wept, and immediately phoned her father.

'Look for the helpers,' he had said. 'That's what your mother would have said if she were here.'

'His bravery, his integrity puts us all to shame, doesn't it?' continued Barney, slamming down his pint glass and causing the other glasses to tremble and tinkle. 'What do any of us do that counts for anything? Do any of us have true integrity, or are we just self-serving shits, doorstepping victims of crime and road traffic accidents, hoping for a good story and front-page picture to further our careers?'

She glanced at Larry, whose expression was suddenly serious. Somebody sighed. Someone else lit a cigarette. Another ripped tiny pieces off the cardboard coaster.

'Why don't we just talk about *Neighbours*?' said one of the party, to a ripple of laughter. 'Kylie and Jason are leaving the show, you know.'

Barney slapped the table. 'Be serious,' he said, gulping his pint.

Nancy sighed and stared at a framed cricket bat on the wall, signed by cricketer Ian Botham, who had presumably once visited The Eagle.

'He's famous for making everyone feel guilty,' Larry whispered to Nancy, flashing her a brief smile. 'It's his party piece. Mine's fitting a whole orange into my mouth. What's yours?'

She smiled, enjoying the subterfuge.

'I can do a headstand,' she said, 'with no hands.'

Larry raised his left eyebrow admiringly.

'What about you?' Barney suddenly swung round to face Nancy with an angry glare. 'What do *you* do in your life that makes a difference?'

Nancy sucked in her breath.

'Come on!' he said. 'There must be something going on in your tiny world!'

'Hey, hey, Barney, don't be a bully,' said Larry. 'Nancy has only just met us. You'll scare her off.'

Nancy cleared her throat, forcing out an answer. 'I'm a dressmaker, so I don't suppose I do much for the wider world apart from sympathise with the plight of those who are suffering. Within my *tiny world*, I visit my father often and cook for him,' she said. 'He's quite old and my mother died when I was a child, so I make sure he has company and good food. He loves pies. I also have a disabled neighbour – an old lady – and when she goes into hospital I do her laundry, empty her fridge and feed her cats.'

Barney snorted.

'I don't think you're going to change oppression by feeding someone's fucking cats or cooking a pie,' he slurred. 'Jesus Christ.'

There was a silence. Nancy took a sip of her drink. Actually, she wanted to say, in her opinion, sharing food and loving animals was a step in the right direction, wasn't it? She opened her mouth to reply but someone had put money in the jukebox and The Bangles' 'Eternal Flame' came on at full volume.

'Don't underestimate the power of pie,' Larry said, standing. 'Talking of which, Nancy, would you like to get something to eat? I think I'm ready to go. The heat in here is intense, not to mention the company.'

Nancy agreed and stood up. Barney suddenly got up from his chair and pushed past Nancy while heading towards the bar, knocking into Larry and sending the remainder of his pint flying all over him.

'Thanks, Barney! Why did I bother getting changed earlier?' he said to Nancy, mopping up beer from his white shirt with a napkin. 'Come on, let's get out of here.'

'What's wrong with him?' said Nancy. 'He doesn't seem to like me too much.'

'God knows,' Larry said. 'He gets like that sometimes. Hard drinking, hard talking. Don't take any notice. He seems like an angry young man, but honestly, he's solid gold on the inside.'

They squeezed through the drinkers and left The Eagle. Before stepping outside, Nancy glanced back to see Barney glaring at her through narrowed eyes.

'Ah,' Larry said, gulping in the fresh air in the street, 'I should have taken you somewhere more salubrious. I'm not really hungry; I just wanted to leave.'

He stuffed his hands into his trouser pockets and gave her a sheepish grin.

'Neither am I,' she said quietly. 'I don't care where we go. Why don't we walk?'

The evening was warm, so they walked through the back streets of the town, passing a housing estate where boys were playing a raucous game of football and continued past, to the outskirts of the town. Larry talked about his family, who lived in a hamlet in Surrey, which comprised of just a handful of beautiful, converted thatched-roof cottages lived in by stockbrokers and lawyers.

'Once upon a time I suppose a blacksmith lived in the cottage they have,' Larry explained. 'But my father bought it, extended it and commutes to London every day to work in a bank. He and I are very different. My brother too; he's just like my father. All they care about is money.'

Larry described himself as a 'black sheep' and said he felt his parents were disappointed by him because he was comparatively low paid and didn't share their politics. His brother had a house in London's Holland Park, while Larry lived in a two-bedroom, third-floor flat and was, according to them, wasting his time working on a local rag.

'They don't seem to care that I'm happy being a journalist,' he said, with a shrug. 'I don't want to be at the *Post* forever – I want to see the world – but I like the profession.'

'Being happy is all that matters,' she said. 'If you're happy, then you're the success story.'

'And what about you?' he asked. 'Are you happy?'

'Right now,' she said, 'yes.'

He smiled indulgently at her and reached for her hand. They walked a while longer, their fingers interlinked, until, when it was almost dark, they reached the gates of the local amusement park – which Nancy had visited as a child – where there was a swing park, a rowing lake and huge rides such as a pirate ship and a rollercoaster. The huge black constructions were ghostlike in the quiet darkness and a shiver of fear – or excitement – made her stomach flip.

'Let's go in,' he suddenly said, jumping the fence. He held his hand out, so that she too could clear the fence. Nancy didn't break rules.

The worst crime she had ever committed was shoplifting a packet of Munchies from the corner shop when she was twelve. And that was under duress. But, because she wanted to please Larry, she cleared the fence without more than a moment's hesitation. It was thrilling.

They ran across the park towards the rowing lake, hand in hand, two figures cloaked in moonlight. The air was soft and warm on her skin. When they reached the lake, Larry grinned at her with a smile that said: *Come on, we're going in.* She gave a nervous nod.

He stripped off his clothes, down to his underpants and though tiny, faint alarms were ringing in her head along with warnings from childhood – don't swim in lakes, think of the old rusty machinery lurking in the weeds, you'll catch your death – she also undressed down to her underwear. He seemed momentarily embarrassed at her partial undress, which she interpreted as appreciation. She was slim, with a good pair of legs, a smooth complexion and glossy hair. Standing in her gleaming white underwear, she felt lit from within.

'It's beautiful in here on a hot night like this,' he said. 'Literally like swimming through the moon. Hold my hand.'

The lake was still and black, the moon reflected perfectly in its centre, like a giant pearl was floating there. She took his hand.

'Have you done this before?' Nancy asked, suffering a dip in her excitement level – who else had he done this with?

'Come on,' he said, ignoring her. 'I dare you.'

'Oh God it's chilly,' she gasped, wading into the water and watching the ripples reach the reflected moon. 'What if someone spots us? We'll be front-page news!'

'Nobody will see us,' Larry said. 'Come on, it's my birthday.'

She dipped her shoulders under the surface and swam, by Larry's side, to the middle of the lake. With every stroke, the water glittered as if all the stars had dropped out of the sky and into the lake. Every now and then, Larry turned to grin at her. She grinned back with gums and teeth.

'I feel so naughty,' she said. 'I'm loving this.'

'You have to take a risk every now and then,' Larry said. 'That's what rules are there for – breaking.'

Nancy's life, where she worked in the bridal shop and sewed until her fingers were sore and lived in a flat-share with girls who left used earbuds and random pieces of underwear in the bathroom, suddenly felt as bland as sliced white bread. She wanted to be more like Larry. When afterwards they sat on the lake bank, sipping whiskey from his hip flask and Larry rested his head on her shoulder, Nancy's entire body flamed. Love, she realised, was this.

That night she stayed at his flat – and slept in the spare bedroom, wearing one of his T-shirts, while he slept in his own room. Before dawn, she climbed in beside him. She was uncharacteristically bold. He was the first man she had ever truly desired. She took a risk and kissed him. They made love. And a baby.

Chapter Five

There are some people who can walk straight past a person in need without a second glance or care. But even as a child, Nancy couldn't ignore the rough sleepers in her town, the one-eyed neglected cat, a crow with a broken wing or the daddy-long-legs with no legs. It was as if the world's weary and wounded were sending signals, like an ultrasonic dog whistle, to stop her in her tracks. Whether it was a fifty-pence piece dropped in a homeless person's hat, a makeshift cat bed erected in the shed or a bird nursed to health in a shoebox, Nancy could not walk by and do nothing. Which perhaps goes some way to explaining why, when she returned to 38 Evelyn Road to feed Prudence, the Lovedays' Persian cat, on the correct day, and she saw Alfie limping along in the street with a cut on his knee and blood trickling down his leg, she told him to come up to the Lovedays' house, so she could quickly clean the grit out of it for him, before he went home.

'What are you doing in this road anyway?' she asked, washing the cut with water in an outside tap around the back of the house and patting it dry with a tissue from her bag. 'Shouldn't you be at home by now?'

Alfie shrugged and scratched at a scab on his other knee. He wasn't listening. Instead, his eyes were on the impressive swimming pool in the beautiful garden, his mouth hanging open.

'These people,' said Alfie in a shocked whisper, 'must be absolutely loaded.'

She followed his gaze. The pool shone with the reflection of the house and trees. Clouds floated on the surface of the water. Three striped sunbeds were lined up on freshly mown, bright green grass, and beyond them, a pagoda laden with plump pink roses offered shade. It was impossible to believe there were any woodlice under the terracotta planters, ants nesting in crevices or slugs chewing through leaves. The garden was as precise and neat as a paint-by-numbers kit. A small miracle of horticulture. Nancy was struck by the comparison with her own unkempt garden.

A light breeze sent ripples across the water, making the house reflection tremble, as if the bricks might crumble. It jolted Nancy into remembering why she was there. Squeezing the key in her hand, she smiled at Alfie.

'Money isn't everything,' she said. 'Look, Alfie, I need to feed the cat. You better be on your way. Will you be alright walking from here? When you get home, don't put a plaster on that cut, just let the air to it. But keep it clean.'

Alfie nodded and blinked his huge eyes at her. 'Please can I stick my feet in this pool first before I go? Please? I want to see if my skin turns blue,' he said. 'Then we can walk back together. We live virtually on the same road. Please? My dad won't be home yet anyway.'

A small smile crept across Alfie's lips. On the back of his school sweatshirt there were the markings of a child-sized footprint, as if someone had walked right over him. A realisation hit her.

'Did someone push you over today, Alfie?' she asked. 'Is that how you got this cut on your knee?'

He shrugged and stared at his feet. Eventually he lifted his chin and squinted at her.

'It was just a normal day at school,' he said. 'You know what it's like.'

She ruffled his hair affectionately and thought about her own day. Before dawn, William had brought a common frog into her bedroom, bullying it behind the wardrobe until it squealed like a baby. She'd never known, before that day, that frogs could actually scream. At school, the company Nancy had booked for the summer fair – Animal Magic – who were bringing snakes, barn owls, millipedes, guinea pigs and tortoises for the children to see, had called to check whether there was sufficient shade available in case of hot weather. She had gone outside to check with George, who was busy mending a section of guttering.

'Like animals, do you, Nancy?' said George, wiping perspiration from his brow as he scrutinised the printout. By late morning the sun was scorching hot. 'I've seen your advertisement for cat-sitting. What a good idea.'

'Yes,' said Nancy, 'I particularly love cats. They're loving, loyal creatures.'

He nodded, fixing her with pale green eyes.

'I've noticed that gold cat on your desk,' he said. 'The one with the little beckoning hand.'

'It's a maneki-neko,' she said. 'A Japanese charm that's meant to bring you good luck and happiness.'

'I reckon you're a good person if you like animals,' he said. 'People who like animals are generally nicer than those who don't. In my opinion.'

George was beaming at Nancy and she swallowed hard, wondering how to react. There was something she liked about George. He had a kind heart. He was the sort of person to help old ladies across the road. Untangle a dog's lead from a bicycle wheel. Save a child's life. But his attention made Nancy nervous.

'So, do we have enough space and shade available?' she snapped, without intending to. She cringed, feeling increasingly uncomfortable. 'I need to call them to confirm,' she said more politely.

George gave a little shake of his head and returned his eyes to the printout.

'Yes,' he said, with a lopsided grin, 'we do. As far as I'm concerned, if Mr Phillips approves, you can get them booked in. And, Nancy?'

She had turned to go, but turned back. He handed her the printout.

'Yes?' she said.

'I hope the cat charm works,' he said, with a tender smile. 'I hope it brings you luck and happiness. If it does, I want one too.'

Confused by George, she had trotted away from him like a frightened deer. She sighed at the memory. Goodness knows what he thought of her. Mad cat lady probably.

'Yes, I do know what it's like,' she said to Alfie, now, with a sigh. 'Okay, Alfie, dip your toes in while I quickly feed the cat. I'll be two minutes, then I'll see you get home safely.'

Alfie didn't need to be told twice. He pulled off his socks and sat by the edge of the pool, dangling his skinny legs in the water, a big grin on his face, while she went inside to find Prudence. Indoors was just how she imagined it would be – kitchen islands topped with great slabs of veined marble, completely clear of cookery books, or condiment pots. There were no handles or knobs on the cupboards and all the utilities were built-in and hidden. Entirely knob-free. There was nothing to suggest anyone ever cooked.

She tried another room, wondering where the cat was sleeping, and opened the living-room door. Decorated in a minimalist style, above a hanging polished-steel fireplace straight out of a sci-fi movie was a giant studio photograph of a young, red-haired, freckled boy, aged perhaps four, and staring at a point in mid-air, where someone might have been waving a teddy around. She recognised him as the Lovedays' son Stuart. He was in Year Four – the same year as Alfie.

Moving through a dining area, equally sublime with a table that would seat at least twenty people for a feast and bright contemporary artworks on the walls, Nancy's curiosity got the better of her. Glimpsing out of the window to make sure Alfie was okay – he was still dangling his toes in the water – she slipped off her shoes and tiptoed upstairs. The carpet was a mattress underfoot. The doors of the massive bedrooms were open. They were all remarkably tidy, even Stuart's bedroom. She peered inside the master bedroom, heart thumping, trying to imagine the sort of people who would live in such a well-groomed, minimalist and spotlessly clean house. The closet, just a tiny bit open, had rows of pressed clothes hanging, arranged in colour order, from white to black. She crept inside, pulled a leopard-print silk scarf from a basket of neatly folded scarves and draped it around her neck. From a line of expensive-looking shoes, she pushed her feet into a pair of too-small, high-heeled red sandals and quickly pulled a black faux-fur jacket off the hanger and slipped it over her shoulders. She stared in the mirror, shocked by how the clothes made her look older – as if she was being erased. She narrowed her grey eyes, wondering how it was that your appearance could radically change without you really noticing. One day she had been young and attractive, the next, she felt almost invisible. It was like opening your bedroom curtains one morning to discover it had snowed overnight, utterly changing the view.

'What are you doing?' she muttered to herself, when a noise from outside disturbed her. Quickly, heart racing, she took off the clothes and shoes and put them carefully back. She turned to go back downstairs, noticing a door to a room which, unlike any of the others, was closed. Wondering if Prudence was trapped inside, she gently pressed down on the handle and peered beyond the door.

'Oh my gosh,' she gasped, gaping at the room, which looked as though it had been ransacked by intruders. She blushed crimson, feeling as though she had just seen a complete stranger in the nude, yet she couldn't rip her eyes away from the chaos. The bed was unmade, with the duvet stretched across the floor, and the wardrobe door was open, with a trail of clothing spilling across the carpet. Molehills of underwear and stockings and damp towels peppered the floor. Books – mainly self-help titles – open with their spines bent, littered the bedside table and windowsill, gathering dust. A dressing table was covered in make-up bottles, brushes, open red lipsticks and mascara wands. An empty wine bottle lay on its side by the bin, as if someone had swigged it and tossed it aside without caring where it might land. Newspapers and unopened letters were fanned out on a bedside table, encrusted with dark red rings from the bottom of a wine glass, and packets of medication, with a time and date for different pills of some sort, lay empty and discarded. A pregnancy test box jutted out from under the bed. Nancy flushed with embarrassment and moved quickly to close the door when something on the windowsill, a photograph in a bright red frame, caught her eye, as if the person in the picture had beckoned her over.

Stepping, gingerly, deeper into the room, the mirrored doors of the wardrobe startling her with her reflection, she moved towards the photograph, her stomach doing the loop the loops of a gigantic rollercoaster. Staring at the picture, she felt as if she might collapse. There she was. Beatrice. That delicate, beautiful, exceptional girl's face – beaming – as if nothing had ever happened. Why the hell was she here? It didn't make sense. Snatching it from the wall she carried it to the window and held it up in the light to make absolutely sure it was Beatrice. It was. Of course, it was. There was only one Beatrice.

'Darling girl,' Nancy whispered, staring at Beatrice's large brown eyes – Larry's eyes – under perfectly arched eyebrows. The pink swimming costume perfectly fitted her tall frame. Pink painted toenails to match. Skinny legs and pointy elbows, just like her dad. A delicate necklace of alphabet beads spelling out her name fastened around her neck. The sweetest smile in the world. An enormous lump swelled in Nancy's throat, her chest fluttered with palpitations and her knees weakened as her mind scrambled to make sense of what she was seeing. She had tried to hide from the pain, yet here it was in her hand. Fresh and raw as ever.

Chapter Six

Nine months after their midnight swim in the boating lake, Nancy and Larry's baby girl was born at 10.23 p.m. on 28 March 1990, in the maternity ward of Northampton General Hospital. They named her Beatrice Anne Jones. The delivery room was crowded with strangers: student midwives and junior doctors in newly laundered uniforms. They broke out into a round of applause when Beatrice tried out her lungs after a long moment of terrifying silence.

'Her lungs are in fine working order,' said the senior midwife as she checked the wall clock to record the time of birth. At that exact moment, the clock hands rapidly spun anticlockwise. She was later informed that the clocks across the hospital automatically synchronised twice a day, but Nancy had believed it to be an auspicious beginning. Or was it a warning?

'Bloody hell, I need a drink after that!' exclaimed Larry, while Nancy wept with joy and relief as she held their tiny, perfect daughter in her trembling hands. She gazed into her daughter's eyes, dark as that rowing lake, and had a sensation of sharp focus. That, despite the number of people in the room, she and Beatrice were alone together, as if on a tiny sailing boat in the middle of the ocean. Just the two of them under the moon and stars.

'So, now it all begins?' Larry said, bemused. 'Fatherhood? Christ, I hope I'm a better father than my own dad. He doesn't give a shit about me because I don't drive a sports car or belong to a golf club. And my mother has told me, to my face, if she could have her time again, she wouldn't have kids. Talk about messed up. It's a wonder I'm as sane as I am.'

The midwife glanced at Nancy and raised her eyebrows, but Nancy was not fazed. She'd heard it all before during the last nine months. Larry had tried out every excuse in the book for potentially failing at parenthood before it had even begun. Nancy decided it was a defence mechanism and had, over the months, gently reassured him that he would do a great job.

'What if I drop her?' he worried, when he held Beatrice in his hands, so very gently for the first time. Staring at his tiny daughter, he wore an expression of total surprise that remained on his face for years. A tear slipped down his face, clinging to his unshaven chin.

'I'll try to get it right,' he told Beatrice in a private whisper. 'I'll do my best.'

Nancy didn't think she had or could ever love two people more than Larry and Beatrice. The realisation gave her a sudden sense of dread. She would have to do everything in her power to protect them. It was her job to take care of them.

'I must tell everyone that she's here!' Larry said, rushing out to phone their friends and family. While he was gone Nancy and Beatrice were moved to another ward, with other new mothers and their babies. The beds were partitioned by flimsy blue curtains and you could hear everything that everyone else said. Birthing stories were recounted and repeated to anyone who would listen. Some mothers were singing to their new babies, others chatting to each other, stunned by birth. One, with empty arms, was weeping.

'I found Barney,' said Larry, when he returned with a string of happy messages from friends and family, and Barney in tow, who had brought with him a Tupperware of home-made pasta Bolognese and a bottle of red wine. 'He's going to take some photographs of Beatrice.'

Barney leaned over Nancy and Beatrice and kissed them both.

'You smell of beer and cigarettes,' Nancy commented, watching him throw off his long overcoat and toss it over an important piece of medical equipment.

'What do you expect? I've been nervous as hell for you!' he replied. 'Dutch courage. Let me get some photos of you and the baby.'

The two men enjoyed the food and wine sitting on the end of the hospital bed, talking in hushed voices about what was happening at the *Post*, while Nancy held and studied every inch of Beatrice and experienced love at first sight for the second time in her life. Barney had also bought lilies, but wasn't allowed to bring them into the ward (Bolognese but no flowers! he protested), so Larry put them in a vase and placed them on the ledge outside the window, so Nancy could still appreciate them through the glass.

'Your dad's a romantic fool,' Barney told Beatrice, 'isn't that right, Nancy?'

'Yes… yes, he is.' Nancy nodded in agreement, feeling desperately, uncontrollably happy. She had landed on her feet with Larry, hadn't she? Yes, the pregnancy had been a total shock to them both. A meteorite. They hadn't even been an official couple, but Nancy had felt sure they could make a go of it. Larry had taken a whole lot of convincing, but Nancy had known she had enough love in her heart to make it work. Larry had gradually come around to the idea and read the pregnancy books, attended antenatal group and at home *was* romantic. In his flat, which Nancy had moved into, he would turn off all the lights, put on his favourite Nina Simone CD and instruct Nancy to listen. Wake her early to watch the sunrise. Lay out blankets on the roof terrace in the early evening, serving Nancy and their friends drinks with hunks of cheese and bread. She never knew what trick he'd pull from his sleeve next. Even on their wedding day – admittedly a hastily arranged event when she was four months pregnant – he had surprised her by being so nervous he had gripped her lace sleeve too hard, pulling a hole in it. To console her, he'd ripped a hole in his own sleeve too. God knows what the registrar must have thought.

'I crave adventure,' he had told Nancy on their wedding day and often since. 'I want my life to be exciting. Marriage doesn't need to change that, does it? We don't have to be conventional, do we?'

She shook her head defiantly, swept up in his appetite for life, but also felt a flutter of unease.

'Your father is the salt of the earth,' he had said once after they visited Ted with baby Beatrice one Sunday afternoon. They had sat in front of the gas fire surrounded by her mother's old porcelain figurines of Siamese cats, watching the snooker while eating slices of Battenberg cake. 'But shouldn't he use his retirement to do something exciting?' Larry had continued. 'There's a big world out there and it would give him a purpose. I don't want life to pass me by, Nancy. I want to travel and work all over the world. Run with the wolves. I crave—'

'Adventure,' Nancy had finished for him, blushing with half-fury, half-embarrassment, new baby Beatrice in her arms. Larry didn't understand that when her mother Elsie had died all those years ago, her father had fallen into a black depression. His life drained of reason. A young girl herself, Nancy had helped him find reasons to get out of bed. She had stepped up her rescue missions to save injured birds that she found in the garden, encouraging him to help look after them. She had told him about an allotment that she had heard was up for rent, where he could grow vegetables. She had borrowed comedy films from the library to cheer him up after her grandmother had told her that a man had entirely cured himself of cancer by laughing. Slowly, he had realised he had to get up: for Nancy. It was enough, she wanted to shout at Larry, that her father managed to put one foot in front of the other. It was enough, she wanted to say, that her father enjoyed his Battenberg slices and snooker programmes. But she remained silent, leaving Larry alone with his dreams, like a boy with a kite.

Larry loved Beatrice passionately, anyone could see that, but he was overwhelmed by the chaos that having a baby created. He seemed affronted by Nancy's swollen breasts and their tendency to spray, like a garden hose, at any given moment. His bachelor pad was turned upside down and inside out. Their VW Beetle filled with blankets and rattles and lost knitted booties. He didn't understand it when Nancy wept for no apparent reason – but then again, neither did she.

Sometimes Larry invited friends from the *Post* for a party – Barney and the others brandishing bottles of beer and takeaway curries and cigarettes – energetically debating the poll tax riots or the election of the new prime minister John Major. Nancy had nothing to contribute. The outside world seemed quite irrelevant. All she wanted to do was sleep and take care of Beatrice.

She once heard snatches of conversation from two girls who worked on the newspaper, coming from the kitchen, when they thought she was feeding Beatrice in the bedroom. 'Do you think Nancy trapped hi… trust him to stick by… shotgun… old-fashioned… have an abortion?'

She held Beatrice tightly in her arms and blinked away tears. Is that what people thought of her? She tried not to care.

'Where's the old Nancy gone?' Larry would ask, masking anger with a little laugh, so the comment could be construed as a joke. 'I hardly recognise you these days!'

Her hair knotted on top of her head, wearing her comfiest clothing, she wondered how other women coped.

'I'm a bit sleepy, that's all,' she would say, protecting him from the truth. Why did she do that? Some ridiculous knot of pride or fear in her belly prevented her from screaming: I am fucking exhausted, burned out, lonely and scared that you have never really loved me like I love you.

Instead she sipped strong coffee and tried to be the pre-baby Nancy that Larry preferred. At night, she paced around the flat with a fitful Beatrice in her arms, trying not to wake Larry, who had to be at work early and was grumpy when sleep-deprived. With sore, dry eyes and a loneliness growing around her heart, she stared out of the window and watched the town at night. Other people, going about their lives around the edges of the day, had no idea she was there. Were they lonely too?

'Maybe try having a romantic evening in, to remind each other why you love one another. Cook something special, buy a nice bottle of wine,' came her friends' banal advice when she hinted that her relationship was under strain. Those friends, without responsibilities, didn't understand the complexity of being new parents. The silent battles, resentments and the gnawing ache of sleep deprivation. Nancy knew Larry had seen too much of her too soon – like bingeing on chocolate fudge cake and wishing you hadn't. They didn't know of Larry's passive-aggressive refusal to admit that parenthood was hard work and that she might need him to acknowledge that and say: 'I love you.' But he never said that, no matter how many times she led by example and littered him with those exact words. So, a romantic evening in it was.

One evening, with Beatrice in a baby bouncer chair next to her in the kitchen and limp with exhaustion from lack of sleep, Nancy cleared up the flat, cooked steak pie, put on Larry's favourite record and went down on her knees to scrub the kitchen floor until it shone – restoring his bachelor pad to how it once was. She was trying to silently say: *I'll do anything to make this work.*

He had come home from the *Post* very late that night, hours after the record had ceased spinning and the pie was stone cold. He walked straight past where she lay sleeping at the kitchen table. As if she were part of the furniture. She had stirred when, a few moments later, he lay a blanket over her. Her heart squeezed: he still loves me. Doesn't he?

Chapter Seven

The photograph of Beatrice in her pink swimsuit still in her hand, Nancy tried to catch her breath. Why was there a photograph of Beatrice in this stranger's house? She felt devastated and furious and frightened all at once. She had to find out why.

Scouring the walls and junked-up surfaces for other clues, her eyes rested on a collage of photographs in a clip frame, leaning up against the white wall. Some of the photographs had slipped their position, half-obscuring others, but quickly running her eyes over the ones visible, she instantly recognised Marcie Jennings. Marcie was Beatrice's best friend from her first day at school. Was this Marcie Jennings' home? Was she Mrs Loveday? Or could this be her parents' home? Or a friend or relation? Nancy felt waves of despair. Trying to suppress rising panic, her eyes settled on another image of Beatrice – with Marcie this time – perched on a climbing frame in a park, one knee-sock up, the other down. Grinning her devil-may-care grin. Nancy could smell the rust of the climbing-frame bars on Beatrice's palms and the sweetness of a Drumstick lolly on her breath. As if the photograph had been taken yesterday.

'Oh my God,' said Nancy, raising her hand to her mouth. 'I can't—'

She forced herself to look at the others. They were all of Marcie. A complete childhood behind glass. Marcie, in secondary-school uniform, standing next to her brother outside the front door of their house. Marcie diving into a swimming pool from a high diving board. Marcie winning a dancing trophy. Marcie with her arm around a black Labrador. Marcie at her graduation ceremony.

Marcie with a rucksack on her back, standing by a forty-foot statue of Buddha, in Sri Lanka perhaps. Marcie bungee jumping over some sort of terrifying ravine. Marcie on horseback. Marcie with a gold dot in her nose, wearing tie-dye trousers sitting outside a yurt with another young woman, making the peace sign. Marcie lying on a blanket in a garden reading a magazine with a space the length and width of a person – the size of a best friend – empty beside her. There were tickets inserted into the frame too. A Coldplay gig in Barcelona, London Underground and Paris Metro tickets, a restaurant bill from the Grand Central Oyster Bar in New York. Memorabilia of a life well lived.

Nancy wanted more. With trembling hands, she couldn't stop herself yanking open Marcie's drawers, greedily searching. If there were other photographs of Beatrice, she wanted to see them. Flicking through address books and certificates, she found handwritten letters tied with a ribbon, postcards written in blue fountain pen, a strip of passport photos and packets of pills. Sertraline. Valerian. Bach's Rescue Remedy. Lavender capsules. There was one more photograph – a Polaroid – of Beatrice, at the bottom of one drawer. She was around six years old and grinning to show the gap in her teeth, where her front tooth had fallen out. The Polaroid was sticky and damaged from a half-melted cough drop that had stuck to it. Nancy peeled off the cough drop, rested the Polaroid on her knee and rubbed it gently with her sleeve, trying not to damage it further. Tears streamed down her face. She gaped at the little girl smiling up at her, stroked the image with trembling fingers.

Moving over to the wardrobe, she threw the doors open and began pulling out shoeboxes. She tore off the lids and tipped out the contents, scattering jewellery and payslips and certificates and old bits of make-up and postcards onto the floor. As she worked, searching for she wasn't sure what, more tears fell, blurring her vision, when she happened on a collection of birthday cards, sealed in their envelopes. There was a single letter on the envelope: B.

Ripping them open without a second thought, she hungrily read eight cards, written from Marcie to Beatrice.

'Dear Beatrice,' she whispered, 'Happy Birthday, love from your friend M.'

Nancy felt the walls and carpet and furniture merge, when there was a piercing scream outside. She had completely forgotten Alfie.

'Alfie!' Nancy exclaimed, dropping the cards onto the floor. Unsteady on her feet, she lurched towards the window and, after a second, the world came back into sharp focus. Alfie was clambering out of the pool, wearing just his pants, fear written across his features. To his left, with her back to Nancy, was a woman with chestnut hair, standing by his pile of school clothes. Mrs Loveday. *Marcie.* She had her hands on her hips as she continued to shout at Alfie. Nancy listened to her muffled accusations.

'What the heck are you doing in my swimming pool?' she was saying. 'Who are you and how did you get into my house? You'd better explain yourself before I call the police.'

Nancy cringed as a silent Alfie stared at Marcie, cowering and shivering behind his twiglet arms. In a moment, he would explain that Nancy was in the house and Marcie would come looking.

'Oh dear God, Alfie, why did you get in the pool?' she said, watching him point towards the house. Nancy's heart hammered. She knew she should bang on the window, or rush straight outside and come to sweet Alfie's aid, but she was rooted to the spot and didn't want to be seen or be identified. She'd also trashed Marcie's room. She considered sliding under the bed and hiding there but couldn't desert Alfie. Quickly, she swept the contents of the boxes back inside, in any random order, shoving the opened birthday cards to the bottom. *Did I really just open those sealed envelopes?* Her hands shook. Mrs Loveday, Marcie, was probably perfectly within her rights to get her arrested. Then came the sound of Marcie's voice, calling through the kitchen.

'Hello?' she demanded. 'Are you in there? Hello! Where on earth are you? Come out, will you!'

Quickly, Nancy rescued the sticky photograph of Beatrice, smiling her snaggle-toothed grin and slipped it into her skirt pocket, where it would be safe. She took the deepest breath and left the bedroom, closing the door behind her, clutching the red-framed picture of her daughter in her hand, not wanting to let go.

Chapter Eight

Beatrice's first tooth had come out on a camping trip, when she was six years old. The excursion was supposed to be an adventure that Larry, Nancy and Beatrice could share. The plan had been to drive to a campsite in Lyme Regis, Dorset and spend a couple of nights by the sea, fossil hunting on the Jurassic coast and exploring Golden Cap, the highest point on the south coast. Larry had been working long hours at the *Post* or staying on too long in The Eagle after deadline. He oscillated between being attentive towards Nancy and being in an irritable, dark mood.

He no longer invited his newspaper friends over to the flat. Sometimes she found him perched on the window seat in the living room, staring out at the street below, while Beatrice tugged at his hand, *Rugrats* blaring from the television. His head was in the clouds. Then, he would suddenly snap back into the moment and lift Beatrice onto his lap, tickling her until she squealed.

'I don't feel fulfilled on the newspaper anymore,' he would sometimes confide in Nancy when she questioned him. 'I'm restless. I'm treading water writing stories about what the town council is doing. I need to *do* something, *go* somewhere. The walls are pressing in on me, somehow. I can't breathe. Maybe it's boredom.'

He would say all this, wounding Nancy with every word, yet she would comfort and encourage him. She was strong enough to shoulder his frustration, she knew that. But when the semicircles under his eyes developed a blueish-grey tinge as he struggled to sleep, his clothes started to hang off him when he lost his appetite, and they hadn't had a proper conversation in months, Nancy became seriously worried. A camping trip was the obvious answer. Back to nature, with 185 million years of the Earth's geological history on the doorstep would surely invigorate and stimulate Larry, wouldn't it?

She packed the essentials. Red wine, cheese and baguettes. A book on fossils. A pack of cards. New lingerie. Sleeping bags that zipped up together. Books and colouring pencils and puzzles for Beatrice. Her heart raced with anticipation and excitement. This was just what they needed in order to bond. Larry packed his swimming trunks in a carrier bag and threw on his vintage donkey jacket, tucking cigarettes and a bottle of Jack Daniel's into his big pockets.

'What else does a chap need?' He grinned, reminding her of the Larry she had first fallen in love with.

The ascent to the campsite was narrow, steep and winding. There were times when it felt their old, rust-bucket VW Beetle would topple over. Saucepans bounced up and down on the back seat. Beatrice shrieked.

'Careful!' Nancy said, before she could help it, when they came face to face with a tractor. 'Beatrice, hold tight! For God's sake, Larry, slow down!'

'Why are you gripping on to the seat like that?' he snapped. 'You need to relax! It's just a bloody tractor. Beatrice is fine, aren't you? Stop worrying, for Christ's sake.'

Expletives flew from Larry's lips until they reached the campsite, a small field high up on a cliff, overlooking the English Channel. The view was magnificent. Yanking on the handbrake, Larry surveyed the view and gave a deep sigh.

'Wow,' he said. 'This was worth that deathly journey. What do you reckon, Beatrice?'

Beatrice laughed. Nancy's shoulders dropped with relief. They had made it there in one piece. Outside the car, she pointed out tiny boats on the horizon to Beatrice. White dots on blue paper. You could see for miles around, almost 360 degrees. A patchwork of green fields, beaches and the azure sea. The late sun bathed the cliff edge in shades of toffee and cream, like giant slabs of millionaire's shortbread. It was truly beautiful. Nancy felt buoyant with hope.

'Shall we pitch here?' she asked, gesturing to the shower and toilet block, which was within walking distance. 'If Beatrice needs the toilet during the night, we can get there in time.'

'Ever practical,' Larry said. 'No, let's pitch right by the cliff edge. We can pee outside the tent if we need the toilet, for God's sake! It'll be a better view, more exciting when we open the tent up. Like we're actually in the ocean, on our own raft.'

'Okay,' she said, looking out at the horizon. 'Are those clouds coming this way?'

'No,' said Larry, without even looking. 'Relax, Nancy!'

Once they'd erected the tent – an ancient thing borrowed from Nancy's father, with metal poles, yellowing guide ropes and rusty pegs – Larry got stuck in to the red wine. His lips were soon stained and his mood philosophical. The dark clouds previously sighted rolled in and it began to drizzle. The fire went out. Distant thunder thudded. Some campers took down their tents and drove away. A flash of lightning streaked the sky and thunder clapped so loudly Beatrice put her hands over her ears and cried. Nancy silently panicked. Would they be safe in the tent in a storm? She tried not to worry.

'Remember when we swam in that lake the first night we met?' challenged Larry, when she couldn't help but voice her fears. 'We were different people then, weren't we? We were less afraid of taking risks. I thought I had the world at my feet. Everything changed in an instant when you fell pregnant.'

'You've got the world at your feet,' Nancy insisted, thinking: *The Channel, at least.*

'I feel as though my wings have been clipped,' he said. 'I mean, Beatrice, she's everything now, I get that, she's the love of my life, but I'm just standing still. Maybe we should move abroad? I could get a job overseas. Apparently English journalists are in demand in Australia, or… or… I could take some time out and we could do a road trip around the USA. I've always wanted to go to Los Angeles. I'd like to climb mountains in India. I want to meet hill tribes, hang out in San Francisco with artists and just get away from here. I'm sure you must feel the same?'

Nancy couldn't help laughing.

'I'm serious, Nancy!' he snapped. 'I should have known you wouldn't understand. You're so domesticated and practical these days.'

Rain began to leak through a hole in the canvas.

'I do understand, but I have Beatrice to think about and she's only just started school,' she said, stifling a yawn, not knowing what else to say. Los Angeles wasn't really on the cards right now. She didn't know where the nearest hill tribe lived. How could they even think about moving abroad? Soon she felt too tired to keep her eyes open. Larry was too hot and restless for the zip-together sleeping bags, so she began to fall asleep with one arm draped over her precious Beatrice, rain hammering on the tent, thunder and lightning cracking open the sky.

'Larry?' she whispered, thinking she should apologise for laughing when he'd talked about his dreams. His hunger for adventure was one thing she so loved about him. But Larry was asleep. Or pretending to be.

They woke two hours later without a roof. A ferocious storm and gale force wind had picked up the tent and tossed it over the field. They hadn't pegged it down securely enough and were left exposed to the elements. Beatrice screamed. Larry swore. Nancy wriggled out of her sleeping bag and ran towards the car in her pyjamas, hand in hand with Beatrice, feet sploshing in muddy puddles. The new black lingerie untouched in her rucksack.

'Where are the car keys?' she yelled at Larry.

'In the pocket of the tent!' he shouted. 'Shit! Why didn't you keep them somewhere safe?'

'Me?' she yelled back. 'Why is it my job to look after the keys, for heaven's sake? You drove here!'

'Well you're the practical one!' he roared.

'Perhaps I'm not so practical after all!' she screamed.

The rain was torrential; the wind whistled and rocked caravans dangerously back and forth. Waves belted the beach below. Nancy felt they were precariously close to the cliff edge. Their possessions were scattered over the field and the car was locked. Beatrice threw her arms around Nancy's waist and pushed her head into Nancy's chest.

'What shall we do?' she shouted to Larry over the gale. 'We can't even get in the car!'

Nancy became aware of a voice coming from the darkness – a lady in a nearby tent was calling to them.

'Excuse me. Why don't you come and shelter in here?' she said. 'We have room. You can help us hold on to the tent!'

Apologising and swearing in equal parts, a rain-soaked Nancy, Larry and Beatrice blew into the awning of the family's tent. The family – parents and two teenage children – was Dutch but spoke perfect English. The woman gave Nancy a blanket for Beatrice. The man gave Larry a coffee with a large shot of rum in it.

'Welcome to English summertime!' Nancy smiled, trying to make light of it all and shrug off their row. 'Sun one minute, lashing rain the next.'

She had wanted Larry to laugh along with her. *Let's laugh it off*, she pleaded with her eyes. But he was distant and furious and agitated about the car keys.

'I better search for them,' he said. 'We'll never get back to civilisation otherwise. Whose great idea was this anyway? We should have stayed in a bed and breakfast! I hate camping!'

Nancy cast down her eyes. While Larry deserted Nancy and Beatrice and disappeared out into the storm, Nancy watched the way the Dutch couple interacted, gently touching each other, talking and laughing about whether their tent would hold up in the gale. She felt embarrassed. Her own relationship was not like theirs. Was theirs how a relationship should be? Why was there this growing chasm between her and Larry? She felt as if she was continually trying to catch Larry in a giant butterfly net.

After he had been gone for almost an hour, Nancy apologised. 'I'm sorry,' she said. 'I don't know where he's got to.'

'A bed and breakfast?' the man joked. Nancy frowned and chewed her lip, hoping he was wrong. She blew over her hot coffee, thinking, *I wouldn't put it past him.*

The woman had gently patted Nancy's arm and smiled at her sympathetically.

'It's difficult when the children are young,' she said quietly. 'It gets easier.'

Nancy smiled and stared at the top of Beatrice's head, mortified that the woman, a complete stranger, had noticed the distance between her and Larry, too. Was it that obvious?

'My tooth has fallen out,' Beatrice suddenly announced, holding up a tiny, bloody tooth. The Dutch family broke out into applause, made a big fuss of Beatrice. Nancy smiled. Yes, theirs was how it should be.

The years rolled by. Beatrice grew into a beautiful girl. By the time she was midway through junior school, Nancy had returned to working part-time, and Larry began looking for a job at other, bigger regional newspaper titles. She convinced herself that a new job for Larry would solve his frustrations. Even though he'd been promoted, he was bored and their marriage was suffering. They had slipped into a rut. He needed a new challenge. It happened to even the most well-suited couples.

One evening, after he came home late and she asked him about his day, he sat next to her on the sofa and broke down in tears.

'What's happened? What's wrong?' she asked. She waited to be told something awful but he just buried his head into her shoulder and wept. She had never seen him so upset. There were red marks on his neck, which could only have been fingerprints. Had he been fighting? Mugged? Attacked? What was he hiding?

'Please, tell me,' she said. 'Just get it off your chest. It doesn't matter what it is. You know what we say to Beatrice? Nothing can be that bad.'

'Oh, but it is, Nancy,' was all he would say.

And then, on a cold January day, it all became clear.

She had taken the phone call. A job offer for Larry. Deputy News Editor on a regional newspaper based in Cambridge. He wanted the role more than anything, and so she changed into her favourite red dress and rushed out of the house and straight to the office to tell him in person. She envisaged his happy face. Beatrice was having tea at a friend's house so Nancy popped into an off-licence and bought a bottle of champagne.

She flew into the newspaper office. The receptionist was pulling on her mackintosh and told Nancy almost everyone had gone for the day, probably to The Eagle, apart from Larry who she thought was in the picture library.

'Larry! Larry!' Nancy called, sweeping through the empty newsroom, where Larry's leather jacket was slung over the back of a chair. She stopped when she heard a whispery sound. A sixth sense made her suddenly silent. She didn't need to open the door of the picture library because it was already slightly ajar, and there was the love of her life, in the arms of Barney. They were passionately kissing. She gasped. So engrossed in one another, the men didn't notice her. Her legs turned to liquid. Her heart bombed. Everything suddenly made sense. The doubts inside her took on a brutally solid shape. She quickly retraced her steps through the newsroom and past the receptionist, unable to breathe properly until she was back outside in the rainy street.

'Larry,' she spluttered. 'Larry, Larry…'

Pushing her hand into her pocket, she found the key to Bespoke Bridal and rushed into the studio, where she flung herself onto the sewing table and cried in gut-wrenching, bone-shattering sobs. After a few moments, she stood up, pushing her wet hair away from her face, catching sight of her reflection in a mirror. Her cheeks were streaked with mascara, carefully applied earlier. Squeezing her eyes shut, she wept more tears, until she felt sick to the stomach and utterly empty. Images of Barney and Larry pressed against her eyelids. She stared hopelessly at the bridal gowns on the mannequins all around her.

'Will you,' she cried to nobody, 'love her, comfort her, honour and protect her, and, forsaking all others, be faithful to her as long as you both shall live?'

She lifted an intricately embroidered lace veil from one of the mannequins and inspected her stitching in a detached way, the tiny beads blurring in front of her eyes.

'No,' she whispered, suddenly yanking at the lace and ripping a great hole in her painstaking work. 'Larry Jones will not!'

With the destroyed veil in her hand, her entire body trembled as she slumped down at the sewing table, her head hanging, like a puppet with no strings. Larry and Barney. Barney and Larry. Her marriage was over. Her family ripped apart.

'He's solid gold inside,' she remembered Larry once saying about Barney. Had Larry ever even loved her? Had he ever wanted to father Beatrice? From out of nowhere, Nancy felt guilt rise up in her. Had she forced him to marry her and trapped him with the pregnancy? It was the 1990s, not the 1950s – he could have refused. He had proposed to her, not the other way round. Nancy had given her heart to Larry, to have and to hold until death do them part. But he had dropped her heart from a great height, letting it split open like a watermelon smashed onto concrete.

Chapter Nine

'I tried to strangle him the other night,' Barney told Nancy when she confronted him. They met on a cold afternoon in a dark little bar. Barney ordered two glasses of red wine. The bar was decorated with pages torn from vintage newspapers, novels and magazines. Someone had drawn an illustration of the London skyline over the top. Barney didn't take off his black woollen coat. He wore the collars turned up. As he spoke, Barney demonstrated the strangling motion with his hands and stifled an awkward laugh. Nancy's entire body shook with hurt and confusion.

'Of course, that didn't go down very well,' he said. 'Yet another blot on my copybook. Oh well, it will always be tarnished.'

Nancy wanted to slap his face, to shout, to throw things. The fingerprints on Larry's neck must have belonged to Barney. She couldn't look him in the eye, so instead she gulped from her glass of wine. The liquid gnawed at her empty stomach. Her cheeks flamed red.

'I've been giving him an ultimatum for years,' he went on, suddenly serious. 'You or me. But he wouldn't do it to you, or Beatrice. He can't face disappointing you, or anyone else. He doesn't want to be the villain in anyone's story.'

Was that all their marriage meant to Larry, she mused – an avoidance of disappointment, a keeping-up of appearances? Surely it was more than that. Or was it possible for two people to be held together entirely by the love only one person felt? The certainty she had once felt about their love evaporated.

'We've been together on and off for a long time and way before you came along, but then had a falling-out, just at the time you arrived,' he said. 'I should have left him alone, but I have never been able to. You know what he's like. That grin. That playfulness. We work together every day and admire each other professionally. I'm rather addicted to him.'

He gave a tiny, sad smile and drank his wine. A waitress appeared at the table and lit a tea-light candle, dropping it into a jam jar, humming along to a Moby song. Blithely unaware of what she was interrupting.

'When you fell pregnant he phoned me, beside himself with panic,' he said. 'He was furious with me for falling out with him and I quote "pushing me into her arms". He always blames me for everything. Mind you, I am up for blame. If only I hadn't been so pig-headed and determined for him to come out of the closet, this whole scenario wouldn't have existed!'

Barney's words sliced like daggers through Nancy's heart. Her hand trembled when she lifted the last of her wine to her lips and swallowed it down in one.

'But – but then Beatrice wouldn't be here,' she stammered, tears popping into her eyes, her throat aching. *Don't take away the one precious thing in all this.* Barney reached his hand out over the table and rested it briefly on hers.

'Of course, I would never wish for that,' he said quietly. 'The best thing Larry has ever done is to father Beatrice. I could never be that bitter and twisted. I love Beatrice too, Nancy. It's all a bit of a mess, that's for sure, but Beatrice is beautiful. You must have suspected something was between us?'

Nancy was dying inside.

'I never suspected anything,' she said, embarrassed and flustered. 'The thought never occurred to me… I just thought maybe he was finding family life a bit much. Mundane. Having a child, it… it…

puts strain on a relationship. I wanted for him to be happy. I tried so hard to make it all okay, yet—'

'You're so good and kind and innocent,' Barney interrupted. 'No wonder Larry finds it so difficult to deceive you, but I pity him, Nancy, trapped in the wrong life. Don't you?' He drummed his fingers on the table.

'Imagine how he feels,' he continued. 'He has this ridiculous notion that he wants to keep his relationship with me a secret. It's not easy being homosexual. We've come a long way since the 1950s, but even so. I think it's his father's disapproval he fears the most, though he'd never admit that, of course. He pretends to hate the man, but when his father convinced him to do the right thing and marry you, he did what the old man said.'

Nancy was appalled. Larry's father had talked him into the marriage?

Barney cleared his throat. 'Have you said anything… does he know that you saw us?'

Nancy shook her head. When Larry had returned home that night, she hadn't been able to utter a single word about what she'd witnessed. It made her burn with embarrassment, for him and for her. Did he find her repulsive? Did he close his eyes and think of Barney? She would rather never have to hear the answers. She would rather disappear in a puff of smoke. Instead, she had kept on her red dress and given him the champagne and the news about his job offer, about which he was jubilant, throwing his arms around her and lifting her from the ground. She was astonished by how easily he moved between lovers. Were there others he held in his arms?

'Why didn't you come and find me earlier or call me at the office?' he'd demanded to know, uncorking the champagne. 'You knew how much I wanted this news!' She had mumbled something about wanting to wait until she could tell him face to face. Lies on lies.

'What are you going to do?' Barney asked now, folding his arms across his chest. 'One of us needs to be strong.'

Tears slid down Nancy's cheeks and onto the wooden table. She sighed so hard, the candle flame extinguished. The waitress glanced over and frowned at the inconvenience. 'I don't know,' she whispered into her empty glass, her chin wobbling. 'I don't know.'

Sawing off her own arm with a blunt penknife would have been easier. It was the most difficult decision she had ever made. The words were a lie, but her lie would mean Larry could be his true self. She would do anything for Larry. Donate an organ, including her heart. What effect would his otherwise unfulfilled life have on Beatrice? A miserable father – living a lie – surely equalled a miserable childhood. Her voice trembled when she asked him if they could talk, inviting him to sit with her at the kitchen table when Beatrice was asleep in bed.

'I need to talk to you about something very serious, this… marriage… maybe it's having a daughter so soon after we met, when perhaps we didn't truly know one another… I've found the last months, years even, difficult,' she managed to say without breaking down. She squeezed together her hands and clenched her jaw. 'I've felt us grow apart and suspect that perhaps we want different things. You… your career is important to you and I know you want to travel, even move overseas… but I have different priorities. I think I should move out for a while… a sort of trial separation,' she said. 'I can stay with my father. We'll have to find a way to explain it to Beatrice.'

His reaction was infinitesimal, but in a double-bat of his eyelids – a rapid blink – the relief was clear as glass, and she knew she was doing the right thing. The truth was confirmed. A rock plunged to the bottom of her stomach. She leaned against the edge of the kitchen table until it dug painfully into her ribs. Swiped at crumbs. Slowly, Larry shook his head and stared at the floor. When he looked back up, tears were spilling down his cheeks. She took a deep breath and focussed on the fact that she was doing this for him. She was setting him free and she could, would, must handle this. He pushed a hand through his dark hair, which he was wearing longer now – more like Barney's she realised – and moved towards her.

'But…' he started, unable to meet her eye. 'Where did this come from? I thought you were happy?'

He was going through the motions; she knew it.

'I'm sorry,' she forced out of her throat, 'but it's what I want. I can't be happy, not like this.' She didn't say: sometimes I feel as if you've abandoned me, even though we sleep in the same bed. Over the years, I've never felt as if I was enough for you. I tried to be adventurous or exciting, but I was never enough. I've often wondered if you loved me as much as I loved you. And now I know why I felt that way.

'It can be an amicable separation. You can do your own thing,' she said, her lips trembling as tears fell down her cheek. 'You won't be tied down or under any obligation. You can go to London, Los Angeles, live out all your dreams.'

He glared at her. She shook, not knowing what he was going to do. Embrace her? Rest his chin on her shoulder and thank her? All the unsaid words stretched like no man's land between them. He came closer still and swallowed noisily. He narrowed his eyes and shook his head.

'Fuck you, Nancy,' he hissed, his face ashen. Tears spilled from his eyes. Nancy was horrified. She hadn't anticipated anger. Where was that in this script? Confused, she stood from her chair and staggered backwards.

'I think we will both be happier,' she said, gulping down every instinct in her body that was burning to tell him what she'd seen and what Barney had told her, but she had vowed to herself she wouldn't make him suffer.

'Have you got someone else?' he shouted. 'Are you having an affair with someone?'

She almost laughed.

'Not at all,' she said. 'Honestly, Larry, this isn't about me wanting to be with anyone else. It's about us. I just think we need space from one another.'

'I know you're seeing someone else!' he stormed, thumping the table. 'You must be! This doesn't make any sense otherwise. You've always adored me.'

She was thrown off guard. What was he doing? Creating a role for himself as the wronged party? Wasn't that cruel of him, considering what she was doing for him? She wanted to yell: I'm doing this for you! I'm setting you free! I know your secret!

'Larry, no!' Nancy said, feeling sobs ripping through her. She was defeated, couldn't hold it in any longer. 'You... and Barney, you're... I mean, are you... why don't you admit it? This all must have been so difficult for you... are you... I know you and Barney are more than just good friends. Be honest, Larry.'

She gulped. It was as if she'd ignited his fury with a match. He swung his arm at the fruit bowl on the table and swept it off. It smashed into pieces. Apples and oranges rolled across the floor. Nancy's hands flew to her mouth.

'No, we're fucking well not!' he said. 'What the hell are you talking about? You've lost your mind!'

Longing for his quiet understanding and gratitude, she sobbed uncontrollably.

'You don't know anything,' he shouted. 'I've tried so hard to make this work.'

Nancy felt bewildered and wrong-footed. Did he, in fact, actually love her? Was he angry because he'd been willing to sacrifice a life with Barney, for her? Was it about being separated from Beatrice? Was the thought of eventually confronting his sexuality so terrifying to him? Was he ashamed? She didn't understand. Images of Barney and Larry in one another's arms filled her head. Barney's words of their long-standing secret love affair ran in her ears on loop. All those times Larry was distant and frustrated. Turning his back on her in bed.

'I'm sorry, but whatever you say…' she managed. She had to be strong, even in the face of Larry's denial. For his sake. For her sake. For Beatrice. 'This is the way I want it to be. This is the way it *has* to be. Tomorrow I'm taking Beatrice and we're going to stay with my father for a while. Hate me if you have to, but, Larry, you will only make this worse than it already is.'

'Fuck you,' Larry said. He yanked on his coat and stormed out of the flat, slamming the door shut so hard, a picture fell off the wall. Nancy's whole body trembled. She gripped the table to steady herself.

'Mummy?' Beatrice said, sleepy-eyed from the doorway, holding her teddy, Tabitha, in her arms. 'I had a bad dream.'

'It's alright, Beatrice,' Nancy said. 'Go back to bed. I'll be there in a minute to tuck you up.'

'Why are you crying?' asked Beatrice, worry creasing her brow. 'Were you and Daddy shouting? Why are there apples on the floor?'

'I'm not crying!' snapped Nancy. 'Now get back to bed for God's sake!'

Beatrice flinched at her mother's sharpness and scarpered along the corridor to her bedroom. Nancy squeezed shut her eyes and exhaled in exasperation. Furiously, she swiped at the tears on her cheeks before slowly picking up the pieces of the broken fruit bowl with trembling hands.

Chapter Ten

'I repeat!' shrieked Marcie to Alfie. 'What the hell are you doing in my swimming pool?'

Nancy closed her eyes. She would have to say something, quickly. Explain. Yet her legs were buckling. They were barely strong enough to carry her out of the bedroom at 38 Evelyn Road and into the hallway. Her heart thumped in her chest. In her hand, she clasped the red-framed photograph of Beatrice. Half-running in stocking feet, she moved through the kitchen and into the garden, where Alfie was standing by the pool, dripping wet, skinny knees knocking together, his arms wrapped protectively around his waist, teeth chattering. Dark clouds had blown over the house, making the pool water appear green-tinged and uninviting. In the distance, sirens – not seagulls – screeched. How quickly life can change.

'Mrs Loveday,' Nancy began, emerging from the kitchen door. 'Marcie?'

Marcie spun on her heels to face her. The loose, expensive-looking pale grey linen dress she wore billowed beautifully around her lithe gym-fit body. A fur shrug lay across her shoulders and Nancy's mind returned to her immaculate wardrobe, where Marcie had hung her clothes in colour order.

'I—' Nancy started and then, finding herself lost for words, she stared at the frame in her hand.

Marcie pushed her sunglasses back from her eyes and blinked, deep creases forming on her forehead. She pursed her lips.

'What's…?' Marcie said. 'Could you explain why this child is in my swimming pool? And why do you have my picture?'

Nancy waited. There was a sudden glimmer of recognition on Marcie's face, which hadn't much changed since she was a girl. Chestnut hair framed her piercing blue eyes and the constellation of freckles across her nose and cheeks, so perfectly spaced they could have been drawn on, had not faded. There was a smudge of mascara around her left eye which seemed out of place on her otherwise perfectly made-up face. The room that Nancy had just been in could not have belonged to Marcie. Perhaps it was a junk room, or a particularly shambolic visitor had been staying and always kept the door closed.

'I'm so sorry,' said Nancy. 'I'm—'

'Oh!' interrupted Marcie, the anger visibly draining from her as the realisation dawned. 'Do I know you?'

Nancy's heart raced.

'I'm Nancy Jones,' said Nancy. 'I'm feeding your cat and I saw Alfie in the street and he'd grazed his knee. I was just going to walk him home but said he could dip his toes in the water. I'm sorry to have shocked you.' She held out the frame. 'Mrs Loveday, *Marcie*, I saw this photograph of my daughter Beatrice. Do you recognise me?'

Marcie opened her mouth to speak and shut it again. Her bottom lip wobbled. For a moment, time stood still. Marcie visibly shivered, dropped the bag she carried with a thud and lifted her hand to her mouth. Alfie's lips were turning a shade of blue. Nancy felt a tug of guilt for poor Alfie, who must have been wondering what on earth was going on and who should have been home long ago. With trembling hands, she picked up his school uniform and handed it to him to put on. Slowly, he started to get dressed, his teeth chattering together.

'Nancy? Beatrice's mum?' Marcie said, blinking in the sunlight which thankfully reappeared from behind a cloud. 'Yes… yes… I suppose I do now that you say it… I'm sorry, I'm… this is all a bit… It was so long ago. I was just a child when we last met. I didn't immediately recognise you, didn't expect to see you here.'

Marcie's sentence was broken by long, stilting pauses. She didn't meet Nancy's eye. Nancy thought of the cards she'd written and the photographs she'd kept and her heart broke just a little bit more.

'I'm sorry again,' said Nancy. 'I hadn't realised that this was your home, or that we lived in the same town. If I'd known you were coming back early from your trip, I… we… wouldn't have been here. We didn't mean any harm. Has your trip been cancelled?'

'Yes, yes,' Marcie said, her tone suddenly clipped. 'Gerard and I… we… I had a problem at work that I couldn't ignore, and our plans had to change unfortunately.'

Marcie lifted her chin in defiance. Nancy wondered at the tremor in her voice. At that moment, there came the sound of the electric gates opening and car tyres crunching on the gravel. Muffled operatic music suddenly stopped. A car door opened and slammed shut and footsteps marched up the drive. The front door opened and closed. Marcie tensed and straightened her dress and wiped the smudged mascara from under her eyes. Had she been crying?

'We should go,' Nancy said quietly. 'Quickly, Alfie, grab the rest of your things.'

Alfie gathered his school jumper, socks and shoes in his arms in an unruly bundle. A sock fell to the floor and Nancy picked it up, stuffing it into her pocket.

'Oh,' said Gerard Loveday, when he came outside, glaring at Alfie and Nancy. He was a huge man with thick black hair that was swept back as if he'd been in a wind tunnel. He was above six feet tall with a chest as wide as a car bonnet. His citrus aftershave hit Nancy's nose.

'Marcie?' he snapped. 'I didn't know we had guests.'

'This is Nancy Jones,' said Marcie. 'She's feeding the cat. You should know, you booked her! Why didn't you tell me her name?'

Gerard frowned. 'Why should I have told you her name?' he muttered.

'She brought this… boy… her friend, with her and I interrupted them,' continued Marcie. 'They are just leaving, aren't you?'

Gerard frowned, clearly annoyed. Alfie and Nancy glanced at one another. Nancy nodded and muttered, taking an instant dislike to Gerard. Her legs were shaking. Marcie seemed on the edge of something; losing her temper perhaps, Nancy wasn't sure.

'What have you done with our son?' Marcie asked.

'I've dropped him at my mother's,' Gerard said. 'We need some time. Thank you for your services, Ms Jones, but you won't be needed again. Our trip has been cancelled since Marcie had a change of heart. Please leave the spare key when you go.'

Nancy glanced at Marcie, whose eyes were downcast. She wanted to ask Marcie why she'd had a change of heart, but they both obviously wanted her to leave. She put a hand on Alfie's trembling shoulder to steer him out of the house.

'Yes, yes of course, here is the key,' she said. 'Come on, Alfie. Oh, Mrs Loveday – Marcie – your photograph. Here, I came across it when I was looking for your—'

'Cat,' finished Marcie. 'Here, let me take it.'

She handed the frame over and when Marcie took it from her, Nancy realised her hand was also shaking. Nancy wanted to pull Marcie to her chest and hug her, but Marcie had a rigid smile on her face and was walking briskly through the kitchen, ushering them out. She flung open the front door and said goodbye, without further ado, then couldn't close the door fast enough.

Nancy stared at the closed front door, bewildered. Crunching down the driveway with wobbly-legged steps, Nancy heard Marcie and Gerard's raised voices drifting through an open window. Her head spun with questions, none that she could answer. With Alfie's hand in hers, she realised he was still half-dressed. When they were out into the street, she tried to regulate her breathing and helped Alfie on with his shoes and jumper, dusting gravel from his soles, dabbing the flaming red grazes on his knee with her cardigan.

Gerard's potent aftershave was still up her nose, like two sharp fingers.

'Sorry, Alfie,' she said. 'I didn't realise the lady would come back early. I'm sorry she shouted at you. I think she was just surprised to see you there. You should have gone straight back home; I should have sent you straight back home.'

Nancy silently chastised herself. Alfie nodded once. He put his hand over his eyes to protect them from the glare of the sun that had crept out from behind the clouds and squinted up at her.

'Do you have a daughter, Ms Jones?' he asked. 'You said you had a daughter, Beatrice. Where does she live?'

Nancy took a sharp intake of breath. She opened her mouth but could not trust herself to speak. *It was so long ago*, Marcie had said. Time heals, people had told Nancy, but, in her experience, this great healer called Time was just a sticking plaster over a deep wound that refused to scab.

'Let's get you home, Alfie,' she said, walking on a pavement made of sponge. She looked heavenwards, but there were no signs up there. It was vast and wholly white.

Chapter Eleven

'You need a holiday,' Nancy's father, Ted, had said, lifting up the net curtain at the living-room window of his house to reveal a dreary, rainy day. 'After the last few months, with all the toing and froing with Larry, it'll do you and Beatrice good. I'll be fine here. I'll be able to get down to some serious vegetable growing.'

He had smiled and rested his hand on her shoulder. The skin on the back of his hand was thin as rice paper and his veins protruded like blue shoelaces, but his touch was reassuring – warm and gentle. He was getting old, Nancy had thought with a stab of panic. After splitting with Larry, Nancy had moved in with Ted – back into her childhood bedroom – and Ted had been supportive. At seventy-eight years old, his bones were slightly frail, but his mind strong. His love for Nancy and his granddaughter never wavered and he couldn't do enough for them. He brought them vegetables from the allotment, enormous marrows, earthy potatoes and potent leeks that Nancy cooked for dinner, sunflowers that grew to eleven feet tall, pencil holders and giant dice that he made in his workshop from offcuts of wood. He enjoyed the company, but he clearly worried about Nancy and couldn't understand why she had split from Larry.

'There must be a reason,' he had asked at first, but she – in some kind of loyalty to Larry and his reluctance to admit the truth – refused to elaborate.

When she had bumped into William Green, her childhood sweetheart, in the swimming pool one morning, and they had decided to meet regularly for coffee, as friends, Ted was delighted. He'd always liked William. He was dependable and was from a local, well-liked family of cabinet makers. But William had split from his wife and – suffering with chronic arthritis – had been forced to give up his trade. He had however bought a property on the north Norfolk coast that he was employing other tradespeople to help him renovate. He planned one day to rent it out as a holiday home.

'You and Beatrice could stay for a few days; it's a big place so we wouldn't be treading on each other's toes,' he'd said to her over coffee. 'I'd appreciate your advice on the interiors. You know me, I have no idea about interior decoration. It's beautiful, Nancy. It's at the edge of a tiny village, and the sea is a short walk away. We can pick samphire and go crabbing. The offer is there. No strings attached.'

Not wanting to run the risk of seeing Barney at the *Post* on her way to work every day, Nancy had left Bespoke Bridal and was now working freelance for the costume department of the local arts university. To protect Larry – who was still playing the role of the rejected one – she didn't tell their friends the truth about why she'd left him. She said: 'we grew apart' or 'we had different priorities' and deflected the question that burned on peoples' lips – 'was there anyone else involved?' People could speculate and gossip as much as they liked. Deep in her heart she knew she was doing the right thing.

The school summer holiday loomed and Beatrice, now nine years old, wanted to take her best friend Marcie away with them, so she had a friend to play with. Larry was working for most of the summer at his new job and the arts university's term had ended, so Nancy decided to take William up on his offer. There were no strings attached, but she knew Larry wouldn't see it that way. So, she told Larry about Norfolk but left out the part about William to avoid further impacting on Larry's absurdly dented pride. She arranged it all with Marcie's mother, Elaine, who – with three other younger children to entertain – was happy to let Marcie go. The prospect of a holiday lifted Nancy's spirits. Perhaps the change of scene would help heal her heart. The fresh, sea air would clear her mind.

For years after, forever after, she had longed to return to that moment and instead of accepting William's offer, say: *No, thank you, we won't come*. If only she hadn't packed their suitcases with lightness in her heart as she imagined picking samphire on the muddy, sandy flats, the sun on her back. If only she had stayed at home digging over the allotment with Ted, growing tall, yellow sunflowers. If only.

They had driven into a postcard. The property, at the edge of a tiny old seafaring village and with a spectacular view of the tidal saltmarshes and coastline beyond, had once been the village bakery. Dating from the nineteenth century, with outbuildings arranged around a courtyard, the building was, though in need of some renovation, quite beautiful. In the car, with her elbow jutting out of the window, Nancy was assailed with wistful thoughts of Larry. He would adore this place. If he were here now and things had never changed between them, he'd be whooping, or driving along banging his hand on the horn, laughing loudly at how quaint it all was. In the driver's seat, William was frowning and biting his lip. Anxious, Nancy assumed, about the lack of parking in the narrow lane.

'This looks like something from a storybook!' Beatrice said, her travel sickness instantly forgotten. 'Mum, I want to stay here and never go home!'

'Me too,' said Marcie. 'This is the best holiday I've ever been on.'

'It hasn't started yet!' Nancy laughed, delighted that the girls were in such high spirits. 'We're not even out of the car!'

While Nancy dragged suitcases from the boot and paused to stretch her arms above her head to unravel the knots in her back, the girls disappeared into the building to explore. Occasional shouts of 'Mum!' or 'Up here!' or 'You won't believe this!' burst from windows and doors where the girls had discovered concealed cupboards behind wooden panels, cosy nooks and crannies, fireplaces, beamed ceilings and a welcome basket filled with cakes and biscuits.

'They love it,' she said to William. 'Thank you for having us to stay. I'll do whatever I can to help while I'm here.'

When they walked into the property, he rested his hand on the small of her back. Nancy didn't move away. It felt familiar and undemanding. William was a comfort, like a pair of slippers. 'I know how difficult it is when a marriage crumbles,' he said kindly. 'Try to relax while you're here. Your room is at the back, overlooking the garden. The girls' room adjoins yours. Mine is at the front on the right side. You might want to unpack. If you need anything I'll be in the kitchen, trying to kick the boiler into shape. We could drive to the beach later or I can show you the village. There's a fish and chip shop that sells the best fish, with batter bits too. I can't resist them.'

The bedroom was basic but cosy. Nancy ran her hands over the old wooden furniture. It had belonged to the previous owner and perhaps the owners before that and wore the marks and scratches of other people's lives. She unpacked her clothing, a selection of colourful dresses, and opened the top drawer in a chest of drawers and found a Dick Francis novel curling at the edges, a stamp and a coin. It gave her a reassuring sense of following in a long line of others. Yes, she had a broken heart, but so did many others. She could recover from this and love again – one day – couldn't she? Despite the awful year she'd had, she felt a tiny spring of hope in her heart.

Looking out of the window, she saw the girls flying around the garden, doing cartwheels, like spinning tops on the grass. Their cheeks were the colour of cherries. They swept their hair back from their eyes and lips, giggling. She scanned the environment for any dangers, but there were none. The garden was walled and beyond the wall was the church, where rabbits hopped around on the grass. She smiled, happy to be there.

The strong, fragrant smell of cannabis smoke suddenly hit Nancy's nose and she looked down from the window to see William sitting on a bench, inhaling from a long joint. She bit the inside of her cheek. Friends of Larry's had smoked, but she never had. She didn't particularly mind about William smoking – he was an adult – but the girls were there, in view. Couldn't he wait for the evening, when they were asleep?

'You don't object, do you?' he said, noticing her staring down at him. 'It really helps my painful joints like you wouldn't believe. More than the painkillers I've been prescribed and less damaging to my liver.'

Nancy chewed the inside of her cheek. She had to say what she thought – the girls came first, always.

'Maybe just not around the girls though, if you don't mind?' she said, with an uncertain smile. 'I know this is your house, but they are at a funny age. Impressionable. Marcie's mother wouldn't like it, I know that much. She'd think I'd taken her daughter to a drug den!'

Nancy's laugh came out as an awkward bark. She hated to be a prude. William grinned up at her, put out the joint and placed it on the edge of a window box, where rosemary and mint were growing.

'You know what I'm like,' he said. 'I hardly ever touch a drop of alcohol. It literally helps with the pain, but sure, I'll keep out of view of the girls. I understand what you're saying.'

Sudden giggling in the near distance and the sound of footsteps running up the winding stairs interrupted her thoughts. The girls burst into the bedroom, clutching a bunch of lavender picked from the garden.

'Can we go to the beach?' Beatrice said. 'William says it's five minutes from here!'

'What's that weird smell?' said Marcie. 'It's gross!'

'Nothing,' said Nancy, shutting the window decisively.

'Are you okay to drive?' Nancy asked William, when they clambered back into the car with swimming costumes, buckets and spades, sun cream and towels. 'I've read that cannabis can affect your perception of time and speed. Not stoned, are you?'

She was half-joking, half-serious, a niggle of anxiety knotted across her shoulders.

'No!' said William. 'Don't worry, Nancy, I'm still boring old William. A puff or two helps my pain, that's all. That's what my ex-wife didn't like about me. She said I was too boring.'

'You're not boring, William,' Nancy said. 'Buying an old property in north Norfolk is hardly boring. I admire you.'

'What's cannabis?' Marcie interrupted. Nancy glanced at William, but he just smiled, adjusting the rear-view mirror so he could see Marcie.

'It's a kind of medicine I take sometimes to help me with my arthritis,' explained William. 'It fights pain and inflammation. A lot of research has gone into—'

Before William could continue, Nancy moved the rear-view mirror back into place and interrupted.

'Let's get to the beach, shall we?' she said, watching William massaging his thumb joint, which had swelled significantly and was clearly stiff.

'We should stop off on the way to pick up a picnic,' she continued, keen to get off the subject of cannabis.

'I want to get to the beach, not to the shops!' said Beatrice, in her best moan. 'Can't you go to get the food later, Mum? Please?'

'I can go and stock up on provisions if you like,' said William, looking at Nancy questioningly. 'While you have a rest on the beach?'

'No, it's okay,' said Nancy. 'Let's go to the beach and I'll pop back to the shops and pick up lunch. You've done all the driving so you can rest while the girls have a run around. I can see you're in pain. But, girls, you have to absolutely promise to stay out of the sea until I get back, okay? We need to suss out the currents and tide here, and I need to make sure you two are one hundred per cent safe.'

'Yes!' said Beatrice. 'We'll stay out of the sea. We'll dig sandcastles instead. Okay?'

'Perfect,' said Nancy, turning to grin at her daughter, who was beaming with happiness.

The beach was a beautiful, seemingly endless unspoilt stretch of pale golden sand, backed by undulating sand dunes sprouting marram grass. Pine trees infused the air with a heady fragrance and the sea shimmered in the sunlight. There were a few families with windbreaks and brightly coloured parasols in the distance, confetti decorating the beach, but otherwise the sand was empty. Again, Nancy was struck with thoughts of Larry. At this moment, he would probably strip off his clothes and race into the sea, diving into the waves without a second thought for jellyfish or rip currents. But was he, at this moment, with Barney? She sighed.

William carefully laid out his towel and brushed the sand from his feet before he slowly – and painfully – sat down. He took off his glasses and cleaned them, grinning up at her. The girls were running around on the sand with their arms in the air, pretending to fly, madly laughing. Nancy tried to commit their happiness to her memory.

'Are you sure you don't want me to go for the lunch?' said William.

'No, you rest. I'll be twenty minutes,' she said to William, who was suppressing a yawn. 'I'll get something for tonight too. It's the least I can do to say thank you. Look at the girls – they're in their element! Don't let them into the sea until I'm back though, okay? There are no lifeguards on this beach. And tell them not to talk to strangers.'

William's glasses had slipped to the end of his nose. His hands had frozen into a claw shape, but he tried to hide them behind his back. 'Don't worry. I'll be here reading until you get back and we'll stay on the beach,' he said.

Nancy said goodbye to the girls, who were grabbing their buckets and spades and heading off down the sand. 'Not in the sea!' she yelled after them. 'And don't talk to any strangers.'

She returned to the car and quickly drove to the shop in a nearby village, picking up cheese, fresh, warm bread rolls, plump, fragrant tomatoes, biscuits and bottles of water. She also chose vegetables and pasta – planning a simple pasta recipe for dinner.

On the walk back to the car, she was held up by a crowd of people who were standing on a bridge. Trying to push her way through she saw that they were watching some sort of charity duck race in the stream below, as hundreds of yellow plastic ducks were released into the water to a round of applause and cheering.

'Excuse me,' she said repeatedly, weaving her way through the crowds, worrying about how long she had been away. They'd all be hungry. She hoped they'd remembered not to go into the sea. William would never let them. He had always been one of the most sensible people she'd ever known. Larry was different. Restless. Perhaps that was why she had fallen so desperately in love with him. Her heart suffered a sudden, dreadful dip. Having to let Larry go hurt so much some days she could hardly bear it.

Finally back in the car, she headed towards the beach. Reflecting on the months since she had left Larry, she instructed herself to try her hardest to enjoy this week and help William with his house. She owed him. Beatrice needed to see that her mum could be happy. That she and Larry separating didn't have to mean the end of the world.

Closer to the beach now, she indicated left into the parking area, where at the end of the track she saw an ambulance and, in the sky to the west, she became aware of an air ambulance helicopter. Grabbing the picnic, she locked the car and half-walked, half-ran towards the spot on the beach where she'd left William and the girls. As she moved closer, hair flying into her eyes in the wind, she felt dread creep up her skeleton. She increased her speed and then dropped the ungainly picnic on the path and ran as fast as she possibly could, stopping briefly to shield her eyes from the sun with her hand, to try to make sense of what she was seeing.

'Oh no, no, no, no,' she muttered as she continued to run towards a group of people gathered around the towels where the girls and William were camped. The air ambulance had landed further down the beach and two paramedics were running from it, towards the towels, where there was already an ambulance and a crew working on someone collapsed on the floor. She found herself begging, wishing, praying that this was all for a stranger. Perhaps someone walking past had collapsed near their towels. A broken ankle. A jellyfish sting. Something he or she would easily recover from. Perhaps it was William's arthritis. Could it flare up suddenly? Not Beatrice. Not Marcie. This couldn't be about the girls. Not the girls. Please, please, not the girls. And then William's head popped up from the crowd of people. He saw Nancy and yelled at her to hurry. His face displayed sheer terror. She ran towards him, horrified sobs erupting from her throat.

'Make way,' William said to the crowd. 'Please make way. This is the girl's mother. MOVE OUT THE FUCKING WAY! Nancy, Nancy, it's Beatrice, she— The paramedics, they're with her. It's Beatrice, she's not… she's not… breathing.'

Nancy's entire world collapsed in on itself as she pushed herself through the onlookers and fell to her knees. Beatrice, her beautiful daughter, was lying on the sand, unresponsive, her face covered with sand. Her eyelids were closed, her body limp. A paramedic was trying to resuscitate her, performing CPR. There were medical bags, a defibrillator, valves and masks around her – alien equipment – but as the minutes ticked slowly by, it was clear to all that Beatrice was gone. Twenty minutes later, the paramedics made the grave but inevitable decision to stop trying. The ambulance crew confirmed that Beatrice was deceased, and the bottom fell out of Nancy's world. She had left them on the beach with just a bucket and spade, less than an hour ago. Now, her daughter was gone.

Nancy opened her mouth and covered it with her hand and screamed until her throat was raw. William put his arms over her shoulders. He too was crying.

'My daughter,' she wept, brushing Beatrice's hair from her head. 'My precious baby girl.'

People drifted away from the scene, horrified and in tears. Marcie sat in silence, wrapped in a foil emergency blanket a paramedic had given her, her face white as snow. William paced up and down the sand, his thumb and forefinger pressed into his eyes, either side of his nose, his glasses abandoned. Nancy would not let go of Beatrice. Whatever anyone said, she would not let go.

William tried to explain what had happened.

'The girls found a hole near the dunes… someone else must have dug it before and – and not filled it in,' he stuttered. 'They came running back to tell me they were going to dig more and make a house and decorate it with shells. I didn't think anything of it. I could see them digging! The sand flying up! That's all they were doing! Playing in the sand. Then, Beatrice apparently jumped into the hole and sand collapsed over her. Marcie screamed that the sand was over her head and tried to pull her out. I ran down and tried to pull her out too – I dug at the sand with my hands. My fucking useless hands! I couldn't do it.' William held up his swollen hands and let out a strangled sob. 'The sand kept falling in. Someone else helped. A man walking past. Eventually we got her out, but it had been too long. She must have breathed in the sand. I tried to resuscitate her, to clear her throat, but it was too late. Someone must have called the emergency services because they were here straight away…'

William's entire body was shaking.

'I'm so sorry,' said a paramedic. 'Sand is so dangerous. There should be more signs up on the beaches.'

Nancy stared at the young woman blankly. Couldn't understand why she was talking about signs. 'We need to get your daughter to the local hospital,' she said. 'We'll travel by road.'

'I shouldn't have gone to the shops,' Nancy said, wild with shock and grief. 'I shouldn't have gone. I should have stayed here and watched them. If I hadn't gone this wouldn't have happened. How could I have left them? What was I thinking? I should never have gone. Why did I go?'

'Nancy,' said William, grabbing Nancy's hand. 'I am so sorry. My hands. They didn't work. I wasn't watching closely. I think I fell asleep. I didn't think—'

Watching her lifeless daughter being carried on a stretcher to the ambulance was as if her heart had been torn from her body. She knew she could not exist on this earth without her. Beatrice was her reason to be. Her everything. Though Nancy was quiet and numb as she held her daughter's cold, limp hand, inside she was screaming and roaring and writhing in agony. The pain and sorrow she felt was excruciating. She glared at the sand in Beatrice's hair, poking out of the top of the sheet covering her. Inside the ambulance, a paramedic gently wrapped Nancy in a foil blanket as she shook uncontrollably and clung on to Beatrice's hand as tightly as she could. Deep down she had registered that her daughter was no longer alive, but still she refused to let go. The paramedic would later have to prise off her grip. Beatrice was dead, but Nancy was waiting and wishing and longing for her to wake up. 'Please wake up,' she whispered, her teeth violently chattering.

Thoughts of Larry exploded into her head. How could she ever tell him? Warm tears dripped from her eyes, as she stared on in disbelief. 'Please wake up, darling girl. Please wake up.'

Chapter Twelve

'Are you even listening?' said Alfie, tugging on her hand. 'We're here, at my house. You've gone into a trance. I was telling you about Harry Potter. You know the owl, Hedwig? She was played by seven different owls in the film and all of them were boy owls. Did you know that?'

'Hmm?' said Nancy, blinking in sunlight. She had walked Alfie home in a daze; thoughts of the beach in Norfolk and Beatrice and Marcie spinning crazily in her head. They stopped outside Alfie's house, the garden of which backed onto her own, and Nancy became aware of Alfie's dad flinging open the first-floor window.

'I was just about to phone the effing police!' he said. 'What's he been up to now? Christ almighty, Alfie, you're going to give me a heart attack one of these days!'

'She walked me home, Dad,' said Alfie. 'The woman from over the fence.'

A neighbour's net curtain quivered, and Nancy flushed with embarrassment at the prospect of her presence causing a scene. You couldn't not know each other's business unless you conducted your entire life in whispers. Alfie's father thundered down the stairs before appearing at the door, a wiggly vein protruding from his bald head. Dressed in black shorts and a T-shirt with a logo on the breast pocket, he marched towards her. She braced herself for shouting. He was powdery with cement dust or flour, Nancy wasn't sure which. Cooking smells wafted from the kitchen. Nancy was looking at him, but not really seeing – her head still pounding with the shock of discovering the photograph of Beatrice.

'I cut my knee and she cleaned it up for me then walked me home,' said Alfie. 'Sorry I'm late.'

'Who's "she", the cat's mother?' Alfie's father asked, unknowing of the truth in his words as he held out his hand to Nancy. 'Sorry, love, what's your name? We've spoken over the fence, but I don't actually know your name. That's the way of the world these days, though, isn't it?'

'I'm Nancy Jones,' Nancy mumbled. 'I saw Alfie had hurt himself, so I helped him and walked him home. I'm so sorry he's late. You must have been beside yourself with worry!'

He wore a tattoo down his forearm: *Rose*, it read, next to an ink drawing of a rambling rose.

'I'm only just home myself,' he said. 'I'm Jonah, by the way. It's a bit of a nightmare juggling everything now that my wife, Rose, has gone off. Doesn't want to know me at the moment. She's taken our twins and our pug with her, but left me and Alfie to fend for ourselves! Says she needs "space".'

He laughed but wasn't actually laughing. Nancy felt a rush of sympathy. If only people were like cats. Rescuing cats was relatively easy. Even the most damaged ones could be helped.

'I expect you want me to sort that fence out,' he said. 'It's collapsed again, hasn't it? We need to get a new one sorted, but money is a bit tight and—'

He let his sentence drift, sighed and pushed his hands into his shorts pockets.

'No, no,' Nancy said. 'Not at all. You've seen the state of my garden, I'm sure.'

'I'll sort the fence one day,' he said. 'I'd invite you in, but I'm not a very good cook. Fish fingers tonight.'

Defeat shone from Jonah's eyes, and Nancy wanted to say she loved fish fingers and he should see some of the dinners she cooked – sometimes just a bowl of Angel Delight for dinner – to bolster him, but all energy had drained out of her. Instead she gave a slight shake of her head and pushed her hands into her pockets, feeling the sticky Polaroid. At home, she would sit quietly and gaze at it. Remember every detail.

'I'd better get going,' was all she could think of saying. 'Bye, Alfie.'

'Bye, Ms Jones,' Alfie called. 'Thanks for the swim. What a pool!'

'What are you on about swimming for?' Jonah said. 'Come on in, son.'

Nancy waved and walked home via the quay, where the curly-haired painter was taking shelter in the bandstand. Rain had begun to fall, ricocheting noisily off car bonnets like marbles released from a net in the clouds. Nancy didn't mind.

'Nice weather for ducks!' the painter shouted, lifting his hand in a small wave. She smiled briefly and wasn't aware of his gaze resting on her as she walked. Her mind was with Marcie and the memory of the last time she'd seen her all those years ago. That dreadful day she'd accompanied her home from Norfolk, without Beatrice. Marcie's mother, Elaine, had been waiting outside her house, standing by her Volvo, arms folded. Nancy had anticipated a sympathetic look. For her friend to hold out her arms, invite her inside and embrace her. Yet she'd snatched Marcie and held her so tight, Marcie yelped. Nancy's arms and heart had never felt so empty in the face of Elaine's full ones.

'On the phone, Marcie said the man, William, who was looking after them was stoned and had fallen asleep,' she said once Marcie was out of earshot. 'Were you aware of that? Do the police know?'

Nancy wasn't sure what Elaine was doing: blaming William? She had wanted to pull her jumper up and over her head and hide. From Elaine, from the world.

'Nothing to do with William, he wasn't…' whispered Nancy. 'I should have stayed on the beach. I was responsible for them. I left them there, just for a few minutes, but I should have thought harder about the dangers—'

Nancy had broken down into tears. Elaine rested her hand on Nancy's back, but gingerly, as if Nancy's grief was contagious.

'But Marcie said that William was meant to be looking after them,' Elaine pressed on. 'You trusted him to watch them and he didn't. I can only imagine the pain you're in and why the hell was he smoking cannabis? What sort of bloke is he?'

Nancy recalled William's expression of pure agony when he'd recounted what had happened.

'Oh shut up, Elaine,' Nancy said. 'You don't know what you're saying.'

She never saw Marcie or Elaine again – not even at Beatrice's funeral. But she wasn't surprised about that, not after the newspaper printed Elaine's version of events. But now, here, today, the past had arrived in her present.

'I'm home,' she said now to her cats, as she opened the gate and ducked under a wayward bramble and darted up the garden path towards the house, with Elsie and William hot on her heels, Tabitha emerging from under a hedge. Her fluffy entourage detested the rain. Their bright eyes lifted her spirits.

'Come on in,' she said, unlocking the front door and letting the cats inside first. They meowed their hellos, like a choir warming up their voices, before standing to attention with their tails wrapped neatly around their legs. 'Better out of the rain, isn't it?'

Inside, the house was silent apart from the battle of a moth trapped in a lampshade. Nancy caught the moth in her hands and released it from the window, then went into the kitchen. Her teacup was exactly where she'd left it that morning. The cereal packet too. She made a big fuss of the cats, stroking each of their heads, their ruffs, under a chin here and an ear there, finding a smile for each of them. 'How are you, Bea darling?' she asked quietly. 'How was your day?'

Ted jumped on the kitchen countertop and enthusiastically licked his paw as if it were covered in the cat equivalent of chocolate, while William found happiness in a corner chasing a spider. When Nancy put down their food and cat milk, Tabitha raced towards the milk and lapped it up so quickly it splashed over the edges.

'Table manners!' Nancy said, suddenly aware of the shrill sound of her own voice. Quickly making herself a piece of toast, she ate half of it standing up, leaning with her back against the countertop in the fading light, her lanyard still on. The bread stuck in her throat. Shadows from the garden crept across the kitchen walls. Pouring herself a glass of cold water and watching Ted drinking from the dripping tap, her thoughts clung to Marcie. Her daughter's best friend lived in Christchurch. The last person to have spoken to Beatrice, to have seen her grinning in her flamingo-pink swimsuit, fingernails painted to match, plaits flying up in the air like ropes, hair that smelled like shortbread, that sweet necklace she so loved. An urge to hold Beatrice in her arms made Nancy double over. She clutched the photograph in her pocket.

Uncomfortable in her damp clothes, she wandered out of the kitchen and up the stairs towards the bathroom without turning on any of the lights. She would have a bath.

On her way to the bathroom, she paused outside a spare bedroom. Ted and Elsie came too. From the look of the wallpaper and carpets, it had belonged to the children of the elderly couple who had lived there before her. The curtains had remained closed for years; the air was perfectly still, trapped. *Why do I not come in here? Why do I leave the curtains shut?*

Perhaps she didn't want the world to look at her life. To a stranger, her house would be like opening a food cupboard and finding just a couple of old, out-of-date tins in its depths.

'I should open these curtains,' she said, moving towards the window. She pushed her hand into her pocket, ready to look at the precious Polaroid, when there was a knock at the door. Ted pricked back his ears and Elsie stopped washing her tail. Nobody knocked at this time of the day. Ever.

Nancy peered out of the window and saw the top of Mrs Loveday's head. Marcie. Nancy froze. All the blood in her body rushed to her ears; the sound of crashing waves.

Chapter Thirteen

'Coming!' she called, her voice tremulous. At the sudden shout, Tabitha flattened her body, crept under the bed and lay still and flat as a slipper. Ted deftly leaped onto a chest of drawers, his ears at right angles to his head. Nancy trembled. Catching sight of herself in an oxidised mirror, she saw a pale, rain-bedraggled woman with an expression of terror on her face, lanyard swinging maniacally round her neck. Hair had fallen from her tortoiseshell hair combs in the rain, and her chest was sprinkled with crumbs from the toast. Sighing, she averted her eyes from her reflection, before straightening her back and shoulders.

'I haven't even changed,' she whispered to Elsie. 'What do I look like?'

Elsie blinked. Hand on the wooden banister, she travelled downstairs, with Tabitha at her heels, ready to face any trouble. Her mind spun. Had Marcie discovered that Nancy had ransacked her drawers? The memory made her forehead prickle with sweat. Quickly, she pulled off her lanyard and brushed the crumbs from her top, before opening the door. A rumble of thunder sounded in the distance and drops of rain fell onto the ivy clinging to the walls by the front door.

'Hello, Mrs Loveday... Marcie,' she said. 'How can I help you?'

Marcie had re-made her face with smoky eyeshadow that accentuated her bright blue eyes and pale pink lips. She had also changed into a green dress that clung to her lithe frame. Her hair was beautifully styled. Over her shoulder she carried an expensive-looking leather bag from which poked a bottle of wine. She smelled divine – of violets, iris and vanilla. Nancy longed for a trapdoor to open up beneath her feet, or to be able to fold up and in on herself, like a Pac-a-Mac. William, appearing by her side, sniffed Marcie's shoes with deep suspicion.

'Don't look so worried!' said Marcie. 'I didn't think you were in. There are no lights on. Are you saving on electricity?'

'No, I mean… yes! I mean, no,' said Nancy, blushing. 'I… I… isn't it dark? Looks like it's about to pour again. I'll put some lamps on.'

Nancy turned away from Marcie, leaving her on the doorstep, and moved inside towards the hall table lamp, fingers fumbling for the switch. Marcie cleared her throat, raising her shoulders up to her ears, as she tried to protect herself from the impending rain.

'May I come in, do you think?' she asked, placing one foot across the threshold, which sent William rocketing past her and out into the garden, where he flew up a tree and balanced precariously in the high branches. Nancy almost cricked her neck when she turned back to Marcie to apologise. 'Yes, yes, of course,' she said. 'Come in, I'm so sorry. I'm um, you've taken me slightly off guard.'

Don't be so silly! Nancy reprimanded herself as Marcie came inside, scanning for somewhere to put down her umbrella, settling for a dark, cobwebby corner where, unbeknownst to her, Tabitha was now crunching on a moth.

'I brought you a small gift, to apologise for today,' Marcie said, handing Nancy a bunch of tulips, 'and I thought I should pay you for the cat-sitting, because it was unfair of us to cancel you without any notice.'

She gave Nancy an envelope with money inside. Nancy handed it back.

'Not at all,' she said. 'I didn't even feed the cat. Couldn't find her! We'd only just arrived when you came home. I said Alfie could put his feet in the pool and I shouldn't have done. I don't think he'd seen a pool in a garden before; he was very impressed…'

Nancy was saying all the wrong things, so she stopped speaking. They stood together in the dimly lit hallway for a moment. Nancy held the tulips awkwardly.

'Thank you,' she said, 'for these.'

Marcie smiled brightly and craned her neck to try to see over Nancy's shoulder, into the living room.

'Shall we sit down somewhere?' Marcie asked. 'That is, if you have a few moments free?'

Nancy almost laughed. *Yes!* she wanted to holler. *Yes, I've got the whole evening free! I'm always free!*

'I'm not really geared up for guests,' she said. 'I would have run the hoover around if I'd known you were coming. The cats… they're moulting at the moment!'

'Oh, don't worry,' said Marcie. 'I think you saw the state of *my* bedroom.'

Nancy dropped her eyes. Shame coursed through her. How could she have rummaged through Marcie's belongings like a crazy interloper? She hoped they didn't have CCTV inside the house, or a nanny cam. Imagine that such a thing should exist!

Closing the front door, Nancy quickly gathered up the pile of post advertising pizza delivery and tree surgeons and guttering experts from the hallway floor and shoved them into a drawer. She wished there was a vase of glorious sunflowers on the hall table. A big mirror perhaps, to reflect the light. The smell of something delicious cooking in the oven. Music gently playing.

'Come through to the living room,' Nancy said, gesturing towards the room, but Marcie was already halfway there.

'What a lovely old place,' Marcie said, sinking down onto the sofa. It was the polar opposite of Marcie's sleek, minimalist home. The cats had disappeared to their various favourite spots – inside the washing basket, on Nancy's pillow, to the top of the wardrobe, inside an open drawer – but tufts of their hair drifted like tumbleweed across the living-room rug. In contrast to Marcie's walls, which displayed studio photographs of her son, and bold, modern abstract artworks, Nancy's paintings of countryside landscapes or horses in fields seemed terribly outdated. She needed to redecorate, buy a few new pieces of furniture. Something. Why hadn't she done something about it before now?

'I'll make a drink and put these in water,' she said to Marcie. 'Would you like a tea or coffee?'

Marcie held up her bottle of wine.

'I brought this,' she said, 'if you have a couple of glasses?'

Nancy blanched. There was not a single wine glass in the house.

'I'll see what I can find,' she started, backing out of the room and going into the spartan kitchen, where she put the tulips in water and stared blankly at the two tumblers and one mug on the draining board. With shaking hands, she picked up the tumblers, dipping her nose inside to ensure they smelled okay – at least they were glass.

'I hope these will do?' she said, returning to the living room, where Marcie was perched on the very edge of the sofa, with Tabitha, newly arrived and sprawling out beside her, licking her tail. William, who had returned indoors, used the edge of the sofa as a scratching post. The upholstery fabric had been ripped to smithereens, revealing the bare bones of the sofa.

'I don't have anything—' Nancy started.

'They're fine,' said Marcie with a tight smile. 'To be honest, at this stage in the day I'd be happy to forego a glass completely.'

Marcie laughed at her own joke, while Nancy poured a glass of wine and shooed the outraged Tabitha from her spot on the sofa with a silent 'sorry'. Marcie's eyes travelled around the room. Painted deep red, with a floor that had been varnished in mahogany decades previously, the room was perennially dark. The sofa wrecked by the cats' claws, a writing desk, small television and a lamp. A clock that no longer worked was on the mantelpiece, permanently at 8.05, which seemed as good a time as any. A row of Siamese cat ornaments, which had belonged to Elsie, Nancy's mother, looked on, frozen. There was a small bookshelf filled with books. A basket for logs and kindling. In the corner was a table with her Singer sewing machine on it, covered with an old blanket. Marcie was out of place. Too stylish, too contemporary and too sleek – an iPhone in an antiques shop.

'This is a remarkable property you have here, on a generously sized plot,' said Marcie. 'You could really do something with it.'

'Yes,' said Nancy, following Marcie's gaze to the high Artex ceiling and to the wide, deep skirting boards. 'I haven't got around to it, yet.'

'How long have you lived here?' Marcie asked.

'Almost thirteen years,' said Nancy. The tips of her ears were ablaze. William yawned. Marcie had a sip of her wine, and though Nancy didn't ever drink alcohol these days, she had one too. The wine exploded flavour on her tongue.

'I am sorry about earlier,' Marcie said. 'I can't imagine what you thought of me today. I was shocked when it was you, Beatrice's mum, after all this time—'

Nancy swallowed. Aware that she must hold herself together, no matter how she actually felt inside, she nodded. Marcie smiled sadly and held her head on one side.

'It was a big surprise to see you too,' said Nancy. 'I had never imagined I'd meet you again, though I have thought about you and wondered how you were getting along. What brought you here?'

'My husband, Gerard, who you've met,' Marcie said with a slight frown. 'We met at work. He was my boss. To be honest I didn't like him at first. I was only nineteen. I had dropped out of university and he seemed so arrogant and ruthless in the way he conducted himself, but after a while he became a challenge. Someone I wanted to conquer. We run a furniture business together.'

She gave a rueful smile and took a sip from her glass.

'We were living in Kent and had our son, Stuart,' she said, 'then, how shall I put it? Things happened, and we decided to relocate to the south coast. We moved last year. Thought Stuart would like to grow up by the sea and St Joseph's seemed to be a good school. A fresh start for us all. We needed a change. *I* needed a change.'

Her smile was thin. She tucked her hair behind her left ear, revealing a red blemish on her skin that she had tried to cover with make-up. Noticing Nancy's eyes on the mark, Marcie quickly untucked her hair again.

'You're obviously doing very well for yourselves,' said Nancy, not knowing what to say. 'You have a beautiful home. It's like a showroom!'

'Ha!' Marcie said, pouring herself more wine. Nancy's thoughts dashed to the chaotic bedroom in Marcie's house – was it really hers?

'I sometimes think my marriage is rather like a showroom,' she said darkly. 'But let's not talk about me. Did you stay in North-amptonshire for long after…? I always thought you were a fabulous mum. You made Beatrice those brilliant costumes for the school plays. I was so jealous! We all were! Do you still sew?'

Nancy shook her head and shrugged, embarrassed, her eyes travelling to the sewing machine covered with a blanket. She felt a deep sense of longing. Flashes of ribbon and fabric and sequins popped into her head. Beatrice had been a mermaid, a dragon, a tree and a cat and a wizard, to name a few. Nancy had lovingly made most of her daughter's clothes, including a pair of needlecord dungarees she lived in.

'Not very often these days,' she said regretfully. 'I stayed in Northamptonshire for a while afterwards – then I moved here after my father died and used my inheritance to buy this place. He used to talk about Christchurch because he'd been here on holiday as a boy, so it seemed as good a place as any. There was a Butlin's holiday camp here back then, apparently.'

'And you live here alone?' Marcie said. 'Well, apart from the cats?'

'Yes,' said Nancy, taking a sip from her glass. 'The cats came to me, really. Ted was already here, a stray, or perhaps he belonged to the previous owner. He's an old man now, named after my father, of course. Elsie, from the rescue centre, such a sweet-natured gentle cat, I named after my mother. She has this way of waiting for me at the end of the path; she knows when I'm coming home. Then, I rescued the others as kittens. They needed a home after being dumped in a box on a building site.'

They sat there in silence for a long moment. Marcie took another deep drink of her wine and tapped her empty glass with a long fingernail before refilling it.

'Don't worry, I've got another if we finish this,' she said. 'I've come well equipped!'

Nancy swallowed, realising Marcie intended to stay for longer than a brief visit.

'How is your mum?' Nancy said tentatively. 'Is she well?'

'She died nine years ago,' said Marcie, staring at the floor, before lifting her chin and clearing her throat. 'That's the reason I dropped out of university if I'm honest and ended up working with Gerard. I had a horrible row with her on the day before she passed away and I put the phone down on her. She rang me back, but I ignored the call. Of course, I didn't imagine for a second that I wouldn't get the chance to make it up with her. I bitterly regret that now.'

'Oh, I'm so sorry to hear that,' said Nancy. 'Very sorry. I liked your mum.'

'Thank you,' said Marcie, flicking moist eyes towards Nancy. 'Years ago, I asked her why she stopped seeing you, and why we didn't go to Beatrice's funeral, and she said that she wanted to protect me. She said the sadness you had to deal with had got inside you, like a disease, and that she didn't want me to get that disease. You knew my mother; she didn't mince her words. "There but for the grace of God, go I" she used to say a lot. I didn't understand when I was a child, but I grew to understand. She meant it could just as easily have been me that died that day on the beach. Not Beatrice. But then she wasn't there, so she could never really understand.'

Marcie sniffed. Nancy sucked in her breath. The reality, that Beatrice was dead, when spoken out loud, still shocked her to the core.

'Yes, well, I…' Nancy started.

'How did you cope?' asked Marcie. 'Mother said you spent some time in St Anne's.'

Nancy gave an involuntary shudder at the mention of St Anne's.

'Yes, I was rather unwell for a while, after it happened,' she said. 'I went a bit loopy, ha!'

She gestured in a circular motion with her finger at the side of her head, feeling her cheeks burn. Marcie smiled kindly.

'I think I went a bit loopy too,' she said. 'Beatrice was my best friend.'

Nancy managed to smile and gulped down the tears that were burning at the back of her throat. She repeatedly smoothed the fabric of her skirt with her palms. Her body burned and shivered simultaneously. The walls pressed inwards.

'I'm sure it must have been a terrible time for you,' Nancy said, her eyes misting over. 'I'm sorry I never saw you again, after – but your mother didn't want…'

She let her sentence drift and fiddled with the zip of the cushion. 'Hot in here, isn't it?'

'I'm alright; I like to be warm,' Marcie said. 'Did you have treatment in St Anne's? Did you get help?'

Help. Did she get any help? This was the question that she couldn't answer. The help she had gotten was less like help and more like imprisonment. The ward she was on initially had been locked and there were locks on the windows, so you couldn't open them more than a centimetre. Her bedroom window opened enough to stick out a finger, or the tip of her tongue – that was all.

'When I was committed to the psychiatric ward it wasn't through choice,' said Nancy finally. 'My friend, he… William actually, well, he was worried about me and I was sectioned, or whatever it's called.

Makes me sound like roadworks. Ha! Perhaps that's what madness is like in your brain – roadworks. Maybe "detained" is a better word. Then I was a long-term patient in St Anne's, which wasn't a party, but I don't suppose it was ever meant to be fun, else people would be queueing up to go! Ha! I was sometimes allowed out for a few hours, or for a day, but I would just wander around the streets or go and have a slice of chocolate cheesecake and a strawberry milkshake at a coffee shop. There was a lovely girl in there, behind the till. She always smiled and said good morning to me and would I like my usual? As if I was perfectly normal! She was so kind. I wish I could tell her how kind she was. I was in and out of St Anne's for several years. I really lost it for a while.'

Nancy's hands were trembling so much, she had to sit on them. It had been years since she had spoken about any of this and now she was opening herself up like a book to Marcie, Beatrice's best friend. The whole experience felt utterly surreal.

'I've not spoken about this in a long, long time,' she said. 'When I started to feel a bit better I moved here and decided it was probably better not to talk about it all. It's difficult to explain you've lost your career, your husband, your daughter and your mind without driving people away. I've never got close enough to anyone to want to open up in that way. And I know people will want to know the details about how Beatrice died. I find it difficult to say out loud. The thought of the sand, it's still impossible to—'

Nancy stopped speaking, gave a small shake of her head and shrugged.

'You literally don't know what life's going to throw at you, do you? I never thought I would get past what happened—' said Marcie, stopping suddenly, her eyes dropping to her sandals, one of which William was now licking. 'But I vowed that I would live my life twice as hard, for the two of us. I used to look at myself in the mirror and say: *Failure is not an option, Marcie!* I would take every opportunity that came my way and succeed in everything

I did. I would have adventures for Beatrice. The ones we should have had together.'

Nancy smiled. 'That's an admirable way to be,' she said. 'Beatrice's dad was like that, wanting life to be an adventure.'

'What happened to him?' said Marcie. 'Are you in touch?'

A memory of Larry's face, incandescent with rage and grief, spitting words full of blame and accusation, when she'd returned from Norfolk, felt like hands around her throat.

'He… he…' Her words failed her. She couldn't go down this road. 'Let me see if I have any biscuits,' she said, jumping up from her chair and rushing out through the door and into the kitchen, calling behind her, 'You must be hungry?'

'No, no,' said Marcie, 'I'm really not—'

Nancy quietly closed the kitchen door behind her and picked up Tabitha, who had trotted in with her. Leaning back against the door, she held Tabitha's plump, warm furry frame next to her chest and closed her eyes, instructing herself to take deep breaths.

'Oh, I can't do this,' she whispered to Tabitha, who pushed her smiling face against Nancy's chest and purred. There was a tiny tap on the kitchen door and Marcie pushed it open.

'I can see talking about this is painful for you,' Marcie said gently. 'You must be lonely in this big house without a partner, or a family. I know you have cats but…'

Nancy smiled. She had long ago accepted she would not love again. Couldn't love again.

'The cats are my family,' she said. 'They call me the cat lady at school, but it's not like I hoard them or anything crazy! Some of them haven't had the easiest of lives themselves, so we understand one another. It's hard to explain. I love them.'

Nancy shrugged. Marcie gave Nancy a sad smile.

'I've been called much worse than cat lady!' said Marcie, with a burst of laughter. 'Why don't you talk to me about Larry? I remember there was a newspaper article, with unkind quotes from

Larry and my mother. I remember the reporter being in the living room and my mother telling me to go upstairs. I've often thought about that. I should have walked in and told my mother to shut up. She had no right. She wasn't even there. I should have done something, but I didn't.'

A cloud passed over Marcie's features. 'You must have felt like the world was against you,' Marcie said. 'No wonder you ended up in St Anne's.'

Marcie's concern and the wine reached inside Nancy's chest and loosened the tight grip on her heart. She had kept her secrets folded up inside herself for so long, like an ancient road map, but Marcie, standing before her, was part of that map. Their lives had diverged, but their stories were intertwined, their paths converging then, and again now. She felt herself unlock a little and all the words she'd held back for so long rush into her throat at once.

Chapter Fourteen

Beatrice was nowhere to be found. Whatever room Nancy searched, when she returned home from Norfolk, Beatrice was nowhere. For just a moment, sometimes, she thought she heard Beatrice's delicate fingers grace the keys of the piano, her voice calling out 'Mummy' in the middle of the night, or a splash of water coming from the bathtub at bath time. 'Ssshhh,' she told her dad, lifting her fingers to her lips, 'I think she's here.' Her eyes would widen as she strained to listen.

'She's gone, my love,' Ted would say, holding Nancy in his arms, his eyes glistening with tears. 'Beatrice has gone. She's with your mother now, I'm certain of it. Your mother will take care of her.'

Nancy longed to open her mouth and scream until the veins in her neck protruded and she drowned in the sound. But she crept around the house like a thief, making no noise at all. She stared blankly at Beatrice's possessions: copies of Enid Blyton's Malory Towers books, her beloved raggedy teddy bear named Tabitha, a Girls' World head, notebooks filled with beginnings of stories and drawings of animals, small boxes of fabrics and ribbons and buttons she'd loved playing with. A spray of peacock feathers in a vase Beatrice had used as wizard wands.

After a while she couldn't look anymore. Carefully packing Beatrice's things into cardboard boxes, she wound tape around them and wrote labels such as 'schoolwork' or 'clothing' or 'toys' on the side in black marker pen.

The day the newspaper article came out, Nancy was obsessively researching opportunities in VSO projects in far-flung, unstable destinations. The further away, the higher the risk, the better. Rwanda. Uganda. Afghanistan. Mozambique. She would devote her life to helping others on the other side of the world.

'Would you look at this?' said Ted that morning, holding the newspaper in his trembling hands. Nancy watched his face turn a shade of grey. He screwed up the newspaper into a ball, hurling it towards the fireplace and missing, before marching out of the house and slamming the front door so hard the windows shook, still wearing his slippers.

Nancy retrieved the article and carefully smoothed it out, reading the story of a local girl who had tragically died from sand asphyxiation on a picturesque beach in Norfolk in an incident the coroner had recorded as accidental death. However, wrote the reporter, Nancy Jones, the mother of the girl, who had filed for divorce from her apparently heartbroken husband, former *Post* reporter, Larry Jones, had – unbeknownst to him – taken their daughter and her friend Marcie Jennings on holiday with her reportedly drug-taking lover, William Green. There were quotes from Larry saying it was irresponsible of Nancy to not disclose the whole story to him, Beatrice's father, about going away with William.

'I can't understand why she didn't tell me,' said grief-stricken Larry Jones. 'Was she running away with this man? I would have thought twice about letting Beatrice go if I'd known the whole story. Now she's gone forever.'

Marcie's distraught mother, Elaine Jennings, was quoted as saying that she had been horrified to learn that the man who Nancy had 'recklessly' left in charge of the girls was allegedly under the influence of illegal substances. 'Of course, I feel very sorry that she's tragically lost her daughter,' Elaine said. 'But when I think about what could have happened to my own daughter without a responsible adult there to take care of her, I feel sick.'

There was a line at the end. *We tried to contact Nancy Jones, but her father said she was unwell.*

Nancy had thought about the newspaper on the breakfast tables of everyone in the county. There would be people on the bus reading it, men and women in cafés, in their work restrooms, crunching on their cornflakes, or sipping from their mugs of tea, reading it out to their pals. It would be on the dashboards of white vans, wrapped around people's fish-and-chip suppers, the words on everyone's lips.

'The newspaper article twisted everything,' Nancy told Marcie. 'They just blew up a situation. Made something of nothing. Caught Larry when he was raw with grief and traumatised. Your mum, when she was in shock. I can see that now.'

Nancy paused to take a drink of her wine. The alcohol was loosening her tongue.

'William smoked cannabis to help with his arthritis, but it had nothing to do with what happened,' she explained. 'Besides, he wasn't responsible for Beatrice and you. As much as I knew and trusted him, I still shouldn't have left you both; I should have been more careful. It's true that I hadn't told Larry about William, which was stupid of me. I didn't want him making the wrong assumptions about our relationship. But it just made him angrier. I'd been careless, he said, with the most precious person in the world. Careless and selfish. How dreadful I felt. Careless with my darling daughter. And the way she died, my God, I still cannot bare to even think—'

Nancy took a deep breath. Marcie closed her eyes for a long moment.

'It all got a bit too much for me,' said Nancy. 'I needed time away from my father, who I shouted and screamed at, poor old soul. I went to stay with William – another mistake.'

Haltingly, Nancy told Marcie that at William's house, she had tried to end her life. When he went out, she dragged a razor across her wrist. She bled so much she thought she must be dying. The bed and the carpet were soaked in blood, but William had forgotten his wallet and discovered her, bleeding and unconscious, and called the ambulance. Paramedics rescued her and took her to hospital. A surgeon sewed her up. She apologised all the way through her recovery. Sent the surgeon flowers. Suffered guilt for wasting his time, when other people – injured children, for God's sake – probably needed him. When she returned to William's flat, he had ripped up the bloodied carpet and replaced it with a new one. He had also washed the wall and repainted it, so there was no trace of horror.

'Poor you,' Marcie said, when she finished. 'You poor thing.'

'I never thanked William for getting rid of the blood,' Nancy whispered. 'What a dreadful job that must have been. I wish I had thanked him.'

Soon after, she was admitted to a psychiatric ward. William visited at first, but then wrote to say he was moving away and could no longer see her.

'I ate the letter!' she said. 'That's how loopy I was! I ate at least half of it before a nurse intervened!'

Marcie giggled.

St Anne's was bewildering. The women were separated from the men, but they were allowed to mix in the scrub of grass that called itself a garden, and for art therapy sessions. A patient had obviously found it therapeutic to snap all the pencils into pieces, because they were barely big enough to grip on to, which was terribly frustrating if you wanted to draw, but mostly the patients sat about doing nothing.

'It's a five-star hotel compared to some I've seen,' a middle-age woman called Lindsey, another inmate, had told Nancy. Lindsey's daughter occasionally visited and once brought her mother a bag of satsumas. Nancy was sitting in the common room with them when Lindsey peeled and began eating a satsuma, pulled a horrid face and complained that they were all shrivelled up and tough. 'It's not satsuma season, you silly little bitch!' she had said, hurling the fruits at her daughter. Nancy's heart cracked into a million pieces. She smiled at the girl, trying to comfort her with her eyes, but received an evil glare in return. She didn't talk to Lindsey again.

'Having Beatrice offer me a satsuma,' said Nancy, 'ripe or sour, was beyond my wildest dreams.'

Nancy couldn't stop talking. She told Marcie more. How the psychiatric nurses were, in contrast to the patients, relentlessly cheerful and Nancy suspected that some of them had their hands in the happy-pill cabinet – one for me, one for the patient, one for me, one for the patient – but she liked their whistling, singing and laughing. One of them had showed Nancy photographs of her backpacking travels and she was flabbergasted by all the countries the nurse had visited in the time that Nancy had been shuffling around the ward in her slippers or sticking a finger out of the window to touch the fresh air.

'I wasn't allowed to have anything sharp in my room, so when I wanted to cut my fingernails, someone had to sit with me,' said Nancy, shaking her head. 'My whole body used to burn in embarrassment. I was a professional dressmaker, for goodness' sake, surrounded by sharp things!

'Sometimes I had a one-to-one with a psychiatrist who expected me to open up,' she went on. 'But I couldn't. I decided to keep it all inside, locked up, so there could be no more misinterpretation of events. Beatrice died a horrible death because I wasn't there watching over her. I could never forgive myself, so what was the point in asking others to?'

Nancy paused for a sip of wine. 'I was in and out of St Anne's like a yo-yo,' she said. 'When my dad died of a heart attack he left me his house and his savings. Before his death, he wrote a note that said: *Put up with what you can't change and change what you can't put up with.* That really shifted something inside me. I thought, *I've got to do something.*'

'Good God,' said Marcie. She poured herself another glass of wine. 'I had no idea. Did Larry visit you during that time?'

Nancy shook her head. 'Larry and I were in touch a couple of times and then through a solicitor for our divorce. I think he threw himself into his job.'

'And you?' asked Marcie.

'I didn't have much of a plan other than to move here and to find a job,' Nancy said. 'I was drawn to working with children, probably because of losing Beatrice and wanting to help others in some small way, and then there were the cats to rescue. As I said, Ted was waiting for me when I arrived, and I thought my father probably had something to do with that, from the other side. Silly, I know. My gosh, I must stop talking. I don't know what's happened to me.'

Ted jumped up onto Nancy's lap and purred loudly, rhythmically pressing his paws into her thighs. Marcie smiled and pushed her feet neatly together, deep in thought.

'You should contact Larry,' Marcie said after a while, 'and William. They both must feel awful about what happened. Send an email, just to reach out. If my mother's death has taught me anything, it's that you shouldn't put things off.'

'There's nothing Larry could say to me, or that I could say to him that would change anything,' Nancy started. 'And William wanted to put me and the past behind him. He moved away, put distance between us. I respect his decision. Besides, I don't know their email addresses, or where they live.'

'Google them! Larry will want to know that you're okay,' said Marcie. 'Perhaps if he hadn't been so cruel to you, you wouldn't have ended up in hospital for so long, and here, living like this.'

Marcie instantly cringed. 'Sorry, I don't mean anything by that,' she said. 'But you seem so lonely here, rattling around this house. You should be out and about enjoying yourself. You're not an old woman yet!'

Nancy was stung by Marcie's words, yet she was only stating the truth. The thought of ever facing Larry again was overwhelming. Of course she had searched his name on the internet once or twice and seen his byline on various newspaper websites, but she had never contacted him.

Exhausted by laying herself open, Nancy wanted to change the subject.

'How about you, Marcie?' she said. 'You've made the right choices, grasped life with both hands?'

'I have taken every opportunity, yes,' Marcie said slowly, 'and despite the ups and downs, I do love Gerard and, of course, adore Stuart. They keep me in line and on track. I have a tendency, occasionally, to go a bit, how shall I say it, wayward.'

'Oh?' said Nancy. 'Why do you think that is?'

'Various reasons,' Marcie said, her voice faltering. 'Moving here was supposed to be a fresh start, but I… oh never mind. Failure is not an option! Forgive me, I've drunk too much wine again!'

Marcie's hands were suddenly up over her face as she tried to stop herself from crying. After a short hesitation, Nancy got up from her seat and moved over to the sofa, where Marcie was sitting.

'Don't cry,' she said. 'Perhaps it's me talking about Beatrice, going on like that. You should have told me to shut up.'

'No, no,' said Marcie, 'I'll be fine in a minute.'

Gently, Nancy put her arm around Marcie's shoulders and Marcie rested her head on Nancy's shoulder. They sat together for a long moment, in a slightly awkward half-embrace. Nancy briefly closed her eyes, wondering if this was what it would have felt like to put her arms around Beatrice if she had still been alive. While Tabitha sniffed Nancy's glass, Ted lay down on the floor near Nancy's feet. Keeping an eye on proceedings. Standing guard.

Chapter Fifteen

Wine-stained glasses. Crumpled blankets on the living-room floor. Cushions that, when disturbed, effused the faint scent of violets and vanilla. A new contact in her mobile phone. The morning after Marcie's visit, the cats paced. Unnerved by the slight change in Nancy's demeanour, Elsie's anxiety levels were sky high. The heavy, deep red velvet curtains were her refuge. She refused to come out from behind them, but when the fridge opened and closed, or the biscuit box was rattled, the curtains undulated, a paw or whisker emerging. In all the years of Nancy living there, nobody had ever stayed so late, and they certainly hadn't left a wine bottle in the wastepaper basket or Nancy, fully dressed and blinking in the darkness under a blanket on the sofa. Late-night cat milk served daily, in five blue saucers, forgotten.

'Don't be like that,' Nancy said to William and Ted as they communicated their discontent by staring blankly at the wall, backs turned. 'How do you think this feels for me? I've been totally thrown off balance. Did I do the right thing, Ted, by talking to Marcie? I feel strangely exposed.'

She picked up Ted and tickled him under his tiny white chin. His vexation gave way to loud purring.

'I'll take that as a "yes",' she said, kissing the top of his head. He pushed his face against hers. All was forgiven.

Walking to St Joseph's that morning, Nancy felt as though she was a ball of string that was beginning to unravel at dangerous speed. As if someone had clamped their hands over her eyes, spun her round and pushed her towards a cliff edge, while wearing roller boots. She couldn't believe that Marcie lived in the same town. What if she had never started cat-sitting? Would she never have met her?

Marcie had been so warm and understanding the previous evening, but her comment about contacting Larry wouldn't leave her alone. How could that ever be a good idea? The very thought made her faint. And why had Marcie suddenly become so upset? Was talking about Beatrice again too painful for her? The poor girl had witnessed it happening. She must have been traumatised.

Breathing deeply to calm her thoughts, Nancy walked towards the quay, passing the curly-haired artist painting at his easel. He was waving enthusiastically at her, so she slowed slightly.

'Would you give me your honest opinion?' he said, taking off his glasses to squint and observe his painting. 'I can't get the damn thing right. I'm trying to capture the quay when it first comes to life in the morning, but does that sunrise look more like a poached egg to you?'

Laughing, he glanced at Nancy, who was squinting at his painting.

'What do you think?' he said. 'Can I expect a call from the Tate gallery?'

He laughed again. He had a very deep, comforting voice and a slight Scottish accent that made your bones sit up and listen when he spoke. He wore a loose blue shirt, jeans and black boots. By the side of his chair was a thermos flask, and a sausage roll in a paper bag from Greggs. She stared at his painting, which, in her non-expert opinion, portrayed what the quay would look like through a misted-up windscreen. She noticed his rather smudged spectacles and wondered if therein lay the problem.

'It's very... atmospheric,' Nancy replied, wishing she had some-thing more insightful and encouraging to say. She admired him, coming here each day at the crack of dawn. 'You're very dedicated. I wouldn't know where to begin.'

'Too much time on my hands,' he rumbled, rubbing his forehead with his paintbrush in his hand and leaving a streak of purple in its wake. 'I prefer getting up and out of the house and being here, watching the town coming to life in the morning than…'

He let his sentence float between them, unfinished. Nancy cleared her throat, and though she had questions she wanted to ask him, partly to hear his voice again, she was too preoccupied. She had stayed up so late talking to Marcie and had not been able to get to sleep once she'd left. Marcie had been the first person in years that Nancy had spoken to properly about the past, and she now felt vulnerable, like a person standing on a remote moor with nothing and nobody around them for miles and miles. There was something about this man's eyes, and the way in which he was looking at her, that suggested he might have been standing on that same moor once upon a time.

'Terence English, in name only,' he said, holding out his hand. 'I'm Scottish, as you might have guessed. From one end of the country to the other, all for love, of course.'

'Nancy,' she said, briefly placing her fingertips in his. 'Keep up the good work, won't you? You're very good.'

'My old dad used to say: "Never give up on something that you can't go a day without thinking about", which I've lived my whole life by.'

He gently squeezed her hand, before releasing it and returning to his work.

When Nancy arrived at school, bleary-eyed and five minutes late, Frances was waiting by her desk, holding an envelope and pointing at her wristwatch.

'Someone else has been asking about cat-sitting,' Frances said. 'One of the mums from Year Three. She said she was a friend of Marcie Loveday and has left you an envelope with her keys. Do you think you could sort out a different system, Nancy, maybe out of school hours? I don't believe being your personal assistant is in my job description.'

Frances handed Nancy the envelope and then squirted her nasal decongestant up her nostrils in two irritable bursts. It was Friday morning. Frances was always prickly on a Friday. Friday was Frances's Monday. Nancy gave an apologetic smile and pushed one of her hair combs, which had slipped from her hair, back in place.

'Thank you,' she muttered, taking her seat and rearranging her folders so she could hide behind them. She peered inside the envelope. There was a Yale key, with a rubber red coating and a plastic fob and a note with an address, phone number and message: *Please feed Titus next weekend. Sally Mills (friend of Marcie's). PS beware the neighbour's dog – barks and bites ankles.*

Nancy looked up again and noticed Alfie coming through the reception doors in tears, with the neck of his jumper stretched over his shoulder, as if someone had been trying to strangle him. Nancy's heart sank. She doubted Alfie had spoken to his father about what was happening at school, so who was listening to him? Nobody, she feared. She saw it in the playground every day: busy parents on their mobile phones. Children on mobile phones themselves. Everyone seemed awfully busy talking to anybody but the person standing next to them. Every child needed someone to listen to them and if Nancy could lend a child her ear, she would. She got up from her seat and left the office to approach Alfie. Another tut from Frances stuck to her back like a dart.

'Alfie?' she whispered, not wanting to draw attention to him in the corridors thick with children, pushing and shoving each other out of the way. 'Can I speak to you?'

Alfie shrugged and straightened out his jumper, wiping what looked like spit off his shoulder. She pulled him into the small medical room – essentially a large toilet and the first aid kit – closed the door, poured him a glass of water and handed him a flapjack from her bag. His knee jogged frantically up and down as he swallowed the food.

'Do you want to tell me what's happened?' Nancy ventured. But Alfie shook his head.

'I'm used to it,' he said, with a mouth half-full of flapjack. 'It's my own fault.'

'No,' Nancy said. 'No, it's not your fault. Have you spoken to your dad? Or one of the teachers? If you can tell me a name, I can help.'

As she spoke, she was aware of the shadow of a male figure through the frosted window in the door, pausing to glance in, before walking past.

Alfie stared at the floor. He kicked at the dustbin with his toe.

'Alfie?' she asked. 'Is there something else?'

'I haven't got a costume,' he said, screwing up his face, 'for the fancy dress fundraising day. Everyone else is planning something. The winner gets a ticket to the Harry Potter studio tour during the summer holiday. I would love to go there. Someone in Year Six took five of his friends there for his party!'

Nancy saw the disbelief in his eyes that such incredible things could ever happen.

'Maybe I won't come in to school that day,' he said.

Air escaped Nancy's lips as she shook her head with a sigh.

'You have to come to school,' said Nancy. 'You need your education. What fancy dress costume would you like?'

'I want to be Hedwig,' he said. 'The owl from Harry Potter. I'd love to be an owl. Flying over the town at night, making no sound with those amazing wings. A predator with superpower hearing. She was played by seven different owls in the film. I read about it. Remember? I told you about it.'

Nancy smiled. 'I remember,' she said. 'I'll have a think about what you could do for a costume.'

A flash of excitement appeared on his face.

She glanced at her watch and said: 'You'd better get to class.'

The excitement disappeared. Nancy only wished she knew how to keep it there permanently.

*

In the corridor, there was a sharp tap on Nancy's shoulder. She turned to find the headmaster, Mr Phillips, standing with his head to one side, as if confused. A tuft of black chest hair stuck out of his top button and more emerged from the bottom of his shirtsleeves.

'Could I have a word please?' he said.

'Yes,' Nancy said, immediately worrying that she had done something wrong. The Animal Magic people she'd booked for the summer fair had cancelled, the school lunch wristbands mixed up, her data entry wrong. Or was it the cat-sitting poster in the staff room? She would happily take it down – it was Emma who insisted it stayed on the wall, for heaven's sake.

'Come through,' he said. Since her interview almost a year ago, she had barely spoken to him beyond being present in the team meetings. Until now, she wasn't even sure he remembered her name.

He ushered her into his office and gestured for her to sit down on the chair on one side of the desk. She sat very still and straight, with her hands on her knees. He pulled on his left earlobe, which, she noted, was much smaller than his right earlobe. Did he pull at it to lengthen it, or to distract people from noticing the difference? Either way, she politely averted her eyes.

'There's been a complaint, Ms Jones,' he said. 'About your conduct at school.'

The blood drained from her face and she felt light-headed. She enjoyed this job. In this job, there were children who needed her help. A smile. A packet of crisps. A friendly hello. It helped her to help them. She held her breath.

'An anonymous person has reported you giving food and money to Alfie Payne, on more than one occasion,' he said. 'Is this true?'

Nancy thought about the children she had helped since starting at the school. Besides the washing of clothes, she'd given out bits of food or occasionally a bar of soap. Word had got around the playground that she was the person to go to. She didn't ask questions.

She just recognised that some children's lives weren't easy – and helped in the smallest way.

'Yes,' Nancy said. 'Just the odd sandwich, flapjack or banana. I gave him a pound once when he didn't have money for non-uniform day. Alfie lives in the house at the bottom of my garden, so I feel I know him a little bit.'

Mr Phillips sighed and stood from his chair. He stared out of the window, with his back to Nancy.

'You might remember from your safeguarding training that you must never give gifts to the pupils. I know these are small things, but we have procedures in place, Ms Jones, for children in need,' he said. 'For instance, the canteen has jacket potatoes for children who arrive with no lunch, and for people in really difficult circumstances, there is Food Bank Friday, where children can pick up a parcel of food for the weekend. If you identify a child is vulnerable, the safeguarding officer must be informed. Otherwise we can run into difficulties, such as masking neglect. You also need to be aware of boundaries.'

Nancy thought of the blown-down fence between hers and Alfie's garden.

'It was just a few snacks,' said Nancy, 'and some help with his uniform. The safeguarding officer is aware of Alfie, but I saw he was upset this morning and I just thought I'd—'

'We also have a uniform scheme,' interrupted Mr Phillips, 'where we can provide pieces of uniform for those in need, but, in all these cases, there's a procedure and paperwork that must be filled in, so we can document it all and offer better support. It all has to be done properly. You can't just do your own thing without informing anyone. What if you decided to give the child money and they spent that money on alcohol or drugs? That could get you into serious trouble. We are a team and we all have our students' best interests at heart. Do you understand?'

Nancy's cheeks flamed with embarrassment. She felt dreadfully ashamed.

'I'm sorry. I wanted to do something helpful, that's all, and I feel particularly sorry for Alfie,' said Nancy. 'I think he's getting bullied.'

'Why on earth hasn't this been reported?' he said. 'Do you know who the perpetrator is? I will not tolerate bullying. I had to put up with it at school because my teachers were ineffectual in dealing with it, and I will not put up with it in my school.'

He pulled hard at his left earlobe.

'No,' Nancy said. 'He won't tell me. I've reported it to his teacher, but with no evidence of who's doing it, there's not much to say.'

'If he does tell you,' Mr Phillips said, 'please inform me right away. And from now on, please stick to the existing school procedures with regard to food and uniform assistance. Thank you, Ms Jones. I think that's everything for now. By the way, you have something on your top. A bird's feather perhaps? Unless it's a brooch.'

Nancy's hands flew to her top, where she extracted a small feather, probably something one of the cats had dragged in. Her cheeks turned the reddest of reds, but it gave her an idea for Alfie's costume. She opened her mouth, thinking she should ask Mr Phillips if it would be acceptable for her to make Alfie a costume, but thought better of it.

'No, not a brooch, thank you,' she muttered, quickly reversing out of the room, half-bowing. Closing the door behind her, she put her hands over her face for a moment and sighed.

Returning to her desk, she found there was another envelope on her desk – a Jiffy bag this time.

'A lady called Marcie delivered it,' said Frances through gritted teeth. 'Probably yet another cat-sitting request. As I said, if you could sort out a different system…'

Nancy checked inside the envelope and her heart lurched. It was the red framed photograph of Beatrice that she'd discovered in Marcie's house, carefully wrapped in bubble wrap. She brushed her fingers on the bubble wrap. If only you could do that with people too – surround them with bubble wrap. There was a note she almost didn't see, with one line written on it. *I looked on 192.com last night and I found Larry's address! I'm so glad we have met. Marcie x*

Nancy shoved the envelope deep into her bag and straightened her back. She tried to concentrate on her work, but words and numbers swam across the screen. The thought of contacting or seeing Larry again was too much. Something that Terence, the painter, had said burst in her head: "Never give up on something that you can't go a day without thinking about." She rubbed at her eyes, waiting for clarity. None came.

Chapter Sixteen

Nancy saw Marcie before Marcie saw her. With Bea balanced on her shoulders, Nancy was looking out of her kitchen window and noticed Marcie seated in the driving seat of her lime-green Mercedes, rhythmically tapping her temples, cheekbones, chin and collarbone with her fingertips. Her lips were moving as if she was holding a conversation. Nancy assumed she was talking on speakerphone, on her mobile phone, rather than to herself? It was a gloriously sunny Saturday morning – the sun burning gold and round like a new one-pound coin in the sky. The seagulls floated above the quay, strategically placed to target picnicking day-trippers. There were signs up now, erected by the council, warning visitors about the dangers of aggressive seagulls, but they didn't take a blind bit of notice. Neither did the visitors. Tourists were too interested in the twenty-three flavours of ice cream on sale in the ice-cream parlour. Housed in what was once a boatbuilder's shed – when the town had a thriving boatbuilding industry building yachts and dinghies – the parlour was rarely without a queue in summer.

When Marcie suddenly turned her head in Nancy's direction, Nancy ducked, sending Bea flying. She landed on her feet, as cats do, and flopped on the cool kitchen floor, rolling over to show her belly.

'Sorry, no time to play, Bea! Out of the way, Marcie's coming!' she said, picking up a disgruntled William from a sunny spot on the kitchen table. He complained with a meow in a minor key. Elsie, curled up on a kitchen chair, climbed onto the table in his place, basking in his patch of warm sunlight, but Nancy lifted her off too.

'Excuse me, Elsie dear,' she said, 'I'm expecting a guest.'

She placed a bunch of green grapes into a bowl and placed the tulips Marcie had brought her in a vase on the table next to them. Standing back to admire her work, she noted how nervous she felt. Since she'd opened up to Marcie, Nancy had felt a slight shift in her mood. Could it be the beginning of a friendship? The thought made her heart leap. A close friend had seemed out of the question until now, but because Marcie knew everything already, Nancy didn't need to dread the questions about her past. Marcie had taken an interest in Nancy's well-being, and it delighted Nancy that she cared enough to do this.

When the doorbell rang in two short bursts, she ran to the door, almost tripping over Tabitha, whose favourite game was to stretch out like a draught excluder in front of Nancy – be it when she was halfway down the stairs or carrying heavy rubbish bags outside to the bins. Opening the door, expecting to see Marcie, Nancy found Alfie standing there instead, a tiny black kitten's head poking out from his zipped-up hoody. He must have come through the garden, over the collapsed fence. He hopped from foot to foot and looked around him nervously. As if detecting his agitation, two magpies atop a telegraph pole screeched in a raspy chatter. The kitten disappeared inside Alfie's jacket.

'Dad says we can't keep it any longer!' he burst out. 'We've only had him three weeks, but now Mum's gone, we can't waste the money on the cat food or vet bills. Can you take him? Please? I know you like cats.'

'Oh, Alfie,' she said, glancing over his shoulder to see if Marcie was in sight. She wasn't.

'Please?' he said, his eyes filling with tears.

'Don't cry,' said Nancy gently. 'It's okay. Maybe I should go and speak to your dad?'

'No,' Alfie said. 'He'll get mad with me. Please, just take him.'

The kitten poked his head out of Alfie's jumper once again. Nancy's heart melted.

'Come in for a moment,' she said, opening the front door. Alfie rushed into the house and stood still as the stocks in the hallway, his eyes moving from left to right in his head, as he took in the expanse of Nancy's home. She remembered from her own childhood how strange it was to see a person who was usually at school out of school and in their own environment. Incongruous somehow. Glancing down, he unzipped his coat and the kitten flew out.

'This is Batman,' he said. 'My dad got me him a few weeks back but now it's too much for us to keep him—'

Alfie fell silent and took a deep, raggedy breath. 'Dad was going to take him to the Cats Protection centre, but I thought of you. If you look after him, one day I can get him back.'

His eyes flew to the grapes and rested there.

'Please can I have some grapes?' he said.

'Yes,' said Nancy. 'Has Batman had his jabs?'

'Yes, and he has one of those chips, so he can be scanned,' Alfie said. Nancy picked up Batman. In comparison to her other cats, he was absolutely tiny. Batman squeaked a meow and stuck out his tiny pink tongue. Nancy smiled.

'I'll take care of him,' she said. 'Just while you get yourself sorted. I'll have to keep him away from the other cats for a bit though. They might try to fight him.'

Alfie demolished a handful of grapes but kept staring at the front door, as if someone was waiting for him.

'Are you alright, Alfie?' she asked, tickling Batman under the ear. 'You'd better get home or your dad will wonder where you are.'

'That woman is outside,' he said. 'That swimming-pool-house woman. I thought she was going to shout at me again. Is she going to shout?'

At that moment there was a knock at the door and a muffled 'Hello!' A waft of violets, vanilla and iris permeated the door. Nancy smiled reassuringly.

'This is her,' she said. 'She's my friend. She won't shout at you.'

Hearing the word 'friend' escape her lips made Nancy blush. It had been so long since she'd had a friend. Was she speaking out of turn?

Observed by Elsie, Nancy put Batman carefully down on the rug in the living room, closed the door so he couldn't escape and none of the other cats could get in, and let Marcie in. She entered, smiling – and placed her bag down on the hall table, popping her car keys down next to it. The keyring was a large personalised square plastic fob – an option when you order school photographs – with a photograph of Stuart inside. She noticed Alfie had stopped chewing his biscuit and was gawping at the keyring.

'That's my son, Stuart,' said Marcie. 'You might know him from your school? You're probably in the same year. So, I was passing and thought I'd stop by for a chat, Nancy. Thought you might like the company. I didn't realise you already had someone here.'

Marcie was put out, and Nancy tensed. Alfie's jaw had dropped so his half-chewed grapes were visible to all, and he was standing absolutely still. Nancy frowned.

'Alfie has just delivered a kitten to me,' she said. 'I've agreed to take care of it for a while until Alfie's family get sorted out.'

It was as if Alfie's feet were glued to the floor as he continued to stare at the keyring. Nancy cleared her throat.

'I think Alfie might assume you're still angry with him?' she said to Marcie, who was dressed in black. Nancy hoped she had a hair and fluff remover tucked into her bag.

'Not at all,' Marcie said, her eyes flicking from Nancy's face to Alfie's. 'Ancient history.'

Alfie didn't flinch. His complexion had gone from pale to white. He looked like his legs might buckle beneath him any moment. Nancy felt guilty – Marcie must have terrified him when she found him in the swimming pool.

'There's nothing to worry about,' said Nancy, puzzled by Alfie's behaviour. 'Perhaps you should take another few grapes and get back home to your dad? I'll take care of the kitten. Marcie, you go through into the living room, but keep the door pulled to. I'll get us some tea and say goodbye to Alfie. Watch out for the cat hair on those black jeans. Elsie and Ted are moulting.'

'Don't worry, I have my lint roller!' Marcie said.

Alfie grabbed Nancy's hand and yanked her into the kitchen, where William had resettled himself on the kitchen table, his tail draped across the grape bowl. Alfie's face was terror-stricken. He started to tremble as he pointed through the open kitchen door, angrily jabbing his finger into thin air.

'It's him,' he said. 'That's Stuart.'

'And?' said Nancy.

'Stuart is…' mumbled Alfie. 'Stuart is the one who punches me and strangles me and kicks me in the back and takes my crisps and spits on me. Yesterday he told me that when we have swimming lessons at school, he'll try to drown me. He said everyone hates me and wishes I was dead. He says I stink like piss and that I'm a chav.'

Nancy swallowed. The sun suddenly disappeared behind a cloud and the kitchen was cast into shadow. Marcie's son was bullying Alfie?

'Are you sure?' she said. Alfie nodded.

'Definitely sure,' said Alfie, staring at the floor. 'One hundred and ten per cent sure.'

'Nancy?' Marcie called through from the living room. 'This kitten is climbing up your curtains. Do you want me to get it down?'

'No, I don't mind,' Nancy called. 'Kettle's almost boiled! I'll be right through. Make yourself comfortable!'

Her hands were trembling. Nancy forced a smile onto her face and patted Alfie on both shoulders, as if she was plumping up a cushion. She reached into the cupboard and pulled out a plastic bag, into which she stuffed the grapes. Mr Phillips's voice popped into her head, reminding her about procedures for donating food. Boundaries. She handed them to Alfie.

'Let me think about what we should do,' she said. 'You get off home and don't worry. I will help you.'

Batman clung to a curtain with his tiny white claws while Nancy handed Marcie a cup of tea, in a blue porcelain teacup and saucer that had belonged to her father. Marcie took a sip, the cup rattling against the saucer as she placed it down. Nancy caught sight of Marcie's hand fluttering like the wings of a small bird, but Marcie quickly put down the cup and folded her arms, tucking both trembling hands out of sight.

The tinkling sound of the china took Nancy flying back through time, briefly, to perch in her father's old house. He'd insisted on drinking from that teacup, even when his old hands trembled like leaves in the breeze. She cringed at the memory of how she'd treated him after Beatrice had died. Nothing he could do was right. Grief had stolen her kindness for a while. She'd never had the chance to thank him for standing by her.

'Do you mind that lad stopping by here?' said Marcie. 'Isn't that a bit strange? Him coming here? Does his dad mind? I shouldn't think the school would like it.'

'He only popped in to give me the kitten,' said Nancy. 'How can I not help him when he's asking for help? It's not easy for Alfie at the moment, as his mum has left home. They live at the bottom of the garden – their garden is over the fence. We're neighbours really. He's not having the happiest time at school either.'

Nancy stopped short of elaborating on why. Marcie did an upside-down smile – one of those which shows unspoken uncertainty. Nancy's mind was frantic with how to tell Marcie about Stuart. Where are the words for that news? *Your son is making another boy's life utterly miserable. I need to tell the headmaster about what your son is doing. Your son is a bully.* Her stomach churned. Unable to find the words, she watched Batman navigate the curtain rail with skill, hoping that perhaps Alfie had made a mistake and it wasn't Stuart at all.

'We had a therapy session last evening,' Marcie burst out. 'Gerard and I – at great expense.'

Nancy focussed on Marcie, who she sensed was about to tell her something important. She would tell her about Stuart later, when the time was right. The kitten was carefully descending the curtain and climbed up onto the chair beside her, curling into a tiny ball.

'Oh,' said Nancy. 'How did that go?'

Marcie shrugged. 'I did most of the talking,' she said. 'Gerard had one foot out of the door the entire time. He doesn't think it's necessary for him to be there.'

'Doesn't that rather detract from the purpose of marriage counselling?' Nancy asked. 'If only one of you is there?'

'Exactly,' said Marcie. 'The trouble is, he has something on me, something that he won't let go, which is causing problems. We had a dreadful row afterwards! It's a bloody good job we live in a detached house. We go hell for leather when we argue.'

Nancy frowned, confused by Marcie. On the one hand, she seemed like a strong, confident woman; on the other, extremely vulnerable. Producing her hands from her sleeves, she took another sip of her tea. She was still shaking. Marcie reached into her handbag and pulled out a tiny pot of Rescue Remedy. She squirted it on her tongue and smiled briefly at Nancy.

'I don't really need this,' she said. 'I just rather like the taste! Did you find marriage challenging, when you were married? Gerard is not particularly sympathetic when I'm less than one hundred per cent firing on all cylinders. In his mind he's blameless, and that's why he doesn't want to go to therapy. I, on the other hand, am trying to do everything I can to make this work. I'm even having lessons in tapping therapy. It helps you get over your fears. You should try it.'

'I'd like to,' Nancy said. 'You'll have to show me.'

'Okay,' said Marcie, lifting her fingers to her face to demonstrate. 'So if you're feeling anxious, you tap here, and here and here on the meridian tapping points, while thinking about your anxiety and then you "tap them away". See? Have a go.'

Nancy tapped at the points Marcie showed her and smiled.

'Try it when you next feel stressed,' said Marcie. 'Anyway, Nancy, I hope you don't mind that I found Larry's address. Can I ask, why did you separate?'

Nancy opened her mouth to reply, but no sound emerged. She tapped her cheekbones. Marcie laughed.

'I'll butt out, shall I?' Marcie said.

'No, no,' said Nancy, finding her voice. 'It was complicated, really. I was passionately in love with Larry. He was "the one" and all that, for me, but as time went on I realised we wanted different things from life.'

'I understand that, but it's a shame you never speak,' Marcie said. 'I think that would have made Beatrice unhappy – she loved you both so much and hated it when you split up – so, I've been thinking, perhaps you and I should take a trip to see Larry. I would like to see him again too. You were both a part of my own childhood. After Beatrice died, I never saw either of you again. I'd like to see him too.'

Nancy blinked. Hearing that Beatrice had been so upset by her and Larry's separation broke her heart, but the idea of seeing Larry again felt ludicrous.

'I'm beginning to realise that facing the difficult truths in life is the only way to move forward,' said Marcie. 'There's a reason the two of us have met, don't you think?'

'It's too difficult with Larry,' Nancy said. 'I have, over the years, considered contacting him, of course, but when it comes to actually picking up the telephone, I simply can't.' She shook her head. 'I just can't,' she emphasised.

Marcie gave her a small smile. 'Think about it,' she said. 'For Beatrice. He was so easy to find, online. Beatrice would be so pleased.'

Nancy chewed on the inside of her cheek, feeling a myriad of emotions. Breaking the tension, Marcie suddenly stood up and opened her bag, pulling out a selection of paint sample pots.

'I also had a brilliant idea that I could help you decorate. Here, we have Hortense, Milk Thistle and Whisper. Or if you prefer greens, Acorn, Drizzle and Hidey Hole are nice. I'm working part-time at the moment, so we could go together and buy the paint one day?'

'You didn't need to do that,' said Nancy, flustered. The house had been as it was for a long time. The thought of change made her slightly uncomfortable, but Marcie's interest was both startling and flattering.

'I'd really like to do this,' said Marcie. 'This house would be beautiful with a lick of paint, but it's too much to do on your own. If Beatrice were here, she'd be helping you. It's the least I can do for her. I owe her this much.'

Beatrice. *I owe her this much.* Nancy was struck by Marcie's words. It hadn't occurred to Nancy before that perhaps Marcie felt guilt too. A kind of survivor's guilt perhaps? Nancy felt a delicate thread of attachment growing between them strengthen. Nancy had lost her daughter, Marcie had lost her mother. Could they perhaps help one another? Nancy stroked Batman's little paws with her finger. He had bones like dressmaking pins.

'It's… very good of you…' she mumbled. 'I suppose the house is looking quite tired.'

The thoughts of Stuart bullying Alfie and contacting Larry swirled in a dust storm in Nancy's head, and she couldn't make sense of any of it.

'She'd be here in her dungarees probably,' said Marcie, with a laugh. 'Can you imagine?'

An image of Beatrice snapped into Nancy's mind, as clear as if she was actually in the room. The vision took her breath away. Dressed in her favourite dungarees over a red-and-white-striped

T-shirt, Beatrice's arms were tanned. Her hair, the colour of corn, was in plaits. She had on her pretty alphabet bead Beatrice necklace, as always. In her hand, she held a paintbrush and from her lips shone the most glorious smile. Briefly, the sun came out and blazed through the window, making the walls of the living room glow a dazzling red.

Chapter Seventeen

It wasn't long before Nancy witnessed Stuart, with her own eyes, bullying Alfie. At 3.10 p.m. on Friday, when she was leaving the school grounds, she saw Stuart punch Alfie in the back, sending the poor boy ricocheting across the playground. Stuart had then sprinted out of the school gates to his father's waiting car before Nancy could react.

'Alfie!' she called, as he picked himself up off the floor, but Alfie merely glared in her direction before running home himself.

Now she didn't know what to do. Speak to Marcie this weekend or wait until Monday and report what she'd seen to Mr Phillips? Her mind buzzed with difficult questions and so having to feed Sally Mills's cat, Titus, was a welcome relief from her muddled thoughts.

Sally's home was in the centre of town, on a cobbled street not far from the Priory church and quay, bang in the middle of a little collection of pubs, restaurants and takeaway food shops, where office workers congregated to toast the weekend. Though it was early evening, the sun was still very warm, so people sat at tables outside bathed in golden light – women with bare, sunburned shoulders holding fishbowl glasses of wine, and men in short sleeves with their shirt collars open.

'Shouldn't have worn this cardigan,' Nancy muttered to herself as she walked past the revellers, clutching her bag close. Striding through the streets with purpose, she walked as if she had no time to stop. Not that anyone noticed, she realised. If she suddenly smashed a hammer into a shop window and stole a television, and any of the pub-goers had been asked to give an eyewitness description of her for a photofit, she would bet that none of them could. She felt she had become quite invisible – but hadn't that been her wish? To live under the radar.

Occasionally, though, she longed to revert to the person she had once been. Stopping briefly outside a dress shop, she dared to look at the price tag on a red dress displayed in the window. She baulked at the price, knowing she could make one herself for half the cost. She had sewn a red dress or two for herself in the past. She'd been wearing one on the first day she met Larry. Wouldn't it be wonderful to make one again? One that complimented her figure now that she was in her fifties. She sighed. Why would she ever need a red dress? No doubt it was a ridiculous thought.

Head down, she continued on her way and arriving at the address, a top-floor flat above an art shop, in a listed building on a site which, centuries ago, was once a hospital for lepers, Nancy entered the building and went upstairs to the flat, quietly unlocking the front door, to find Titus sitting on the doormat, purring like a drill. He was an enormous cream cat, a Ragamuffin breed, with beautiful long hair and paws as big as a baby's hands.

'I knew you'd be hungry,' she said, patting his head, her eyes running over a wicker basket of boys' school shoes and women's sandals and a pair of men's running shoes under a selection of coats and bags hanging from hooks. In the hallway, there were numerous plants on a telephone table and shelf: aspidistra and fern, aloe, spider plants and a collection of cactuses in small, colourful terracotta pots. From the ceiling hung a paper lantern lampshade in orange, which matched the flecks of colour in the plush wool carpet. Halfway along the corridor was a stained-glass window, which cast rainbow colours onto the white wall. It was carefully and thoughtfully styled. Nancy slipped off her shoes.

'Where's the kitchen, Titus?' she said quietly, following the cat up the hallway to search for the kitchen, where she expected a note – and the cat food – to be.

Pushing open a door that was pulled to, she froze and gasped. Her hand flew to her mouth. On the far side of a massive living room was the disturbing sight of a half-naked Gerard Loveday making love to a half-naked woman – who Nancy quickly calculated was Sally – on the sofa. Titus stared. Everyone shrieked. Nancy instantly reversed out of the living room and ran towards the front door.

Pulling on her shoes and struggling with the lock for a moment, she flung it open before running down the stairs, one hand on the banister, and down into the lobby area. She was propelled through time to when she discovered Larry and Barney in the picture library at the *Post*, and her legs gave way. She gritted her teeth, willing herself to get out of the building so she could blot the image from her mind, but she couldn't unsee what she had seen. Marcie. Poor Marcie. What about Marcie?

Before she reached the front door, her bag caught on the ornamental end of the banister, preventing her from escaping before a barefoot Gerard caught up with her, his skin dewy from his physical exertion on the sofa. His belt hung from his trousers like a dead snake, his shirt half-unbuttoned. Nancy didn't know where to look. Repelled and desperately hurt for Marcie's sake, she refused to meet his eye. He reached out his palm towards her, as if she was a wild cat that might bite him. She certainly felt tempted.

'Ms Jones,' he said calmly. 'Our paths keep crossing at the most inconvenient times. Marcie has told me all about you and how you know one another, so I'm very sorry you had to see this. It's very complicated, as I'm sure you'll understand life can be…'

He pushed his hair back behind his ears. Behind him arrived a woman, wrapped in a big fluffy white dressing gown, with her hands pushed deep into the pockets.

'Sally is a friend,' Gerard insisted. 'She's going away tonight for the weekend with her two sons, as you know. They're with their dad at the moment and I popped in to talk to her about a business matter before she left. We had a glass of wine and things got a little out of hand.'

Nancy knew she was supposed to say something. 'Spare me the details' or similar. But she couldn't speak.

'Why were you here?' said Sally. 'I said to feed Titus on Saturday. Did Marcie send you to spy?'

Gerard sighed. 'Did she?' he said angrily.

'No, no, of course not,' Nancy uttered. 'I just thought the cat would be hungry. You said you were going away for the weekend. I thought that meant he would be hungry. I was thinking of the cat. I just wanted a walk… something to do… such a lovely evening…'

Sally and Gerard exchanged a doubtful glance. Gerard grabbed Nancy's hand.

'If you care about Marcie at all, you must not tell her about this,' he said. 'She won't cope with this.'

He released her hand and, without saying anything else, returned upstairs to the flat, trailed by Sally – apparently Marcie's friend. Turning to leave, her bag tightly under her arm, Nancy paused and rested her forehead against the wall, horrified by what had just happened.

'Do you still want me to feed Titus?' she called up the stairs.

Sally's head popped over the banister. 'No, I bloody well don't,' she said. 'Leave my keys on the doormat! I will not be recommending your service!'

Nancy placed the keys on the mat and opened the front door, closing it quietly behind her. Outside in the street, a beautiful sunset had turned the clouds apricot. Laughter erupted from the groups of office workers. Shaken and deflated, Nancy took a deep breath and walked to the quay. Her mind reeled. It was full of information that concerned Marcie. Information she wished she never had. Stuart was bullying Alfie. Gerard was having an affair.

'What shall I do?' Nancy said to nobody. Marcie had come into her life unexpectedly. They were united by Beatrice's death and

Nancy felt strangely protective of Marcie. She didn't want to lose her as soon as she'd found her – but did she have a moral duty to tell her about this? Was it possible that Marcie might never speak to her again? It was widely known that the messenger was routinely shot and killed.

Nancy stopped at a bench and sat down. Her heart was going too fast. She told herself to calm down. What was the best thing to do? She knew that she couldn't ignore what she'd just witnessed – that wouldn't be right. She would have to speak to Gerard, tell him to admit to Marcie what he'd been up to. Then she'd have the facts. She deserved the facts. If only she'd known earlier about Larry and Barney, maybe her life would have turned out differently.

What was wrong with people? Why were some intent on destroying other people's lives? Or perhaps it was more complicated than that. Perhaps all marriages were complicated. Who really knew what went on in other people's lives, behind closed doors and curtains. Did you ever really know anyone?

'Maybe it's better not to try,' Nancy sighed.

Out of the corner of her eye she noticed Terence, the painter, abruptly stand up from his seat and grab his canvas from his easel. He hurled it onto the pavement and stuck his foot through it, ripping a great hole in the middle of his painting. His hair stood up wildly from his head. Nancy held her hand to her chest. He stamped on it once more for good measure and kicked the broken pieces, before reluctantly picking it up and throwing it in a litterbin. Obviously raging, he threw his tubes of paints and brushes into a plastic carrier bag and collapsed his easel before stomping off down the road with it under his arm. Nancy felt desolate. Terence was a beacon of hope. She longed to run after him or call out that his paintings were very good and that him being there each day, trying hard to create something and never giving up, was remarkable.

Opening her handbag, she pulled out a piece of paper and a pen, scribbling a note saying: *Never stop painting!* She walked over to the bandstand, where he usually set up his equipment, and tucked the note into the railings, hoping that by some small miracle he would read it, the next time he came. If he ever returned.

On the way home, she chose a different route, avoiding the people in the bars and restaurants, the red dress. She longed to be at home, with her cats, so that she could think about what to do. But when she arrived home, Gerard had got there first. Waiting by her front door, he stood in a strange pose, with one leg up on the wall, as if kicking the house. His expression was thunderous. As she approached him, her heart thudded. Ted appeared, rising out of the long grass like a stalking tiger, and ran towards her, meowing loudly. She stroked Ted's head, ignoring Gerard.

'Don't look now, Ted,' she said, 'but there's an idiot on the doorstep.'

On reaching him, she didn't stop, but instead walked straight past and pushed her key into the lock.

'Ms Jones,' he said. 'I meant it when I said you need to keep this to yourself. Do you understand how important this is? I need your word that you won't tell Marcie. We're going through something at the moment and this would be too much for her.'

Nancy imagined herself answering back and telling him what she really thought of him, but she opened the door and tried to close it before he could say anything else. He put his foot in the way of the closing door.

'You *have* to promise me,' he said. His face was red, the veins in his head pulsating like jellyfish tentacles. 'Promise me, you idiot woman!'

Nancy was frightened, but also furious.

'I will not,' she said. 'You must tell her yourself, or I will.'

'Keep your bloody nose out of my business!' he shouted.

Gerard's shout gained the interest of Alan, the neighbour, whose head, in a rare sighting, popped out from behind an azalea.

'Nancy?' he called over the fence. 'Is everything alright over there? Is that man bothering you?'

Gerard suddenly shifted his foot from the door and reversed down the steps, turning on his heel, his fists clenched. Head bowed, he marched down the garden path, pushing bushes and branches aside, snarling and swearing at the neighbour and leaving the gate swinging in his wake.

'Fine yes, thank you!' she squeaked to the neighbour, before quietly closing the door and slumping onto the floor, in the exact same position, she realised, as Marcie had been sitting in when she had first clapped eyes on her.

Elsie, Tabitha and Bea ran towards her, climbing onto her lap, kneading her legs and purring loudly, pushing their bodies close to hers, circling until comfortable. Stroking their soft fur in the gloomy hallway, Nancy felt grateful for their affection. She firmly believed they knew when she needed their love. They were also hungry.

Pushing herself up into a standing position, shaken by the evening's events, she went into the kitchen and, without turning on the lights, gave the cats their dinner. Though she was slowly introducing Batman to her other cats, he was still nervous at mealtime, so she moved his saucer away from the crowd, to give him space. Staring out of the window, while the cats concentrated on their saucers of food, she caught sight of the beautiful white cat confidently tightrope-walking the fence again, his or her tail upright, boldly approaching the house. She opened the window, silently beckoning him or her to bring his or her good luck to the door.

'Come on, come here, kitty,' she called in a high voice. 'Come closer.' The cat stopped and stared at her for a long moment, as if communicating a message, before turning away.

Chapter Eighteen

Something had happened to Nancy's tongue. One of the cats must have got it, because she couldn't find the words to tell Marcie of Gerard's infidelity, or about Stuart's bullying ways. Sitting in Marcie's car – on their way to Homebase to purchase paint – waiting at the traffic lights and staring out at billboards advertising the tiger enclosure at Marwell Zoo, Nancy was silent. She pushed the cuff of her sleeve up and down, foot tapping in the footwell. Her hands were clammy and her mouth dry. She glanced at Marcie and felt her stomach somersault again. The time had to be right, the environment appropriate. You couldn't just blurt out huge, life-shattering things while waiting for the traffic lights to change, could you?

'What a dickhead,' Marcie muttered, tucking her dark hair behind her ear, revealing a gold earring in the shape of a lightning bolt. She was having a battle of some description with the male driver of the black car in the next lane. Drum and bass pumped out of his car's speakers at such volume Nancy's skeleton vibrated. People in other cars pretended not to notice, but Marcie was taking issue with him. She lowered her window.

'Is your music loud enough?' Marcie shouted. The male driver, who looked about fifteen years old, didn't acknowledge Marcie, so she turned up the volume on her own car stereo until it drowned out his. Nancy couldn't stop herself putting her hands over her ears. She wasn't used to such loud noise and it made the situation feel even more disjointed. Marcie then lowered all the windows, so the other driver couldn't fail to hear the ear-piercing crescendo of Puccini's *Madame Butterfly* playing on the stereo – Gerard's choice. Nancy sucked in her breath as the opera singer's voice swept through the car. Even with her hands over her ears the song made every hair on her body stand on end and tears spring instantly to her eyes, as if the music was a giant spoon stirring up her insides.

'Bloody men!' Marcie hissed, stamping her foot on the accelerator, revving up her engine. 'They have such an arrogant sense of entitlement.'

The man gave her the one-finger salute and so, the second the lights turned green, she put her foot flat on the floor and raced ahead of him, breaking the speed limit by at least 20mph, with a cowgirl 'yee-haw' as she left him for dust. Nancy clenched her teeth, resisting the temptation to close her eyes tightly shut. There was a wildness to Marcie – a deep-seated streak of anger or frustration – that unsettled Nancy.

'Idiot!' Marcie muttered, continuing to drive too quickly. 'Arrogant fool.'

Nancy worried for the lives of slow-moving pedestrians – or a cat that might run across the road at the wrong moment.

Screeching to a stop in the car park, Marcie turned off the engine and slumped her shoulders with a sigh. The disturbing image of Gerard and Sally exploded into Nancy's head once more and her heart squeezed. Perhaps she should just say it now?

Marcie grinned at her, raising her eyebrows.

'Marcie, I—' started Nancy, but Marcie interrupted.

'I know I was driving too fast,' said Marcie, resting her hand on Nancy's arm. 'I shouldn't let other people bother me. I've always been too quick to flame. I see red mist! Let's go inside and choose some paints.'

'I don't know how to say—' Nancy tried again. But Marcie shook her head and raised her palms, interrupting her again.

'I don't want you to thank me,' she said. 'As I explained, I want to get to know you better. It feels right, after all these years, to have met you again. Beatrice would have liked us to be friends, I'm one hundred per cent sure of it.'

'Marcie, I…' Nancy started.

'What?' Marcie said. 'What is it?'

Nancy took a deep breath. Stalled. Another breath. 'I… I… saw a red dress in a shop in town and it made me think I'd like to try making myself a dress again,' she gabbled, blushing madly at her own inadequacy. 'I've got a pattern at home; I just need the fabric. Perhaps we should go to the fabric shop, in town, after this. I mean, if you have time?'

Marcie reached over and took Nancy's hand in her own. She squeezed it.

'I'd love that,' she said. 'What a fantastic idea. You should definitely start sewing again.'

Nancy pushed her head back into the headrest, feeling hopeless. But would there ever be the right moment to throw another meteorite into Marcie's life? Was it really her place? Perhaps their marriage was their business, and she was only poking her nose in where it wasn't wanted? But what if Gerard continued to be unfaithful to Marcie and thus deceive her? She couldn't stand by and let that happen.

'Come on,' Marcie said. 'Let's raid Homebase.'

In the paint aisle, Nancy was overwhelmed by choice. The paints had multiplied since the last time she'd looked. She stared blankly at a family tree of whites: Beige White, Canvas White, Cream White, Dream White, Maypole White, Old English White, Sail White, Serene White, Sherbet White, Stone White, Summer White, White Glove and on, stretching across two shelves. How could there be so many shades of the same colour?

Marcie paced up and down the aisle, pausing occasionally to check colour charts or compare and contrast paint brands, unaware of Nancy's conundrum. With just a few words, she was going to destroy Marcie's marriage.

'I think Sunrise would work well in your hallway,' said Marcie, holding up a tin of yellow paint. 'It's cheerful but not too bright. I wanted to paint our house this colour, but Gerard wanted something more neutral. Calming. He's very into neutral and all that decluttering movement. He's a slave to minimalism.'

Nancy thought of the room she'd discovered in Marcie's house, filled with Marcie's belongings. She opened her mouth to say something – anything – but Marcie was already on her way to the till, a 2.5 litre tin of emulsion in each hand, lifting them up and down on the way, as if they were weights. Now, she was chatting away to the sales assistant and Nancy loathed herself for not knowing what to do for the best. She despised her inability to confront difficult issues head-on. Who was she protecting in this situation? Marcie or herself? The realisation that she was actually protecting Gerard made her sick.

Walking out of the shop, Nancy grabbed Marcie's arm and made her stop.

'Marcie, wait…' she started, feeling the blood drain from her face.

'Fabric!' Marcie said. 'Come on, let's go and see what there is. I might ask you to knock up a dress for me too.'

Nancy sighed. It was useless. She would have to give up trying for the moment.

With the paint left in the boot of Marcie's car, Marcie linked her arm through Nancy's and they walked into Christchurch. It reminded Nancy of being a schoolgirl, walking home from school with her best friend, a bag of sherbet in her pocket. For a split second, Nancy wondered if they looked to strangers like mother and daughter. A shiver of dread ran through her – if she told her about Gerard, would she lose Marcie forever?

'I'll need two or three metres,' Nancy said, when they entered the shop. 'It's been so long since I've been in a fabric shop…'

She stared longingly at the shelves of fabrics, neatly organised by fabric type: dressmaking, upholstery, curtain and craft. Her eyes travelled over the cottons, trimmings, zippers, buttons, tailor's chalk, scissors and sewing kits. She felt like a child in a sweetshop, running her fingers gently over a bolt of velvet. Smiling at Marcie, she lifted a bolt of red jersey fabric from the shelf and an unfamiliar feeling of excitement coursed through her.

'This is perfect,' Nancy said. 'It would hang really well. I've got a pattern with a cowl neck at home.'

'I wouldn't know where to start,' Marcie said, shrugging. 'Are you going to buy it? You should.'

Nancy chewed her lip. One part of her longed to sit down at her sewing machine and create a beautiful dress, but when would she wear it? Those days of dressing up and wearing red dresses were long gone. She pushed the bolt of fabric back onto the shelf.

'No,' Nancy said. 'When would I wear it?'

'We could go out somewhere together,' said Marcie. 'I'd like that.'

An idea popped into Nancy's head.

'Actually, I have been invited to a hen-party thing by someone at work,' she said. 'Perhaps you could come to that with me?'

'Okay, sounds like a deal,' said Marcie. 'I could do with something fun to look forward to. Have a drink. Enjoy myself.'

A shadow passed over Marcie's face and Nancy frowned. She was suddenly reminded of what she had to tell Marcie and she sighed, preparing to leave the shop empty-handed.

'Come on, Nancy,' Marcie said. 'Buy the fabric. You'll enjoy making it.'

Marcie grabbed Nancy's hand and gave it a squeeze. Nancy wished Marcie would stop being so kind. She felt a lump form in the back of her throat. She was beginning to love Marcie, but she was going to have to break her heart.

'When you've paid we'll go back to mine, so I can pick up some painting clothes, then we'll go to yours and get on with the decorating,' Marcie said.

It was hot in the shop and Marcie pushed up the sleeves of her long-sleeved top, revealing her forearms. She flapped her arms around in front of her face, as a makeshift fan, and blew out and upwards, sending her fringe flying up in the air. Nancy noticed small marks or bruises, like smudges of purple chalk on her forearms. It reminded her, with a horrible jolt, of when she'd seen those marks on Larry's neck, all those years ago.

'How did you get those bruises?' Nancy asked quietly. Marcie glanced down at her arms and quickly rolled down her sleeves.

'In the warehouse at work,' she said. 'I was doing some lifting and the ladder closed on my wrist. My job's quite physical at times.'

Marcie was laughing but Nancy saw it, the slight flicker in her eye, the high-alert, stiffening of her back.

While Nancy paid for the fabric, cotton and a zip, Marcie waited outside, claiming she needed air.

'Hot flushes in your twenties; is that a thing now?' she joked, but Nancy saw vulnerability in her eyes. Secrets.

Marcie was quieter on the car journey to Evelyn Road, and Nancy willed herself to speak, yet she still couldn't force the words from her lips. In Marcie's kitchen, she drank black coffee and listened to Marcie's ideas for the redecoration of Nancy's house.

'You again, Nancy,' said Gerard, suddenly appearing sock-footed in the kitchen. He walked over to Marcie, looped his arm around her shoulder and kissed her. Gerard was followed by Stuart, who didn't say hello. It was the first time Nancy had seen him close up and he looked far less intimidating than she had expected from Alfie's accounts. Ginger hair, freckles and a wiry frame, by the way he swung himself around the kitchen, he seemed shy and sullen. Marcie wriggled free of Gerard's embrace and pulled Stuart to her, to give him a big kiss. His cheeks flamed in irregular patches, as if he'd been slapped.

'Mum!' he complained, wiping her kiss from his cheek. Marcie tried to laugh, but Nancy felt his rejection stab Marcie in the heart.

'Excuse me for a moment,' said Marcie. 'Just popping to the loo.'

Stuart also left the room and so Nancy was alone with Gerard. He poured himself coffee, his gold watch slipping a little on his hairy wrist, and leaned against the kitchen counter, taking big glugs from his cup. Nancy could not help but notice his massive Adam's apple protruding from his neck like an elbow. He was so male, somehow. The A in alpha. Trembling in her seat, she felt bewildered and embarrassed and furious by what she knew about him.

'You haven't told Marcie, have you?' she mumbled. 'You know you must, or I will.'

'I meant what I said,' Gerard said very quietly and coldly. 'Marcie must *never* know about Sally. If our marriage breaks down, then she'll lose the house. You know she's already having therapy, for all her "issues". Have you ever seen her doing that ridiculous tapping? We pay a fortune for a woman to come here every week and teach her to tap. Nice work if you can get it.'

'It's rather effective,' muttered Nancy, 'actually.'

He gave a derisive little laugh. It was the way he acted out the quotation marks when he said 'issues' that affronted Nancy. She raised her chin and glared right back at him, feeling increasingly protective of Marcie. Her entire body trembled. She put down her coffee cup and climbed off the breakfast bar stool and picked up her bag. At that moment, Marcie swept back into the room, grinning.

'I didn't realise the time; I'd better go,' said Nancy. Marcie frowned, picked up her car keys, swinging them around her finger.

'I'll give you a lift,' she said. 'No argument.'

Back at home, Nancy told herself it was now or never. Gerard was clearly not going to tell her himself. They were in the garden, Marcie stirring a pot of paint with a long stick to combine the binders and pigment, humming as she worked. Bees buzzed lazily, and William slunk in and out of Nancy's legs, giving her moral support. Nancy now felt certain Marcie would want to know all the facts about her own marriage. If Marcie were Beatrice, she'd want her to be armed with all the information about her husband. *Get on with it*, she thought. Tabitha lay on her back in a sunny spot, warming her undercarriage, playing dead. Garden birds observed her, nervously dipping into an abandoned, water-filled Belfast sink to wash their feathers.

'I've done something a bit naughty,' said Marcie, not looking at Nancy, throwing Nancy off-track. 'But you mustn't be cross. My intention was good.' She lifted her face to the sun, briefly closing her eyes. 'Isn't it hot?' she said. 'We should go for a swim one of these days.'

'What?' said Nancy, her mind racing. 'What have you done?'

'You'll find out soon enough,' said Marcie, opening her eyes and tapping her nose.

Nancy was confused but pushed Marcie's comments aside and focussed. She had a sense of foreboding, already feeling Marcie's absence from her life.

'How well do you know Sally?' Nancy began, her voice wobbling. Marcie paused from stirring the paint and went very still. She looked up at Nancy and narrowed her eyes.

'Why?' Marcie said, a nervous smile playing on her lips. 'Her son is pals with Stuart. We've been out for a glass of wine a few times. She's an architect, very intelligent. She drew up the plans for the new housing estate on the edge of town. We sometimes work with her. Did you feed her cat the other day? Hasn't she got the most beautiful flat? I could be happy living there.'

Nancy nodded. Her hands trembled as she placed the unopened can of paint on the ground. Above, a lone cloud entered, stage left, concealing the sun. She cleared her throat.

'Marcie, I've got something to tell you which is going to be hard for you to hear. I saw Gerard and Sally together,' said Nancy, 'in Sally's flat.'

Marcie stared at her blankly.

'In Sally's flat?' Marcie said. 'When? What do you mean, you *saw* them?'

'When I fed the cat,' Nancy said quietly. 'I arrived, and, unbeknownst to me, they were there too. They were being intimate, on the sofa. Marcie, they were having sex! Gerard pleaded with me not to tell you; he said it would break you, but I couldn't not be honest with you. I knew you would rather know the truth.'

'That can't be true,' said Marcie immediately. Nancy blinked.

'It is true. I saw them with my own eyes. And while I'm telling you this,' babbled Nancy, 'I need to also tell you that Stuart is bullying Alfie, the boy who lives over my fence. I know this must be a shock, a dreadful shock, but it's all true. I haven't known when to say it to you or how to.'

'Why would you want to tell me these things now?' Marcie said faintly.

Marcie stepped backwards, steadying herself on the trunk of an apple tree. She blinked rapidly, then narrowed her eyes at Nancy.

'Stuart wouldn't do that,' said Marcie. 'He wouldn't hurt a fly. He's a gentle thing.'

'He's hit Alfie several times,' said Nancy, 'and apparently he steals Alfie's lunch. I haven't wanted to tell you, but I can't leave it any longer – I'm sorry.'

Marcie shook her head.

'I don't believe you,' Marcie said. 'You must have the wrong child and you must have made a mistake with Gerard. That's my family you're talking about, my boys – my life, for God's sake.'

'I'm telling you the truth,' said Nancy. 'I know it must be hard to hear. I know your life must feel like the bottom has fallen out of it, but, as you've previously said to me, these things are better confronted and dealt with.'

Marcie let out a guffaw, but in a bitter way. 'Are you jealous or something?' she said, swiping at a tear that had escaped her eye. 'Or are you trying to punish me in some strange way for what happened with Beatrice? Are you angry it was her and not me?'

Nancy was horrified, her heart racing. The back of her throat was painful.

'No,' she said, 'of course not. Why would I want to punish you? You're my friend! Beatrice's friend. I wanted you to know the truth. I hate that Gerard is doing this to you. How could he? A beautiful, lovely young woman like you? If you were my daughter, I'd—'

'I'm not your daughter though, am I? So, you waited for how long to tell me this?' she said. 'How long has this been going on?'

Nancy shrugged and shook her head. 'I don't know,' she whispered. 'He threatened me not to tell you, and I might as well say it, I'm worried about those bruises on your arms. Did Gerard hurt you, physically? Marcie, you don't have to put on an act. If you're in difficulty, you can talk to me. I would never judge you.'

William sat down by Nancy's feet, as if he could sense the tension. Marcie glared as she slowly shook her head in disbelief. Nancy shivered –Marcie looked like she wanted to kill her.

'You know what? You can paint your own fucking house,' Marcie said, throwing the paintbrush at Nancy so hard it whacked her cheek. 'You just want to ruin my life because your own life is a load of shit. I don't know what I was thinking of trying to be kind to you!'

'No, no, Marcie, I—' said Nancy, raising her hand to her face, chasing after Marcie as she quickly marched into the house and grabbed her handbag and car keys. Nancy hated confrontation. She was no good at being angry, or at being shouted at. Even as a child, the warning 'if you carry on like this, I will lose my temper', was enough to stop her in her tracks. She followed Marcie as she flew down the garden path, sleek hair swinging, the intoxicating fragrance of iris and vanilla in the air.

'Damn it!' Nancy said as Marcie jumped into her car and roared off down the road, without glancing back. Nancy kicked the gate.

She'd handled it so badly. She was completely hopeless. Marcie was furious with her.

Sighing heavily, Nancy folded her arms and closed her eyes, before returning to the house, where she carefully put the lid on the paint and pushed the pots into the corner of the hallway, where they'd probably stay forever.

'Elsie,' she said, picking up the cat from the stair she was resting on. 'Why do I get everything so muddled up? I've ruined everything!'

Elsie meowed. Tears slipped down Nancy's face as she went over her conversation with Marcie in her head. She kissed Elsie's paw, but Elsie was clearly also irritated with Nancy because for no apparent reason, she stuck her teeth into Nancy's hand.

'Ouch!' Nancy shrieked and dropped Elsie from her arms, waving her hand up and down, before rubbing the punctured skin, cheek stinging from where the paintbrush had landed.

So that was that, she thought, her heart twisting painfully in her chest; she had lost someone else. She sat on the bottom stair, where Elsie had been, and William climbed up onto her lap. She stroked his fur, remembering the day she picked up Bea, Tabitha and William as kittens from the Cat Rescue centre. The fosterer had explained that the three kittens had been dumped in a box on a building site and that it was just a stroke of luck that the builder who found them had looked in the box before throwing it into a skip.

'But I will get her back,' she whispered, 'if it's the last thing I damn well do.'

Chapter Nineteen

Nancy worried for days and nights about her decision to tell Marcie about Gerard. Perhaps it had been the wrong thing to do. Perhaps it was none of her business. She hadn't been able to sleep, and during those sleepless nights she had dusted off her sewing machine and made a red dress out of the fabric she'd bought. A beautiful creation, which hung perfectly on her slim frame, Nancy wished she could show it to Marcie, but that was out of the question. Repeatedly bringing up Marcie's number on her Nokia, but never pressing 'call', she didn't know what to do next. She hoped, with her whole heart, that Marcie would get in touch and so, when an email pinged into her inbox at work one morning with 'Marcie Jennings' in the subject line, her heart sang. But, after scanning the words and reading out loud in an almost whisper, Nancy felt faint.

Nancy,

Marcie Jennings contacted me to tell me you had bumped into one another. Small world! She insists that she would like the three of us to meet up again – says that she wants to talk to us both about our beloved Beatrice. It's difficult for me to leave Hastings at the moment, but you are both welcome here a week on Saturday. It has been many years and though we have not spoken, I have thought about you often, hoped that you had remarried and had more children. I would like to see you again. It might be our last chance before I head off to San Francisco! I have copied in Marcie too. How strange it will be to see you again. Larry.

Larry. Nancy rested her hand on her heart, thinking that it might just burst out of her chest. She scanned the email again, desperately trying not to let Emma and Frances see how agitated she was. She hadn't spoken to him in years and now he was suggesting they meet? For a brief moment, she felt Larry was actually there, his radiant young self, in front of her. What was he like to hold on to? She remembered exactly. Warm, firm, strong, alive, pulsating with energy and restless determination. He had smelled faintly of newspaper print, roll-ups and pubs, but with minty fresh breath, from the Extra Strong mints he munched.

She read the email again, this time noting the absence of To or Dear, or any Love to finish it with. He had, however, said he'd thought about her often. How often was often? she wondered. Every day? Once a year? He'd written it might be the last chance for them to meet before he headed off to San Francisco. Was that alluding to his youthful dreams to adventure around the world? Was he poking fun at himself and referring to a shared experience, or was he actually leaving the country?

Trying to control her breathing, she began typing but the words leaped about the screen. Who would have thought it would be so hard to write to the man she'd married and had a child with?

Larry,

I have thought about you and Beatrice, every day

Larry,

No, I haven't had another relationship, let alone got married or had more children. How could I ever replace the one we had?

Larry,

Are you really going to San Francisco? Can I come too?

Deleting the words, before starting afresh, before deleting again, she squeezed shut her eyes and closed down the email. She had no idea what to say. How could she go to see him in Hastings? She thought about Marcie and her decision to take it upon herself to write to Larry, despite Nancy saying she couldn't face seeing him – a bold move. Was this what she'd meant by being naughty? So, it was perfectly okay for Marcie to meddle in Nancy's life and contact Larry and insist she confront the past, but not the other way around?

And what could Marcie want to talk to Larry and Nancy about, concerning Beatrice? Perhaps she wanted to buy a plaque for a bench or remember her in some way and she wanted their approval. But all of that could be done by email or phone. Nancy sighed. She needed to see Marcie again, *wanted* to see Marcie, but suspected that Marcie was busy hating her.

Opening up the email again and pulling Marcie's address from Larry's email, she quickly typed her a message.

PLEASE MARCIE, RING ME! WE NEED TO TALK! in her most urgent uppercase.

'Nancy!' said Emma from behind her, making Nancy leap off her seat.

'Yes,' she said, spinning round.

'Tell me you're coming tonight,' said Emma, 'aren't you?'

Nancy had completely forgotten about Emma's party. Larry's email had left her wrong-footed, restless and unsettled. Her argument with Marcie had made her feel confused and lonely. She didn't have the energy to make up an excuse.

'Yes,' she found herself saying. 'Yes, I'll come.'

'Good!' said Emma. 'George will be pleased.'

Emma's wink did not escape Nancy, but she ignored it. Her mind was on Larry's email. She read it several times over before the end of the school day, feeling increasingly enraged and oddly powerless. Marcie had cooked up this situation and now she felt at a loss about what she should do. She would have to reply tomorrow.

Gathering her bag, ready to go home, she was thoroughly distracted when Emma reminded her of the evening's plans.

'Seven p.m.,' Emma instructed. 'Arriba!'

Nancy lifted the edges of her mouth into a watery smile and nodded.

Chapter Twenty

Nancy stared at the red dress. It looked like a stranger was standing in her wardrobe, or a version of Nancy from the dim and distant past that she no longer recognised. As a young woman, she had wanted people to notice her. Now, nobody did. She had been foolish to make the dress – and had only done so because Marcie had said she'd join her at Arriba! if she did.

Nancy knew, after their dreadful argument, that Marcie wouldn't come, but there was one, hopelessly optimistic, per cent of her that thought Marcie might still turn up. But even if she did, what would Nancy say about Marcie's decision to contact Larry? Her stomach plummeted. Larry's email, pinging out of the past like that, had totally thrown her.

'Oh, what shall I do?' she said to Elsie, stroking the cat's head. Elsie yawned.

Nancy tried to imagine herself walking into the bar in the red dress; ordering a cocktail – something like a Manhattan or a Long Island iced tea – which would come adorned with a paper umbrella or a sparkler. She'd join the others and make conversation about relationships and work. They'd laugh about school matters: the recent performance by the woodwind group, where none of the young musicians could blow a single note in tune. The audience's shoulders had been visibly rising and falling as they silently suppressed their laughter. By the end of it, everyone in the room, including the children and teachers, were in fits of giggles.

But that wasn't going to happen, because she wasn't going to go. She closed the door on the red dress and sat on the very edge of the bed, hunched over. Marcie wouldn't turn up – she hated Nancy's guts. If she did go she would sit on the edge of the group, leaning in to try to hear snippets of the conversation, paralysed by their intimate discussions of love and relationships. Someone might turn to her and ask about her private life – and her mind would empty of words.

She picked at a piece of fluff on the duvet. Ted stared down at her from the top of the wardrobe in sympathy. 'I'll stay here with you,' she told Elsie, who purred.

She suddenly heard Marcie's voice in her head. 'You should be out and about enjoying yourself.'

It sounded simple enough, but old habits die hard. She hadn't been to the pub in years. But you can't hide forever. Even when you put years and distance between you and the events that sent your life spinning out of control, it's all still there, etched into your memory.

'For goodness' sake, I'm going to make myself go,' she said as William, sick of her indecision, sharpened his claws on a wicker basket in preparation for a night of hunting or fighting neighbouring cats who dared to venture into his territory. Nancy stared at him. If only he'd had a kinder start in life – and hadn't been callously dumped in a cardboard box – perhaps he'd be less aggressive.

Flinging open the wardrobe door, she pulled the red dress off the hanger. Her functional, utilitarian underwear was not suitable really – when she was a dressmaker underwear had been a crucial consideration – but there was nothing much she could do about that now. Slipping the dress over her head, she zipped it up and looked at her reflection. She had done a good job with the dress; it fitted her perfectly. She took a deep breath. It was now or never. Pushing her wispy hair into combs and dabbing a little mascara onto her eyelashes, she said goodbye to the cats and left the house; Elsie settling down on the doormat, slavishly awaiting her return, Batman safely curled up on the top bookshelf, William foraging through the undergrowth in search of unwitting mice to torture. 'Leave those poor creatures alone,' she told him. 'What have they ever done to you?'

Walking into town, she couldn't get Larry's email out of her mind. He had said he'd like to see her again, a week on Saturday, to be precise. Would he really? Tomorrow she would reply and put an end to it all. Yet…

Nearing the bar, she grew apprehensive and her pace slowed. She felt too noticeable in her red dress. Did she look ridiculous? She probably did. She definitely had more in common with the old woman from that poem she used to read to Beatrice – the one who wore purple with a red hat and who went out in her slippers and ate two pounds of sausages in one go. 'Warning' it was called. Beatrice had loved it, even at her young age.

From across the road she recognised the group from St Joseph's framed in the window of Arriba! Industrial-style lights hung on long colourful flexes from the ceiling, over wooden tables. Copper saucepans and strings of dried garlic hung in garlands over the diners' heads. Emma had on a bride-to-be silk sash and a lace veil, pushed back at a madcap angle over her head. The women and George sat in a neat huddle – and she couldn't imagine where she could possibly sit. Behind them perhaps, like on a bus. Suddenly the group broke out into laughter at something. Now halfway across the road, she began muttering to herself. 'I can't go in, I just can't go in,' and decided to go home before anyone noticed.

Quickly, she trotted along the pavement, retracing her footsteps towards home, when she felt a hand on her arm. She spun around.

'I thought it was you,' said George, pulling off his cap, a little out of breath. He smiled. 'Where do you think you're going? You need to come and help me out. I'll get eaten alive if I stay there on my own for much longer.'

Nancy felt desperately embarrassed. She opened and closed her mouth.

'I have a headache,' she spat out. 'And so I thought I should get an early night instead of coming in. I also think I might have left the iron on—'

George glanced at her red dress appreciatively. He smiled kindly and reached out his hand towards her.

'Come with me,' he said. 'I know Emma will be pleased to see you. It'll be a relief for me to have someone to talk to. I can tell you all about my allotment. I've a glut of cucumbers at the moment – they're coming out my ears – if you like them, I can bring some in. Come on, what else are you going to do? We all think we've left the iron on. It's actually got a name – FOLO. I heard it on the radio. Fear of leaving on. There's an acronym for everything these days!'

Nancy smiled, grateful for George's kindness. He tugged her gently towards the bar.

'Take a deep breath,' George said, as he held open the door for her – and Emma and the other ladies shrieked her name. Emma thrust a fruity cocktail into her hand and Frances peered over the top of her glasses at her, before fumbling in her pocket and retrieving her nasal decongestant, which she squirted up her nostrils in two bursts. Nancy caught George's eye and they shared the briefest smile.

'Oh, don't you scrub up lovely in red!' Emma exclaimed. 'More scarlet woman than cat lady tonight! We were just discussing how I met my other half, Nancy. A blind date, would you believe. When I walked into the bar to meet him, I couldn't believe my eyes – he looks exactly like that rugby player that used to go out with Charlotte Church. You know, Gavin someone or other.'

The group murmured with pleasure and approval. Nancy's mind went to Larry, that day on the pavement, when he was sellotaped to a chair. She thought of his email, waiting in her inbox.

'Who are you thinking about, Nancy?' asked Emma. 'Something tells me you're a dark horse. You never did tell us if you've got a man in your life? Or woman, perhaps?'

Blushing, Nancy took a gulp of her drink, feeling the alcohol on her tongue, and shook her head dismissively. Waiting until the other women lost interest and resumed their conversation, she focussed hard on listening to George, who was regaling her with details about his allotment. She drank more while George talked of perennials, pest control and planting. Nancy was grateful for every potato, raspberry and courgette he mentioned.

As the spirits floated into her brain, the alcohol dulled her thoughts of Marcie and Larry and, despite everything, she felt, for the first time in the longest while, like a woman who might wear a beautiful red dress.

Chapter Twenty-One

The sun was setting when Nancy left, bathing the town in a pink and violet wash. She'd managed over an hour in the bar, but found her mind wandering to Terence and whether he'd found her note at the bandstand. Before she slipped out of the bar to check, George offered to walk her home since they lived on the same side of Christchurch. When she refused, he rubbed his perspiring forehead, furiously blinking.

'It's not right, a lady walking home on her own,' he said. 'It doesn't sit well with me, especially if she's swaying ever so slightly.'

'I'm not swaying!' Nancy smiled, though she probably was. She almost went on to tell him she'd been alone for years and every walk she'd done in that time was on her own. Unless you counted Ted as a person. Which, in actual fact, she did.

Outside on the street, she took off her shoes, which had pinched her toes, and removed the combs from her hair. She walked towards the bandstand by the water – silver, pink and still as a pond – and squeezed shut her eyes, trying to clear her head.

Opening them again, she gazed further down the quay, where the reflection of lights from a waterside hotel, The Sailor, had turned the water into spun gold. It was fantastically beautiful.

A sudden lump came into Nancy's throat. How good it would feel to have someone to share this moment with. A person by her side. Would she ever know that feeling again?

The cold air sobering her up, Nancy walked towards the bandstand. She thought about how kind George had been to her that evening, making sure she had a drink and somewhere to sit – should she perhaps have allowed him to walk her home? Perhaps they could become friends. Perhaps they could—

Quickly, she closed down her thoughts. She had long ago given up on love. She didn't have the courage to expose her heart to love again. And love was never easy – she only had to consider Marcie's situation to realise that. Poor Marcie. Her own marriage had cast a lifelong shadow over her future – would Marcie be equally troubled?

'Did Terence find the note?' She spoke out loud, checking the bandstand railings. The note had indeed gone – and been replaced by a torn blue piece of card. She pulled it out. On it, Terence had written a reply. She flooded with excitement. 'Never!' he'd written, with a little line drawing of a smiley face. Nancy's cheeks flamed and, feeling absurdly happy, she pushed the note into her bag when she was suddenly distracted by a rustling coming from a bush. Her heart beating, she stood completely still and looked in the direction of the noise, where she noticed a white bundle underneath the bush.

Still swaying slightly, she moved towards the bush and knelt down to discover the bundle was actually a badly injured, fluffy, pure white cat – the same beautiful white cat she'd seen walking the fences and rooftops of her neighbouring houses. The cat that brought good luck and prosperity to those doors it crossed.

'It's okay,' she told the cat, noticing that the fur on its back and hips was covered in blood. The cat meowed and tried to stand but collapsed. By the look of the poor creature, it had been caught and bitten across its back, perhaps by a dog or fox? She registered how still it was and how heavily it was panting. Nancy swallowed. She could not let the cat die.

'It's okay,' she told the cat again. 'I'm not going to let you die. I'll get help.'

Nancy frantically looked around for something to wrap around the cat's body, so she could pick it up without hurting it further, but there was only silence and darkness. Her phone was at home.

She didn't even have a coat on. Staring at her dress, she made a tear in the skirt and ripped off a length of the soft jersey material, gently wrapping it around the cat and lifting it from the ground. She bundled it into her arms. It rested its head heavily against her arm, like a weary child, and closed its eyes, but incredibly still found the energy or kindness to purr.

'Poor thing, please don't die, please don't die,' Nancy repeated the words under her breath as she walked as quickly as she could to the out-of-hours emergency vet clinic, a good ten-minute walk away. All the way there, she whispered to the cat, willing it to stay alive.

'What do we have here?' the vet said, gently placing the cat down on a table in the consultation room. Nancy quickly explained how she'd found it.

'Poor kitty,' the vet said. 'Looks like a dog bite. They tend to go for a cat's spine, clamp it in their jaws and shake it. I'll put her on a drip and give her painkillers straight away.'

Nancy, trembling, nauseous with shock, waited in silence, staring into the white cat's blue eyes.

'Did you walk here without any shoes on?' said the vet, peering down at Nancy's feet.

'I had stupid shoes on, with heels that are impossible to walk in,' said Nancy. 'I don't normally wear heels.'

'Well you've saved her life, I would think,' said the vet. 'She's a friendly thing, despite her injury. If you hadn't found her under the bush, she may well have died. When injured, cats tend to hide themselves away.'

'I'm so happy I found her,' said Nancy. 'She's such a beautiful creature.'

The vet explained that, like so many pure white cats with blue eyes, she was deaf and might not be so good at escaping danger.

'You don't see many pure white cats like this around; they're often kept indoors,' the vet continued. 'We'll check for a chip to find the owner.' But on finding there wasn't one registered on the system she shook her head. 'No chip. Sometimes owners will ring around the vets if their cat doesn't return home.'

'Can I look after her, if the owner doesn't come forward?' said Nancy.

'You can,' she said, 'but there's a thirty-day window where you have to advertise locally, on social media and with posters, so that you're actively looking for the owner.'

Nancy nodded and gently stroked the cat's head. 'Shall I wait in the waiting area?' she asked. 'I'd like to wait.'

'I'd go home for a cup of tea,' the vet said. 'You've had a shock and your dress is torn… I'll call you in an hour or so when the painkillers begin to work. You can visit her again in the morning if you'd like to. She's a dear little thing, isn't she?'

At home, Nancy changed out of the ruined red dress, put on her dressing gown and sat on the sofa, waiting for the phone to ring. Elsie sat on her lap, sensing Nancy's anxiety, while William lounged on the rug, as if utterly exhausted with life. When the vet phoned, she explained that in the morning she would give the cat an anaesthetic so she could clip off the hair around her hips and investigate the wounds and that, if the owner hadn't come forward by the next day, Nancy could take her home, where she'd have to be kept away from the other cats while she healed.

'She's a survivor,' the vet said, and Nancy's eyes pricked with tears. 'Any ideas on what we should call her? She's a beautiful girl, in good condition with a gentle nature. I'm sure she's been loved and cared for by someone.'

An idea flashed into Nancy's head. 'Hope,' she said. 'How about we call her Hope?'

Chapter Twenty-Two

When Beatrice had been a small girl with pigtails and gappy teeth, Nancy had done everything she could to protect her from life's darkness. When reading bedtime stories, she skipped the pages that told of evil forces, killing or death. Switched off the television when the news came on, turned over the newspaper so she couldn't see tragic front-page imagery of desperate children in war zones. Talked loudly when neighbours argued with each other, or stressed parents in the swimming pool changing room swore at their kids to hurry up, you little shitheads. She even glossed over what she was eating when Beatrice asked where the meat on her plate had come from. 'A happy chicken,' Nancy had said. 'One that had lived a long happy life running around in the fields enjoying the sunshine.' Lies, basically. Silly lies.

Larry had rolled his eyes at her and insisted that Beatrice at least be aware that bad things can and do happen – and that it was an important lesson for her to understand that she should ask questions of the world around her – but Nancy's desire to protect her had been such that she had resisted him. Even when Nancy and Larry split up, Nancy had insisted that Mum and Dad were the best of friends who still loved each other very much, but that they had different interests and hobbies that made living together difficult.

She wondered now if softening all those blows had been a mistake. If Nancy had warned Beatrice that tragic things happened daily, unimaginably awful things, that children died because they got involved in horrific accidents, would she have taken more care on the beach that day? Would she be here now, with Nancy, helping her take care of Hope, this beautiful white cat, which nobody had claimed, and who Nancy was now fostering? Thinking of Beatrice, Nancy remembered Larry's email – how could she forget – but still she hadn't replied. Nothing she could write, or say, seemed adequate.

'Where do you live?' she asked Hope, as she put the painkillers and antibiotics into the cat food, as the vet had prescribed. With half her fur clipped off she made a pitiful sight. 'Who do you belong to? I bet your owner is missing you.'

Nancy gently stroked Hope's soft head and tickled her velvet ears. Hope purred.

'Just you keep an eye on everyone,' Nancy told Elsie and Ted, in the hallway, before leaving for St Joseph's that day. 'Don't let anyone into the room that Hope is in. She needs peace and quiet to heal.'

Sitting quietly outside the living room, side by side as if on a park bench, the two old cats blinked their agreement. 'I'll love you and leave you and come back later then,' Nancy said, blowing them kisses.

At school, Nancy told Frances and Emma about finding the white cat after Emma's party and put out a note on the town's community social-media site, appealing for its owner to come forward. Nancy also printed off some posters to stick up around the neighbourhood. Frances squirted her nose with decongestant, while Emma widened her eyes into perfect circles.

'Do you think that's bad luck?' Emma said. 'For my wedding?'

'I think it's bad luck for Nancy,' said Frances, 'as now she's lumbered with yet another cat. Do you know years ago, in the 1800s, women who kept cats were burned alive because everyone thought they were witches? What do you think of that?'

Bollocks, Nancy found herself wanting to say, but she kept quiet. Instead, she focussed on the newsletter she was compiling. She also kept an eye on the reception doors, wanting and hoping to see both Alfie and Marcie, who had as yet not replied to her email.

'Codswallop,' said George, who was in the office to pick up some keys. 'That's what I think to that, Frances. Anyway, that cat's not the only one who's been in the wars. Did you hear about that lad Alfie Payne's dad?'

Nancy turned quickly, almost cricking her neck.

'No,' she said. 'What's happened?'

'He fell off some scaffolding at work,' said Emma, 'and he's broken his arm and leg. He's a roofer apparently. Called in to say they were in a fix as the mum's gone and so Alfie's at home looking after him. The welfare officer is going to call him.'

'Oh no, oh dear,' said Nancy. 'Poor Alfie. He doesn't have much luck. They're my neighbours, you know. The fence is always down; it's as if we share a garden.'

Nancy stared at the gold Japanese fortune cat on her desk, her mind whirring.

Alfie answered the door immediately. Dressed in shorts and T-shirt, he held a games-console controller in his hand, and from somewhere in the house came the sounds of gunfire erupting from a computer game. From the living room, Jonah, Alfie's dad, broke out into a hacking cough, before calling 'Who is it?' to Alfie.

'Can I come in please, Alfie?' said Nancy. 'I heard about your dad's accident.'

'It's the lady from over the fence,' called Alfie, moving sideways so she could enter the house. 'How is Batman, Ms Jones?'

Nancy closed the front door behind them. A strong smell of menthol hit her nose.

'He's doing fine,' she said. 'And I've got another cat now. A white one, Hope, who's been badly injured by a dog. So, I'm looking after her and helping her to get well.'

'A bit like me and Dad then,' said Alfie, giving her a lopsided grin. 'He's in there.'

Nancy moved into the small living room, where Jonah was sitting in an armchair looking desperately uncomfortable. His left leg and right arm were cast in plaster and he wore a collar around his neck. In his hand, he held a wad of tissues and a pot of Vicks VapoRub. Next to the chair was a walking frame.

'I would get up,' he said, 'but then I might not get back down again. Alfie, get the lady a cup of tea. Please sit down. I apologise for the mess. Can't do much of anything since I fell off a ladder and broke half my bones. I've got a summer cold too. Bet you wish you had half my luck!'

His broken body shook with mirth. Nancy perched on the edge of the squidgy brown sofa, which was littered with letters and magazines and wrappers.

'You must be extremely uncomfortable,' said Nancy, 'especially in this heat.'

Jonah exhaled and leaned his head back in his chair, releasing a cry of pain.

'Alfie's helping me,' he said. 'He'll be back into school tomorrow or the next day.'

Nancy's eyes moved slowly around Jonah's front room. A sofa, a chair, a television set and a shelving unit with various trinkets and framed photographs on, it looked a little unloved. The main ceiling light was on and the curtains were drawn. On the floor was a plate with the crust of a sandwich on it and a banana skin.

'I can't cook a decent dinner at the moment,' said Jonah. 'With one arm and one leg.'

'Is there nobody else who can help? Any relatives?' Nancy asked. 'Is there anyone at all?'

The silence between her question and Jonah's reply was laden with pain. Nancy recognised it exactly and felt instantly guilty. She hadn't meant to make him feel bad about not having a close-knit team of stew-cooking friends and kindly aunts to step in and help. Jonah swallowed noisily, and he lowered his eyes to the carpet.

He was a huge, muscle-bound man, but his bottom lip clearly wobbled.

'My sister might be able to come next week, but nobody local really,' he admitted, clearing his throat. 'I've got a couple of mates from work but…'

Nancy tried to emit her empathy by picking up the plate and carrying it into the kitchen, which was in a worse state than her own. She opened the fridge. It was bare apart from a tub of margarine. Nancy returned to the sofa, feeling desperately sorry for Jonah and Alfie, and before she had time to think it through, or consider the school's take on her actions, she had spoken.

'I know this is completely out of the blue, but you and Alfie could come and stay with me for a couple of days,' she said. 'The fence is down, so you'd only have to walk across the garden. I can cook for you and Alfie, just to see you through this patch, until your sister gets here next week.'

Jonah screwed up his face and looked at her stupefied, as if she had just offered to marry him.

'We're strangers though, Ms Jones,' he said, trying to sit up straighter in his chair. 'We couldn't take you up on that, but it's very good of you to offer.'

'We're neighbours,' she said, her face burning. 'And I don't see you have a lot of choice. You could consider it like a bed-and-breakfast stay. Alfie can go to school then, can't you, Alfie?'

Alfie shrugged. 'I like it at home,' he said. 'I hate school.'

Alfie's eyes were big and lonely. Nancy's heart sank.

'I know that boy has bothered you,' Nancy said, 'but you need your education.'

'What boy?' said Jonah. 'If someone is bothering you, son, I'll break his neck. Just tell me who he is.'

Alfie cast his gaze down. Nancy rested her hand on his shoulder.

'We can talk to the headmaster about it,' Nancy said. 'That's the best way.'

Alfie shook his head again, more violently this time. Nancy sighed. Jonah tried to stand from his chair but couldn't.

'You'll just have to let me help you,' Nancy said. 'It would mean a lot to me, if you would let me. I don't make a habit of this. The school will probably frown on it, I suppose, but they don't need to know. There are so many rules about boundaries, what we can and can't do, but you're my neighbours and you're in need. I feel compelled to help. It just… seems… like the right thing to do.'

Jonah and Alfie looked at one another, perplexed. Alfie started to pull tiny pieces from a slice of bread, pushing the morsels into his mouth.

'She's a helper at school,' Alfie said to Jonah. 'Will there be ice cream?'

'Yes,' said Nancy. 'There will be ice cream. Jonah, please, just for a few days, until there's a better option.'

'She rescues animals too,' said Alfie, pausing from his bread. 'Cats. Let's go, Dad. Can we? I can see Batman then.'

Jonah was speechless. He stared down at his broken limbs.

'I'll have to do something to repay you for the favour when I'm on the mend,' he said. 'Your gardening? I won't lie, I've looked over the fence and have seen that it needs a bit of TLC.'

'What's TLC?' asked Alfie, pushing his glasses up his nose.

'Tender loving care,' said Nancy. 'You must view it as a few days of respite. I don't live in luxury, but you'll have a room, food and company in case you need it. I know how it feels when there's literally nobody to help. It's lonely.'

Jonah and Alfie fell silent.

'If you insist,' said Jonah eventually. 'Just for a few days.'

Nancy nodded, left the house and closed the front door behind her. In the sunlight, she blinked for a few moments, stunned at her uncharacteristic boldness, but she had to help them. Images of herself as a child rushed into her mind; injured garden birds in shoeboxes, a butterfly with one wing, an old teddy bear with no eyes or sugar water for an exhausted bumblebee – she had always tried to rescue abandoned or desperate things. A nurse in St Anne's once said it was her way of taking control after her mother's sudden death when Nancy had been only eight years old. That if she was thinking about somebody else's troubles, she didn't have to think about her own. Perhaps there was truth in those words, or perhaps it was just the way Nancy was: her blueprint. 'Florence Nightingale' her father used to call her, telling her stories about Florence – who, Nancy was thrilled to discover, owned more than sixty cats in her lifetime. The original cat lady, then, if ever there was one.

Chapter Twenty-Three

'And then, one morning, I stood on the back of her flip-flop by mistake, when we were out for a walk, and it just tipped her over the edge,' Jonah said, snapping his fingers on the hand of his unbroken arm together. 'As I told you before, she said she needed space, packed her bag, took the twins and the pug and that was it. Gone.'

Jonah sat in Nancy's kitchen flanked by three cats. He was at the end of telling Nancy his story, and William had slept through the whole thing slumped on Jonah's good leg. Batman nestled into his shoulder, eyes half-closed, and Tabitha perched on the kitchen table near Jonah's coffee, pushing her face into his hand every time he reached for his mug. Jonah was bigger than the fridge and seemed enormous in the small room, like a carved stone statue had been mistakenly installed indoors. The cats gravitated towards him. For such a big, alpha-male-looking man he was surprisingly emotional and honest. Nancy, much like the cats, instantly warmed to Jonah, though couldn't deny feeling envious of how much the felines loved him. Beside him sat Alfie, a grasshopper in comparison, with his great big eyes searching the outside world through the window, as if waiting for something. Or someone.

Nancy had listened carefully to Jonah, who had suffered more than his fair share of bad luck, while stroking Hope on her lap, her front half soft as clouds, her back half clipped and her skin reminiscent of suede. Hope's wounds were healing well and she loved fuss. Rather than be aggressive towards her, the other cats seemed to revere her.

'Enough about me. Have you always lived here alone, Ms Jones?' said Jonah, placing his mug of now stone-cold coffee on the table. 'Must get lonely, does it?'

'Call me Nancy,' she said, fiddling with an invisible mark on the tablecloth. 'I have the cats to keep me company.'

'Never been married then?' Jonah asked. 'Wise woman! Or is there a husband under the patio?'

Jonah cracked up laughing. Nancy sighed. Questions. People couldn't resist. They always wanted to know why there wasn't a man, or any children, in her life. Just cats. A memory of Larry tugged at her hand, pulling her through the door of a random memory that she hadn't thought about in years. They had been out for dinner with friends in a restaurant and Larry had insisted the chef come out from the kitchen to join them at the table, so Larry could thank him for the food and buy him a whiskey. The chef had said it was the first time, in eight years working in that establishment, that a customer had bought him a drink. She had loved Larry with her whole self in that moment. Now, she thought of his email and shivered. She still hadn't replied.

'I was married once,' said Nancy quietly. 'A long time ago, but we went our separate ways.'

Jonah nodded and took another sip of his cold coffee.

'Yes, well,' he said. 'People don't always turn out to be who you think they're going to be, do they? I mean, as I said, Rose, my wife, she's been with me since we were at school. I never thought she'd desert us. I never thought it would turn out like this. We've always been tight. A team, you know? It's weird being on my own. When I wake up, I turn over and think she's there, only to see her side hasn't been slept in.'

He sighed deeply and stroked Tabitha under the chin. Tabitha purred.

'Maybe she just needs a bit of time to go off the rails,' Nancy said. 'We're all so quick to partner up with someone, I wonder if people really know themselves, let alone the other person they pledge their lives to. Would you have her back?'

'Like a shot,' said Jonah, without missing a beat. 'Alfie pines for her. He needs his mum! You know what kids are like! You never had kids?'

Nancy's heart bombed. As if hearing it pounding in her chest like a drum, Alfie looked up.

'She has a daughter,' said Alfie, 'don't you, Ms Jones?'

Nancy was floored by the direct question and felt she had nowhere to run. This was her own fault. She had been foolish to invite strangers in. What did she expect? The answer to Jonah's question was so simple, really, yet when she opened her mouth to reply she couldn't find the words. Never had been able to. Perhaps, as much as anything, it was putting the other person in a situation of having to sympathise, find something appropriate to say, that stopped her from telling people.

'I—' said Nancy. She paused to take a deep breath. 'Yes, I had a daughter. Sadly, she died when she was a child. It was a long time ago but honestly feels like yesterday.'

A tremble in her voice gave her away. Alfie gasped, and Jonah glanced at her, nodding slightly, as if suddenly finding a missing piece in a puzzle.

'How did she d—' started Alfie, but his father silenced him with a glare.

'Ah,' Jonah said gently. 'I'm so sorry to hear that. Can't imagine what that must be like.'

'No,' Nancy said, placing Hope on a cushion and collecting the mugs from the table before setting them down in the sink. 'It was hard. I had a breakdown afterwards. Spent some time in hospital.'

There, she'd said it. Her fingers shook. She ran the tap, grateful for the noise. A tear dripped into the water. She squirted washing-up liquid into the water, leaving the mugs to soak.

'The black dog,' Jonah said. 'It's a bugger.'

She turned back to face Jonah and offered him a small smile, wanting to reassure him that she was okay. He smiled back, with great kindness.

'Shall I show you your room, so you can settle in?' she said, almost adding 'and stop asking me questions'. 'Don't feel you have to be with me, while you're here,' she said. 'I'm very used to my own company.'

The room Nancy gave to Jonah and Alfie was downstairs because Jonah couldn't climb the stairs. It had once been a large dining room, probably used for family dinners, Christmas lunch or for guests who came to tea, but was now never used. The window was vast and had a view of the back garden, which was thick with out-of-control weeds and entangled bushes. Open slightly at the top, fingers of ivy crept inside the window. Nancy caught Jonah's despairing expression – and their eyes met in acknowledgement. Nancy was relieved when he grinned.

'It's like *The Day of the Triffids* out there!' Jonah said, leaning on his walking frame. 'I can do that for you when I'm back on my feet. Dig out the old stuff beyond help and lay seed for a lawn. You've a lovely old place here, you know? With a lick of paint and a prune in the garden, it could be grand.'

Nancy nodded once. She'd seen Jonah's gaze sliding over the ailing interiors too – the chairs from her father's home, with stuffing spilling out of the cushioned seats, the wallpaper peeling, dead light bulbs unreplaced, cobwebs festooned across the corners. Her face reddened. She began to apologise for the state of the house, but Jonah silenced her with a shake of his head.

'No need,' he said. 'You've seen my gaff. Not exactly a palace.'

'A friend was going to help me decorate,' she said, thinking of Marcie with regret. 'But we didn't get very far. I know it's not the best accommodation, but hopefully it will help you get Alfie back off to school until your sister comes.'

She put her hand on her cheek where Marcie had hurled the paintbrush and felt a surge of anger. Why was she blaming Nancy for her husband and son's wrongdoings?

At that moment, Jonah pulled at a piece of peeling wallpaper and a chunk of ancient plaster came with it. He shook his head.

'Thought as much,' he said. 'I can do that for you, Ms Jones. It's the least I can do.'

'Call me Nancy, and do be careful,' she said, waving a hand in the air, gesturing at the walls. 'The whole house might come tumbling down. I suppose I should have paid more attention, but I've had other things on my mind.'

Nancy had made up a sofa bed for Jonah and a camp bed for Alfie in the same room, so he could help his dad in the night should he need anything. Having visitors to stay in the house like this was unprecedented, and Nancy felt waves of mild panic pass over her as she guided them through the downstairs of the house, including the downstairs toilet.

'And that's upstairs,' Nancy said, pointing up the stairs. 'Bedrooms and a bathroom and general storage.'

Alfie disappeared upstairs for a few moments, then poked his head out over the banister.

'What's in this big cupboard up here?' he said. 'Can I hide in it?'

'Alfie,' said Jonah. 'Don't be a nosy git. Get your backside down here.'

Nancy felt her heart fluttering.

'It's just the linen cupboard,' she said, blinking rapidly. 'Please, just…'

But Alfie had his hand on the cupboard handle and yanked it open.

'There's a box in here that says "toys" on the side,' he said excitedly. 'Can I get them out?'

Quickly, Nancy flew upstairs and pulled him away from the cupboard, before slamming the door shut.

'It's private,' she snapped. 'Get away from there.'

All the colour drained from Nancy's face. The cupboard was packed with boxes of Beatrice's belongings. When her father had died, and she'd cleared out his house, she hadn't been able to part with any of the boxes containing Beatrice's things, yet neither had she been able to go through them, so she stored them in the linen cupboard until further notice. Now, it all felt dangerously close to spilling out.

'Sorry,' Alfie muttered.

Stung by the sharpness in Nancy's voice, Alfie moved to another cupboard at the top of the stairs, where, nervously, he put his hand on the door and looked at her. She nodded. Tabitha immediately jumped inside and disappeared into a hessian bag.

'What's in this one then?' he said, pulling some feathers out of a box and throwing them into the air. Tabitha balanced on her back legs and batted them with her paws. Alfie pointed at her and laughed.

'Alfie!' shouted Jonah. 'Get down here!'

'Don't worry, Jonah, that's all my fabrics and feathers,' she said. 'You can look in there, it's just the other one that's a bit private… I used to make costumes sometimes and those are my materials.'

'Are they actually owl feathers?' he asked. 'Hedwig feathers that will make me fly? Will I ever be able to fly?'

What a question, Nancy thought. *And not one I can easily answer.* She and Jonah exchanged a glance; he had made his way to the bottom of the stairs.

'In your own way, yes,' she said decisively. Keen to make up for her earlier flash of anger, she made a suggestion: 'Why don't I make you that owl costume we talked about, for the fancy dress day?'

'Yes please,' he said, throwing his arms around her waist. He looked up at her, full of gratitude, and her heart lifted.

'Okay,' Nancy said. 'Then why don't I measure you up for a pair of wings?'

Jonah shook his head.

'Don't worry yourself,' said Jonah. 'The boy can do without. Alfie, stop asking for things. We're guests in this house – start behaving yourself.'

Alfie kicked the skirting board and stared at Nancy with flaming eyes.

'Stuart was right,' he spat. 'He said I would come to school in my school uniform when everyone else was in fancy dress. He said I was too poor to buy a costume and that my mum had run away so nobody would make me one.'

'I doubt very much that *his* mother is making him one!' Nancy said, trying to imagine Marcie at a sewing machine.

'Who is this lad?' said Jonah. 'I'd like to give him a piece of my mind!'

'He's called Stuart,' said Nancy. 'I have a feeling his own home situation might not be that wonderful, if you see what I mean. It would be a good idea to speak to the Head about it, Jonah, when you're back on your feet.'

Alfie shrugged and screwed up his face, and Nancy checked herself. It was a bit much of her to expect Alfie to be empathetic towards Stuart.

'He's got a costume from the internet,' Alfie said. 'Apparently it cost £50. He said his costume cost more money than I would ever have. He said that my mum was never coming home.'

'The little shit,' Jonah said. 'If I wasn't all laid up like this, I'd be right round their house to tell them what for!'

Nancy felt another rush of anger towards Stuart who, if he looked at his own parents, might get a nasty shock when he realised his own life wasn't so rosy. But mostly she felt cross with Marcie. Why wasn't she taking what Nancy had told her about Stuart seriously? Why hadn't she been back to talk to her, to find out exactly what had been going on? Was Marcie's ego really so fragile that she couldn't accept the truth?

'We'll show them,' Nancy said, ruffling Alfie's hair. She felt a pang of longing for Beatrice. As a child, Beatrice hated unfairness. She would have stood up for Alfie, hands on her hips, telling Stuart to back off. Beatrice had been a gutsy little girl: up trees, jumping off climbing frames, diving into the swimming pool. A breath of air. Much missed.

When darkness fell, and Jonah and Alfie had gone to their room, Nancy knew she would never sleep. She was too aware of other people being in the house. The cats were prowling and sniffing Jonah and Alfie's possessions in the hallway. Instead of going to bed, she returned to her sewing machine, threaded the needle and replaced the bobbin thread, and started to make Alfie's wings. She would sit there until they were made, all night if she had to.

Chapter Twenty-Four

Nancy woke up the following morning on the living room sofa, with feathers in her hair. Alfie was tapping her shoulder and softly calling her name, cajoling her from a dream where she was trying to write to Larry, but her hands wouldn't work. A moment of confusion gripped her while she remembered why Alfie was in her house.

'It's time to go to school,' he said. 'Wake up. It's the fair today!'

Bleary-eyed, Nancy blinked and blew away a feather that was stuck to her lips. She looked at Alfie's huge, concerned eyes and smiled. He instantly returned the smile. Quickly covering the wing she'd made during the night, she stood up and left the room, to first feed the cats, then go and change her clothes. In the hallway, she tripped over one of Jonah's giant work boots – the one he couldn't wear – and from which Batman was poking out his tiny black head. From the kitchen came the sounds of the radio – a station that Nancy had never tuned into before that seemed to be playing heavy metal music.

'I used to listen to this at the end of a shift when I worked nights years ago,' said Jonah, seated at the kitchen table, his broken leg jutting out at an awkward angle. 'Kept me awake on the drive home. Never got out the habit. What do you normally listen to? Let me guess. Radio 2? Classic FM? Radio 4?'

'I don't normally have it on,' she said. 'Sometimes at night we listen to the bedtime story. I don't like to listen to the news.'

'We?' Jonah said. 'As in the royal we?'

'Me and the cats,' she said. 'They love it, actually. They really listen. Ears pricked up, eyes wide, paws crossed.'

Jonah laughed as if she'd said something hysterical. He was freshly washed and shaved and had made a pot of tea. He had also made toast and put slices into the toast rack that Nancy never used and found the marmalade from the back of the fridge. Nancy made a mental note to buy more conserves and cereals. He poured her a cup of tea. 'This will restart your engine,' he said.

'I'm supposed to be looking after you!' she said. 'Not the other way around.'

Nancy blinked, pulling her cardigan around her rumpled clothes, before picking up the tea and taking a sip. She yawned. 'I must have fallen asleep.'

Having other people in the house – besides the cats – made her feel like a visitor herself and she felt unpractised. She wasn't sure where to sit, so she leaned against the kitchen counter, blowing over her hot tea. The house felt different and even smelled different too, of Jonah's aftershave or hair gel. Alfie was giggling, dragging a piece of string from room to room for William to catch. She felt off-balance but strangely alive.

'Come on, Ms Jones!' said Alfie, rushing into the kitchen with his rucksack on his back. 'Or you'll be late and get detention!'

Nancy finished her tea and ran upstairs. In her bedroom, she quickly washed and changed into a beige skirt and white top, and put her hair up in combs. Elsie and Ted were lounging on her bed – they'd had it to themselves the whole night. Listening to the faded voices of Jonah and Alfie downstairs – Jonah was telling Alfie how he should defend himself if Stuart picked on him – she opened the curtains and stood for a moment staring out over the quay. In the distance, she saw Terence setting up his easel. She was relieved that he hadn't given up. He was a part of the landscape and she felt reassured by his presence. Ted jumped up by her side and pushed his head against her hip, purring loudly.

'What do you think, Ted?' she asked him. 'About having visitors?'

He turned 360 degrees, twice, before sitting down. Mulling things over.

Walking to school with Alfie, she listened to him talk about Harry Potter, re-enacting scenes from the book that he seemed to have learned the lines from off by heart. At the school gates, in a scrum of children, they both noticed Stuart's red hair in the crowd. A poisonous red berry. Alfie slipped his hand in hers and physically cowered. She gave his hand a squeeze, then let go and leaned down to his level, watching his eyes dart nervously through the crowd, alert.

'I'm going to sort this out for you,' she said. 'Put it out of your mind.'

Alfie hesitated then nodded, before running into class, head bowed. As he went through the doors, Nancy noticed Stuart stick out his leg to trip him up. Luckily, Alfie saw his leg in time and jumped over it. Furious, Nancy shook her head and, once inside the school, knocked on Mr Phillips's door. Jonah was not in a position to speak to the school right now and Marcie was ignoring her, so she would talk to the headmaster herself. Besides, Mr Phillips had asked her to inform him if she found out more information so she was doing the right thing.

The door opened and Mr Phillips popped out his head, his hair sticking up in strange directions. Another teacher, Miss Colm, was in there with him too. She seemed agitated – perhaps they were in the middle of a curriculum meeting.

'Can this wait until later, Ms Jones?' he said. 'I've just discovered we may not have the correct licence in place for us to be able to sell alcohol at the fair this afternoon. I'm desperately trying to sort it out. Come back and see me later?'

He pulled at his earlobe.

'It's about Alfie—' she began, but the door closed in her face before she had opportunity to continue. Deflated, Nancy returned to her desk, where there was a KitKat waiting for her on the keyboard.

'From George,' said Frances, winking at her. Nancy blushed. 'But before you get too excited, he left one for all of us.'

Frances burst out laughing. Nancy clenched her teeth and forced herself to smile. Out of the corner of her eye, she saw Alfie scampering down the corridor like a frightened kitten. She thought of him and Jonah, how they chatted and laughed and messed about before school. Alfie was like a different boy at home. She couldn't stand for him to be miserable at school. If Mr Phillips didn't have time to do anything about Alfie's situation, and talking to Marcie had been a disaster, she'd simply have to take the whole thing into her own hands.

Chapter Twenty-Five

'If you lay another finger on Alfie,' Nancy said to Stuart, gripping hold of his shoulder, 'I will make your life—'

'You will make his life what?' said Gerard Loveday, appearing by her side like an unwelcome genie from a lamp.

The summer fair was in full swing. The afternoon sun beat down on Nancy's head like a metal sheet. There were excitable children and, with the makeshift bar in full flow, intoxicated parents everywhere. The smell of burnt sausages from the BBQ clung to nostrils and hair-dos and music blared from a PA, while welly wanging was proving popular.

Stuart had come over to have a go on the hoopla, the stall that Nancy was looking after. Nancy knew it was wrong to threaten him. That she was breaking every rule in the book. She knew she should have insisted on seeing Mr Phillips, or waited for him to be free. After all, Stuart was just a child. A confused boy who probably needed guidance himself. Yet she couldn't help herself. She just wanted to warn him off. Slamming the four wooden hoops into Stuart's hand, she snatched his 50p and glared into his eyes.

'Nothing…' she replied to Gerard.

'How do you play?' said Stuart, unfazed.

'Hoop the prize, you win it,' she seethed, folding her arms across her chest.

'Go on something else, son,' warned Gerard. 'Go on! I need a word with Ms Jones, in private.'

Stuart didn't move. After a moment's hesitation, he looked at his dad and dropped the hoops, ran towards Splat the Rat and disappeared out of view. Gerard hadn't moved. He narrowed his eyes and Nancy's heart took a dive. She realised he wasn't finished with her. The seagulls paused in the sky to tread the air and watch. The entire school field seemed to fall silent.

'I know what you were about to say,' he said, towering above her. Nancy tried to make herself taller. 'How dare you speak to my son like that?'

'He's been bullying Alfie for weeks!' Nancy said. 'He has to be stopped! It's not fair!'

Her whole body trembled, her voice raised.

'What proof do you have?' Gerard said.

'Bruises,' she said. 'A bloody nose! Stolen food! Alfie said Stuart had threatened to kill him last week and I've seen him do it with my own eyes.'

The raised voices had attracted the attention of other parents, who were edging closer for a better view. Sally was in earshot and Marcie – an empty plastic glass in her hand – was striding towards them.

'That's playground banter and nothing more,' said Gerard. 'If you say anything else to my son – if you so much as utter a word into his ear – I will not be held responsible for my actions.'

'Are you threatening me?' Nancy said, her cheeks bright red. 'Has Stuart learned his bully-boy tactics from you? Is that how you speak to Marcie? Is that why she has bruises on her arms?'

She knew she'd gone too far. Hardly knew where the words were coming from. Gerard literally exploded.

'You are a lunatic and you will be hearing from my lawyer!' he hissed. 'You've told my wife lies about me, and now you're telling the entire school lies about me. But what else can I expect from a screwed-up old bag like you? It might interest Mr Phillips and the teachers and the parents to know that you were locked up in a loony bin after your daughter died when you left her with some bloke off his head on drugs! You are untrustworthy and unstable! You shouldn't be allowed to work in a school. Does the local authority even know you spent time in a psychiatric ward? She's a danger to our kids.'

Nancy staggered backwards. Gerard's words were like knives through her heart.

'No… no… that's not… true…' she stuttered.

'Isn't it?' Gerard said, looking around him to see who was listening. Everyone seemed to be staring in their direction, lapping up the scandal.

'Marcie told me everything about how you know each other,' he continued. 'Why do you think she lives with all those cats? Nobody will have her! She's totally fucking deranged!'

By now, Marcie had arrived and had heard Gerard's accusations. Yanking at his arm, she tried to pull him away, but he shook her off. Marcie didn't know where to look, but she wouldn't meet Nancy's eye.

'You'll be hearing from my lawyer!' Gerard repeated. But Nancy couldn't listen to another word. Dropping the cash tin and the wooden hooplas on the grass, she pushed past Gerard and the gawping parents and ran towards the school and into the ladies' staff toilets. She flung open the door, stormed into the first cubicle and locked herself inside, the door and lock rattling noisily as she did.

The high windows in the ladies flooded the toilets with bright sunlight and, as she perched on the closed toilet seat, she watched dust particles fizzing in the rays of sunshine and listened to the drip-drip of the water in the cistern. It ponged of disinfectant.

Pushing her palms against her eyes, she bent double and rested her nose in her lap, Gerard's words repeating on a loop in her head. Tears slipped down her cheek and she yanked tissue paper from the holder, dabbing it against her face. She would never be able to leave the toilets. The whole school would be talking about her. Marcie wouldn't even look her in the eye.

'Oh God,' she said, kicking the door with her toe. 'What a disaster.'

Just then the door of the ladies creaked open and someone came in. She lifted her feet up onto the toilet seat to hide, but there was a tap on the door of her cubicle.

'Ms Jones?' asked a gentle voice. It was George. Nancy sighed. 'I know you're in there. I heard what happened and I'm sorry. That's what's wrong with people today – they're so quick to accuse and attack. That man is a thug.'

Nancy didn't say anything. She heard George walk towards the door and let someone else in. From the sound of the heels clip-clopping on the tiled floor, it was Emma.

'Ms Jones... Nancy,' continued George, 'are you going to come out? You must ignore gossip.'

Nancy stayed seated but started ripping up squares of tissue into a million tiny pieces, letting them flutter to the floor like snowflakes, reminding her of a white veil she had once ripped up. The door creaked open again – and Nancy wasn't sure whether someone else had come in or someone had gone out.

'George?' she muttered. 'Are you still there?'

There was some whispering and a cough – definitely Emma.

'Yes, Ms Jones,' he said. 'Are you alright? Why don't you come out now? There are more pleasant places for you to sit.'

George was a genuine, kind man. She wondered what he'd been like as a young person – probably a scout in shorts and cap. The sort of person who would know how to start a fire from a stick and a tinder nest. Nancy couldn't hold it in any longer.

'It wasn't gossip; it's the truth,' she sighed. 'It all happened a long time ago, but it doesn't feel long ago. Gerard was right – my marriage broke down, then my daughter died the most horrible death. I took her on holiday and a terrible thing happened while I went to buy some lunch. I left her with a friend, but I should never have left her, not for a second. After that, I had a breakdown, tried to take my own life and went into a psychiatric hospital. I was in and out of that place for several years. I just kept slipping down…'

The words were tumbling from Nancy's mouth and she couldn't stop. 'I moved here twelve years ago and rescued five cats. I've got two more now. They make me feel less alone. I usually take in the ones who have suffered in some way. I couldn't stand to see Alfie getting bullied anymore. I know there are rulebooks we have to follow, but I need to be able to make some wrong things right. Do you understand? I couldn't not help him.'

There was a murmuring from outside the cubicle.

'But I know everyone thinks I'm crazy,' she continued. 'Unstable, untrustworthy, crazy cat lady, or whatever Mr Loveday says. Well perhaps I am. Perhaps I'm *totally fucking deranged*, George!'

She kicked the door and the whole cubicle vibrated. It was the first time she'd sworn on school premises and she felt terribly guilty. Someone in the room coughed. Nancy frowned. Why didn't they all just go away?

'Why don't you all just go away and leave me alone,' she said, but nobody moved.

'For one entire year I couldn't get out of bed in the mornings,' George suddenly said, in a serious voice she'd never heard before. 'One evening, when I was a lad, I'd had too much beer and got into a fight with my brother. He hit me in the nose, then I punched him on the side of the jaw and he staggered backwards and stepped into the road, just when a van was coming. I ran towards him to try to pull him back to safety, but it was too late. He was hit by the van and instantly killed. I changed the course of our family's life forever that night – and the life of the driver of the van. Our mother blamed me entirely. I spent the next forty years trying to make up for it.'

Nancy's mouth fell open. How little she knew about the people she worked alongside every day. So busy with concealing her own secrets, it hadn't dawned on her that they might have their own.

'Oh, George,' she said, 'I'm sorry.' She put her hands on the door and rested her cheek against it.

'It's public knowledge that's why I don't drink. Never touched a drop since then,' George said, before falling silent. The sound of nasal decongestant being sprayed – two squirts – broke the silence. Frances.

'I had a child when I was fourteen,' said Frances quietly. 'My parents made me give her up for adoption. She tried to reunite with me last year – she's been to university and is now a high-flying criminologist with grown-up sons – but my husband refuses to let our daughters know about her or meet her. It keeps me awake at night. Every Friday night I have a secret telephone conversation with her and I worry about it all day because eventually I'm going to have to tell her that my husband says she's not welcome in our lives, that I have to keep her a secret until my death.'

'Oh, Frances, you never said,' said Emma, who was obviously also in the toilet. 'That's so sad. Well, I might have told you this, but my father is a bloody nightmare and I've just had to tell him I don't want him to walk me down the aisle. He was always in and out of prison when I was a kid and it's been tough and chaotic. I worry he'll ruin my wedding. Life is… I don't know, it's…'

'Bloody messy,' finished George.

'And complicated,' said Frances.

'Not to mention confusing,' said Emma. 'You should have told us, Nancy.'

Nancy's cheeks were wet. After a few moments of silence, she spoke.

'I've always wondered why I ever told Beatrice off when she was a little girl. You know, why I told her off for not brushing her teeth properly, or why I wouldn't let her have more biscuits, or sleep in the tent she made from blankets in her bedroom. She was always so merry and happy, then, sometimes, I was too busy to listen, or snappy – with the person I treasured most in the world. If I could do it all again, have another go, I wouldn't be like that. I would be a magical person who never let her down, who always stood by her side, who ate more biscuits and slept in those tents with her. Side by side, hand in hand.'

Nancy's voice faltered. She squeezed her eyes shut.

'Why don't you come out,' said George, 'and I think we could all do with a strong cup of tea, couldn't we?'

'What about Mr Loveday?' muttered Nancy. 'He'll have gone straight to Mr Phillips. I'll lose my job.'

'Sod him,' said George with heartfelt insistence. 'Come on, I've got some KitKats in the staff room. Mr Phillips needs to hear both sides of the story.'

Nancy slid open the lock on the door and emerged, shame-faced and blotchy. George, Emma and Frances stood there, waiting, their faces full of concern, and for a moment, Nancy felt that precious sensation of being cared about and understood. Emma held out her hand, her bangles jangling on her wrist, took Nancy's hand in hers and led her to the staff room, a small space stuffed with chairs, with a view over the playing field, where the fair was continuing as if nothing had happened. Emma and Frances returned outside to their duties, while George boiled the kettle and put teabags into cups, half-whistling. Her eyes moved over the walls, where there were team photographs of the St Joseph's staff. In the latest one, she was there too, but right on the edge and at a slight distance from the nearest person. Was that her own doing, or had the photographer asked her to stand there? She had a realisation: it was her who put up these barriers, not other people.

'I've put extra sugar in for you – I think you need it,' George said, handing her a warm cup of tea and sitting down beside her, gently touching her arm. The tea felt like the most generous, kind act, and, once again, she felt tears brimming in her eyes. Noticing, George rested his hand on her shoulder, and his touch was so gentle and reassuring that she was overwhelmed by the desire to have more of his warmth. She pushed her head into his neck and grabbed hold of his hand, tears squirting from her eyes. Pushing her cheek up against his, some long-forgotten instinct rushed through her body and she turned her lips towards his—

'Ms Jones,' George said, leaping up from his seat and rapidly lifting his sun hat on and off his head. 'I think you're a lovely lady and that people underestimate you and, well, the only thing is, my dear, that I'm married. I hope you haven't misunderstood my friendship towards you. I've only ever wanted to let you know that you are liked and admired and respected, very much. I wanted to include you. I wanted you to know that you have friends, here at St Joseph's, no matter what you might think.'

Nancy covered her burning face with her hands and bent over her knees, wishing she could roll into a ball and disappear under a hedge for several months, like a hedgehog.

'Sorry,' she muttered, mortified. 'I'm sorry. I've been very upset today. I'll go home. I think I'm coming down with something. The flu. The plague. Something bad.'

She left her cup of tea untouched and, without looking at George again, stood up and rushed out of the staff room and out of the building.

Running away from school, desperate to escape the sounds of the fair, she headed to the quay to clear her mind. Catching sight of her reflection in a window on the way, she was horrified by how wild she looked. Her hair had fallen from its combs and her face was puffy from crying. A stone sank to the pit of her stomach when she thought about everything that had happened. What must George think of her, let alone the rest of the school? She stared at the ground as she walked, unaware of her surroundings.

'Nancy,' a voice suddenly said. 'Why do you look so sad?'

She looked up. Terence. In the breeze, his hair looked to be standing on end. He smiled at her in concern, gently reaching out towards her to guide her to the bench, near his easel. He gestured that she should sit down, which she did, while he unscrewed the cup from his flask and poured coffee into it. He handed it to her.

'It has quite a kick because I make it to my own recipe, which includes whisky,' he said, with a wicked grin. 'Get it down you. Might take the edge off.'

Nancy took a sip to steady her nerves.

'What's on your mind?' he said.

Nancy puffed out her cheeks and stared at the boats in the harbour, with names such as *Wind Dancer* and *Breaking Waves* sign-written on the sides. He gently nudged her arm.

'I've just made a fool of myself in front of the whole school, where I work, and will probably lose my job,' Nancy began, 'and I've lost a new friend who I really liked because I told her the truth about something she didn't want to hear. My ex-husband wrote to me about visiting him and invited me to visit him in Hastings, where he lives, tomorrow. I haven't seen him for over fifteen years, but I've not even replied because I couldn't find the words.'

Terence took a swig of his coffee directly from the flask.

'I see,' he said. 'Does any part of you want to see your ex-husband? Could you go anyway, even though you haven't replied? Tomorrow is yet to come.'

Nancy shrugged. 'I don't think I can see him,' she said. 'It's complicated. We had some… difficult times.'

'Haven't we all,' he said, before pointing at a light-chestnut bird in the distance. 'That's a kestrel. That one's female.'

He fell quiet before turning to her.

'I wouldn't worry about it,' he said. 'Honestly, worry gets us nowhere. It's like banging your head against a brick wall. Just let it go. This too shall pass and all that.'

Nancy couldn't help laughing.

'You're right.' Nancy smiled at Terence and thanked him for the coffee, and for listening. For a second, she felt hopeful, before reality hit – she could never not worry, had never been able to not worry.

'I'm told it's possible, the not-worrying thing,' he said, 'but I've never tried it myself.'

They shared a knowing smile.

'Thanks again for listening,' she said.

'Any time,' he said. 'Any time at all.'

With a heavy head and heart, Nancy continued home and, when at the garden gate, she heard the sound of music blaring from a radio and remembered that Jonah was there. She pushed open the front door, and the smell of fresh paint hit her. Jonah was perched awkwardly on a chair, his plastered leg jutting out at an angle, his broken arm in its sling, but managing to slowly paint the hallway wall with his one good arm.

'You don't like it?' he asked, horrified. 'Oh Christ, have I made a mistake? I thought you had this paint here to get going with the hallway. You said you'd started it with a friend? I wanted to help.'

'I do like it,' she said dully. 'Thank you, Jonah. I've just had a bad day. A very bad day.'

'Can I get you anything?' he asked, but Nancy was already walking upstairs to her bedroom and closing the door behind her. On her bed, Hope was curled up in a tight ball, hiding her face with her paws, protecting herself.

Chapter Twenty-Six

Nancy explained to Ted that she needed a change of scenery, and he listened intently, purring wildly through his little trumpet, while Nancy poured the contents of her heart and drawers into a dusty old holdall, fished out from under the bed, along with handfuls of cat fur. Each time she put an item of clothing on the bed to fold up, William sat on it, as if trying it out for comfort.

'I've really messed things up this time,' Nancy said, stroking Ted's head. He blinked twice.

A pensive Elsie sat silently on the windowsill, paws tucked in as if she was having to sit on her hands to stop her from grabbing hold of Nancy and shaking her. Hope continued to sleep with her paws over her head, blocking out everyone else.

Elsie was framed by the window, through which was a clear sky over the quay. Nancy paused from packing when she spotted a kestrel hovering in the sky, searching for mice or voles in the long grass. The rooftops and windows were ablaze with early-evening sunshine, and the water glittered. She thought of Terence and his wise words. If only she could take them on board and not worry, but the feeling that she must hide or run away prevailed.

'I just need to think about how to handle this,' Nancy said to the cats. 'I've made such a fool of myself!'

Ted meowed several times, then leaped off the bed when there was a clatter from downstairs, followed by swearing. Nancy deduced that Jonah's ladder had fallen to the floor. She froze but heard him laugh and say something to someone – Alfie? – before shouting up the stairs: 'Visitor for you, Ms Jones!' he said. 'Made me fall off my chair!'

'Call me Nancy, for heaven's sake!' Nancy yelled back. 'Who is it? I don't want to see anyone!'

There was a whole lot more clattering as he picked up the ladder and put it back in place.

'What did you say, Ms Jones?' Jonah yelled back. 'On the way up to you.'

Nancy barely breathed as she listened for the footsteps on the stairs. For one dreadful moment she thought it might be George, cap in hand, to repeat that he had absolutely no interest in her whatsoever, thank you very much. Or Gerard, coming to threaten her once again. He might like to try! Quickly, she rearranged the combs in her hair and dried her damp eyes. She clenched her fists. There was a gentle tap on the door and Marcie's voice.

'Nancy?' Marcie said. 'Please can I come in? It's me.'

Nancy's shoulders dropped, and she relaxed her fists. Slowly, she opened the door to Marcie, who shivered in her thin cardigan, her normally made-up face pale as milk.

'Can I come in?' she asked again. Nancy opened the door wide and Marcie stepped in, her eyes on the holdall.

'Are you going somewhere?' said Marcie.

'I don't know where I'm going.' Nancy shrugged. 'Nowhere probably, but after what happened at school, I can't face anyone. I'll probably lose my job. I'm so ashamed and embarrassed. I shouldn't have spoken to Stuart like I did. I'm sorry, Marcie, but I couldn't see Alfie suffer for a moment longer. I feel inexplicably protective of him, like I'm—'

'You're not his mother, Nancy,' Marcie said. 'And you're not mine either.'

'I know that,' snapped Nancy. 'But thank you for pointing it out.'

Marcie sat on the bed and let out an exasperated sigh. She ran her hand through her hair and gave Nancy a quick, sorry smile.

'Forgive me,' said Marcie. 'I'm very stressed. Gerard and I are… as you know, having trouble. Big troubles.'

Nancy didn't say anything, hoping that Marcie would carry on speaking. The silence between them stretched out uncomfortably then Marcie suddenly flung herself backwards onto the duvet and sighed, disturbing Hope from her nap.

'I'm ashamed to say that I think Stuart has probably seen Gerard and I fighting, and he's acting out what he's seen,' Marcie said matter-of-factly. 'Gerard and I have terrible fights – I mean physical fights.'

'Does he hit you?' Nancy asked. 'Is that how you got your bruises?'

Marcie sat upright again and wrapped her arms around her waist.

'It's more me than him,' she said. 'I know that sounds bizarre and not what you expected, but it started out as a silly thing, where I'd slapped him around the face after we had a row and he'd pushed me onto the sofa, but it then got out of hand and we had an actual fight. Now, whenever we have a row, we end up having a physical fight. I know it's peculiar. You're shocked, I can tell. He thinks I have an anger problem.'

'Do you?' said Nancy.

Marcie shrugged. 'Possibly,' she said. 'But if I have an anger problem it's because I can't… I can't…'

'What?' said Nancy. 'Tell me.'

'I can't cope with it all,' said Marcie, her voice cold and flat. 'There you go, I've said it. I. Can't. Cope. Haven't you been waiting for me to say that? That's what he's been waiting for me to say. Bastard. He wants to make it all my fault. Marcie can't cope with life. There's something people love about seeing a successful woman like me fail, isn't there? I'm so despicably weak.'

'You're not weak,' Nancy said, sitting beside her and holding her hand in her own. 'You're brave. Admitting you have a problem is incredibly brave. It sounds complicated, Marcie, your situation.'

Nancy squeezed Marcie's hand. 'You're a remarkable woman,' she added. 'Anyone can see that.'

'I've been holding everything inside for so long,' Marcie said. 'Before I met Gerard I was determined to live life to the full, for Beatrice's memory as much as for me. I threw myself at everything and that included Gerard. I was determined to make him mine and I did. I was only twenty when I fell pregnant and I was determined to be the best mother I could, whilst also carrying on working. I was holding it all together, juggling all these different balls, but I'd have these moments when I'd question every decision I'd ever made. I'd have a drink to blot out the doubts and not know when to stop. As soon as I've had a drink, my mood turns sour and I see red. That's why I got the tapping coach – to help me find a different way to deal with the anxiety. She's good, but there's only so much tapping you can do when you find that your husband is having an affair with your friend.'

'Sally?' Nancy asked.

'It's not the first time,' Marcie said. 'I should have left him the first time around, but I gave him the benefit of the doubt and thought he would change. I thought us staying together was better for Stuart. That's why we moved here. He blames me for driving him into Sally's arms – and says that I'm messed up and not the woman he thought I was. I drink too much, I get furious for no reason… the list goes on. I don't know, Nancy; I'm tied up in knots. I love Stuart and I'm devastated to learn that he's bullying Alfie. I have to get us out of this mess, but I don't know how. I think Gerard and I are going to separate, but the thought of unravelling everything overwhelms me. I'll need somewhere to stay. My mother would have been furious.'

'You can stay here,' said Nancy calmly. 'And I'm sure you can get help for feeling angry, or I can try to help. Do you know why you feel so angry?'

'I… yes, I think… but…' Marcie said, faltering and swallowing. 'There's something I want to explain, to you and Larry. He's expecting us tomorrow, in Hastings, as you know. I replied to him today and said that we'd come. I thought that was why you were packing your bag.'

Nancy froze. She'd spent the morning getting everything ready for the fair; she hadn't seen those emails.

'I can't—' Nancy started, but Marcie interrupted.

'Please, Nancy,' she said, 'will you do this for me? I think all of this stuff in my head, it goes back a long way, to when Beatrice died. I'll pick you up before eight a.m. and we'll drive together and talk about this more on the way. I wanted to help you, but I think what I really need is for you to help me.'

William curled up near Marcie and she leaned over to rest her head in his fur. He half-turned onto his back and purred his deep rumbling purr. Marcie smiled.

'Cats are so comforting,' she said, standing and opening the bedroom door. 'I don't know what I'd do without Prudence. I tell her everything. It's a bloody good job she can't talk! So, I'll see you tomorrow. Thank you, Nancy, for this. I know it won't be easy.'

Nancy's heart was thumping. The prospect of seeing Larry was surreal. After Marcie left, Nancy sat at the window, watching the light fade over the town. She thought about all the parents of schoolchildren in those houses that now knew everything about her. She longed to disappear, but then she'd be letting Marcie down. She'd asked for Nancy's help – there was no way she could turn her back.

Listening to the sounds of Jonah and Alfie watching television downstairs, occasionally discussing something, Nancy checked on Hope and the other cats, then returned to her bedroom, trying – and failing – to picture what the following day would be like. At 9 p.m., Alfie knocked on the door and handed her a piece of cheese on toast – and though she thanked him, she left the plate untouched by the bed. She had no appetite, or energy, only trepidation at what lay ahead. And though it was hard to admit, the tiniest part of her yearned to see Larry again, even if it would be a painful experience.

Nancy pulled the duvet over her, and during the sleepless night, the cats, one by one, came to sit around her, keeping her warm and soothing her, with their affectionate, quiet loyalty.

Chapter Twenty-Seven

True to her word, Marcie collected Nancy at 8 a.m. Nancy had been awake since 5 a.m. and had tried on three different outfits before settling on a linen skirt and top. The streets of Christchurch were quiet, curtains still drawn and lawns shiny with dew. She wished Marcie was driving her anywhere but Hastings, as she longed to go far away from everyone and everything for a few days; up a mountain or into a valley. Anywhere remote. Jonah had gawped at her, incredulous, when she said she was leaving him in charge of the house and cats. She had, after all, invited him to stay so she could help take care of him and Alfie, but Alfie nodded and stood taller and straighter, keen to shoulder the responsibility.

'I think it's about being brave,' said Marcie now, 'and facing our demons.' Nancy wasn't sure who Marcie was addressing but nodded in agreement.

Marcie leaned over and opened the glove compartment in front of the passenger seat. It was stuffed with chocolate-bar and food wrappers, paper coffee cups, black banana skins and several empty packets of cigarettes. A miniature bottle of gin didn't escape Nancy's eye. She was reminded of Marcie's bedroom that she had stumbled on weeks earlier. She clearly had two sides to her personality.

Marcie pulled out a cigarette, put it between her lips, lit it and took a deep, noisy drag.

'My granddad died of lung cancer,' she said, keeping her eyes on the road. 'You'd think I'd give up, but I only smoke when I'm stressed out. Do you mind?'

Nancy shook her head, wound down the window and stared out. Though she had never smoked in her life, for a moment she considered joining Marcie and smoking five cigarettes at once, like a set of nicotine bagpipes. She exhaled deeply, her thoughts returning to St Joseph's and the stories her colleagues had shared with her. It was amazing what people had suffered, but even though they would be sympathetic about Beatrice, how could she ever go back now that she had broken down so spectacularly? Everyone would be talking about her after Gerard had told the world she was deranged, and facing George again was impossible – she remembered the look on his face when she'd cuddled up to him. She wasn't due into work until Wednesday, but on Monday she would phone in her resignation, though Mr Phillips might have already sacked her by then.

'What a mess,' she muttered. Marcie patted her knee.

'You and me both,' Marcie said.

Driving past the quay to leave the town, Nancy sat straighter when she saw Terence setting up his easel, chatting to a cold-water swimmer who pulled on his goggles and swung his arms around in a windmill motion to warm up. Both men were laughing, and Nancy felt a brush of envy. Noticing it was Nancy passing by, Terence raised his hand in greeting and gave her the thumbs up with both of his hands. Nancy raised her thumb too, smiling. A flutter of hope lifted the edges of the blanket smothering her heart.

'Who's that?' asked Marcie, with the cigarette dangling between her lips, switching on the radio. 'Another waif or stray?'

'I don't know him well,' Nancy said. 'He's Terence. We sometimes say hello when I walk past. He paints there most days, near the bandstand, for the shade, I suppose.'

Marcie nodded, accelerating at the traffic lights to avoid a red light, tutting at an ancient driver taking ages to turn a corner.

A few moments of silence passed between them, as Marcie found her way out onto the dual carriageway, which would take them to the motorway.

'How were things with Gerard this morning?' Nancy asked tentatively. Marcie sighed.

'I told him last night that I want us to separate,' she replied, stubbing out her cigarette and popping a mint onto her tongue. 'Twenty-eight, with a failed marriage behind me! My mother would have been shocked. The most important thing is that I have to find a way to keep Stuart protected in all of this. He's the one who has suffered most. His behaviour towards Alfie proves that. God, I'm so horrified about it all. I'll have to find somewhere to stay, until we can sort out what we're going to do. It's Gerard's house; he's the one with bags of money, so I'll probably have to find a small rental.'

'Like I said, you and Stuart can stay with me,' said Nancy without missing a beat. 'You can have the back bedroom and paint it whatever colour you choose. Stuart could have the one opposite.'

'Thank you, Nancy,' she said, turning to smile at her. 'But I'm not sure Alfie will be keen on that idea.'

'Alfie and Jonah won't be there for long,' said Nancy. 'Just until Jonah can move around better, his sister comes, or his wife comes back from wherever she is.'

'She's probably having an affair with Gerard,' Marcie said, laughing bitterly. 'I shouldn't joke about it, should I? You know, I was once madly in love with Gerard, or I thought I was, but he makes me feel like I'm all over the place, though I think it's to do with the past. I don't think I knew what to do with all the grief I had when Beatrice died. My mother didn't talk to me about it. I remember overhearing her say how adaptable I was and that I was coping well, but I wasn't, not at all. I missed Beatrice so much, I used to talk to her in my head and imagine she was in the room with me. I made decisions, for years, based on what I thought Beatrice would do.'

'Maybe we can help each other in all of this,' said Nancy quietly.

'Yes, I think we can,' Marcie said, 'and seeing Larry is the first step in doing so.'

The prospect of seeing Larry again seemed so huge and unlikely – like being told you had to climb Everest in your pyjamas and slippers – Nancy could not believe it would ever actually happen.

'It's all very complicated between me and Larry,' said Nancy. 'A lot of things were said.'

'Yes,' said Marcie, 'relationships *are* complicated. People are complicated. I might only be young, but I have learned that. I'm complicated – at least that's what Gerard says!'

The journey to Hastings passed quickly. They turned off the dual carriageway and passed a sign saying 'Welcome to Hastings' when Nancy's stomach flipped over. She placed her hand on Marcie's forearm.

'Marcie, I'm so nervous I feel sick,' she said. For a crazy split second, Nancy thought about opening the car door and rolling out onto the road. Staring ahead, she noticed a BP garage with a Marks & Spencer Simply Food attached. Nancy looked at the sign longingly. Anything to delay their arrival. She needed thinking time. Perhaps she could escape. Hide in a loo. Anything.

'Can we stop for a minute?' said Nancy. 'I need to use the ladies. Urgently.'

Marcie nodded once and swerved off the road and into the BP garage, leaving in her wake a chorus of bleating horns and silent swear words mouthed through windscreens.

In Marks & Spencer, Nancy's legs wouldn't work properly. They were like wooden blocks beneath her – numb with fear. Sliding her feet along the floor in the sandwich aisle, she glanced at Marcie, who was frowning at her.

'You look like you've got a broom up your bottom,' Marcie said. 'Are you okay?'

'I'm just so horribly nervous!' Nancy said, closing her eyes for a long moment. 'It all ended so badly. I haven't got anything to say to him.'

'Yes, but he might have something to say to you,' said Marcie. 'Come on, let's get a snack to keep us going.'

The fridges hummed as Marcie and Nancy stared at the sandwiches and drinks. Nancy picked up an orange juice and a fruit pot and placed them in a basket. A man reached in front of her, selecting a prawn sandwich and a bag of crisps. Nancy had never felt less hungry.

'Do you think I should take Larry something?' Nancy said. 'A bottle of wine perhaps?'

She moved to the wine aisle, where the labels on the bottles blurred into an unintelligible string of letters. Larry loved red wine. Or he used to, she corrected herself. Perhaps he hated it now!

She picked up a bottle and stared at the description. A memory visited her of Barney coming to the hospital on the day Beatrice was born. Larry had poured her a glass of wine in a plastic cup. She'd only managed a small sip, while the two men enjoyed the rest of the bottle. What was going through Larry's head at that moment? Did she ever really know him? Had he ever loved her? Did he despise her? What if, when he saw her again, he couldn't hide his contempt?

Placing the wine back down on the shelf, she put her fingers on her temples and shook her head.

'Marcie,' she said. 'I don't want to do this. I want to go home.'

'You have to,' said Marcie.

'Why do I?' said Nancy.

The colour drained from Marcie's face, until she was absolutely white.

'I told you. I want to talk to you and Larry,' she said. 'Together. I want it all out in the open. Meeting you, in Christchurch, it feels like the time is right.'

'What?' said Nancy, irritated. 'I can't think of anything you have to say that will change anything at all, Marcie. I appreciate your help, but I think we should go home and get on with our lives and that's the end of it. Beatrice is dead, Larry has moved on, I've got the cats to concentrate on. You've got your marriage to sort out. Full stop.'

Marcie stared at the floor.

'It was me who told Beatrice to jump into that hole in the sand,' she said in a quiet voice. A man with a basket pushed roughly past her and tutted. Nancy wanted to shove him in the back.

'What did you say?' she said, pulling Marcie into the corner of the shop where there were very few customers. A security guard clocked them – as if they were about to stuff several bottles of spirits in their bags.

'I said, it was me who told Beatrice to jump into that sand hole,' Marcie repeated. 'We were just playing, digging the hole deeper and deeper and when we climbed out, decorating it, I said: "Why don't you jump in to the hole and see exactly how deep it is?" And the terrible thing is that she was so sensible, she turned to me and said: "It's too deep; it might be dangerous." I said: "What are you talking about, it's just a hole in the sand?" and laughed, and then she shrugged and held her nose, as if diving into water, and jumped in. The sand poured over her head. It was so fast! I tried to get her out, but I couldn't. I've spent my life wondering if I hadn't told her to jump in, would she be here now? Why didn't I jump in? I wish I had. I wish it had been me.'

Nancy gasped. Marcie and Nancy's hands were tightly clasped together. Another customer pushed past them and grabbed a bottle of wine from the shelf. Nancy didn't even notice. She was paralysed by the knowledge that Beatrice had realised the sand hole was dangerous but had still jumped in. Why did she do it? To impress Marcie? Her first instinct was that it was dangerous. Why did she ignore that?

'I wish with every cell in my body that I hadn't said that to her,' Marcie said.

'You were nine years old,' said Nancy calmly. 'You didn't know what was going to happen. I should have been there, watching you both. It seemed so harmless, out on the beach with just a bucket and spade. You did nothing wrong. You were a child.'

Nancy gave a quick shake of her head.

'I need you and Larry to know how sorry I am,' Marcie said. 'I was too frightened to tell Larry on my own. I wanted to tell you together, but it's all come rushing out too soon – in Marks & Spencer's Simply Food of all places!'

Marcie pushed at an escaped grape with her toe. The security guard had moved closer and was still watching them. Nancy's eyes brimmed with tears. Marcie looked so pathetic standing there, holding her shopping basket. Fragile. Nancy's heart broke. She moved towards Marcie and pulled her close. Marcie sobbed into Nancy's collar.

'It's okay,' soothed Nancy. 'Please, don't cry.'

Chapter Twenty-Eight

'Had to go out. Back later. Larry.'

The yellow Post-it message flapped limply on Larry's front door. It had obviously been written in a hurry and hadn't even been fixed with a drawing pin, or stuck with Sellotape or Blu Tack, so could quite easily have blown away, which made Nancy suspect Larry didn't want this meeting to take place either. If he could put their reunion in the hands of a yellow stickie, he clearly wasn't that interested. And his message included no detail. When did he leave and what time was 'later'?

'Let's go,' said Nancy. 'He's obviously gone out deliberately. I think you can tell him what you told me in a letter, or I can write to him, to explain.'

Marcie was sitting on the doorstep, fiddling with the strap on her sandals and looking, suddenly, like the young girl Nancy had known all those years ago.

Nancy sighed and looked around her. The apartment was a stone's throw from the shingle beach. The elegant four-storey building, with decorative balconies under French door windows, was the colour of clotted cream and, if you squinted, looked like a giant iced cake. Nancy placed her hand over her eyes to protect them from the glare of the sun, to look at the sea. It shimmered in the sunlight and Nancy thought of Terence's efforts to perfectly capture the light at the quay. Suddenly, she longed to be at home with her cats – with all the doors closed and the curtains drawn. Life as she knew it. Safe in her space.

'Marcie,' she said. 'Come on, this is madness. He's not even here!'

Nancy began pacing up and down on the street. Marcie stubbed her cigarette out on the floor, tucked her hair behind her ears and shook her head.

'Let's wait ten minutes,' she said, then, protecting her eyes from the sun, gazed up at the block that Larry lived in. 'How much do you think these seafront properties are worth? He must have done alright for himself, Larry. Oh wait, is this him coming?'

Marcie stood up and gestured, with a nod of her head, towards a man walking up the road, his head bowed. Nancy sucked in her breath. Her heart raced, and she felt as though her head had disconnected from her body and was floating upwards. She would recognise him anywhere – the slightest swagger – black jeans and sleeves of his shirt rolled up to his elbows. He had visibly aged, but not by much. His hair, once dark brown, was now grey. Lines around his eyes that were once faint were slightly deeper.

'Larry,' she whispered, her hands flying to her mouth. It was definitely him. Larry, the man with whom she'd had her beautiful daughter Beatrice. Larry, with whom she had shared a bed for nights and nights, chatting in the darkness. Larry, who had broken her heart. Larry, who had given that quote to the newspaper over Beatrice's death. Was he thinking of their daughter now, as he stared down at the cracks in the pavement? Was he dreading seeing Nancy? Was Barney on the scene? Did he have more children?

Glued to the spot on the pavement, she waited for him to raise his head and notice her. When he did, his pace slowed to almost stopping slap bang in the middle of the pavement. A man jogging past knocked into Larry's shoulder and he staggered back a little, before straightening up. Slowly, Nancy lifted her hand in a hello, her palm waving like a little white flag.

'The plan is that I'm going to leave you for an hour,' Marcie said quietly. 'Then I'll come back to talk to Larry myself. Okay?'

Marcie's words were muffled by the rush of blood in Nancy's ears. She nodded, resisting the impulse to run. Run away as fast as she could. She forced herself to stay put and the closer Larry got, an unexpected feeling of joy bubbled up inside her and a smile crept onto her lips. Images of Beatrice swamped her mind. She shared Larry's dark almond-shaped eyes, his full, handsome lips. Nancy was filled with desperate longing for that once-upon-a-time time – when she had imagined that her life with Beatrice and Larry would be long and happy.

'Hello,' he said, his face portraying a myriad of emotions.

'Hello, Larry,' she croaked as he took hesitant steps towards her. She instructed herself not to cry. Becoming suddenly aware of him watching her, making a judgement perhaps, she worried about what she looked like in her plain skirt, probably covered in cat hair, her flat ballet pumps and her hair pulled roughly back in combs, her carrier bag containing a bottle of wine, swinging from her wrist. She held it out to him, a pathetic offering.

'Nancy, I—' Larry moved towards her, took the bag with a smile and awkwardly embraced her. With his warm arms around her, she closed her eyes. They were both trembling and crying.

'Why don't you come in?' he said, briefly taking both her hands in his. He turned to the front door and put the key in the lock. His hand was violently shaking. She followed him into the hallway, where he pointed at the old-fashioned open lift, with wrought-iron doors and the spiral staircase.

'It's broken and I'm on the top floor,' he said. 'Happy to walk?'

'Yes,' she said, then gesturing vaguely to the beautiful open hallway, bursting with character details muttered: 'It's a nice place.'

She rolled her eyes at her own inadequacy but couldn't find any other words. They walked together up the carpeted steps, as if they were walking the plank. Nancy squeezed her hands into fists as she moved, her palms slippery with sweat. When they reached the top of the staircase, Larry turned to smile, nervously, at her and took a deep breath, then unlocked the door to his apartment, holding the door open for her to enter first.

'Thank you,' she said.

'Through there,' he said, pointing down a long corridor, the walls painted yellow, to the living room. 'I'll put the kettle on.'

Slipping off her shoes, she regretted her skin-tone shoe-liners and padded down the hallway – carpeted in burnt orange – in them, towards the living room. As she moved along the corridor, she registered the rooms on either side – a double bedroom, a study, a bathroom. There were pictures on the walls she recognised that had been in his flat when they were together: a line drawing of a hot air balloon and children playing in the snow, and another of Beethoven's face. He'd found both in a second-hand shop – she remembered how proud he'd been of his discoveries. There were new additions – black-and-white photographs charting his travels to far-flung destinations. Machu Picchu, the Grand Canyon National Park, the Taj Mahal… Larry had clearly travelled the world.

'Travelling was the way I dealt with everything,' he said, following her gaze. 'I became a travel writer instead of a news reporter. You might have seen some of my pieces in the nationals?'

He walked through to the kitchen, which had a serving hatch into the living room.

'I don't buy newspapers,' she said. 'I can't face all the bad news.'

He nodded, while she tentatively sat down in the middle of a huge black leather sofa.

'Careful, there's a crack in the middle of that sofa,' Larry called through from the kitchen. Nancy felt the gaping space in the middle of the sofa – it was completely divided – and frowned.

'I had to saw it in half,' he said, coming through holding two cups of steaming tea. 'The removal men brought it into the hallway downstairs and said there was no way they could get it upstairs. I sawed it in half, put it in the lift and got it up here myself!'

He raised one eyebrow and smiled at her. Nancy returned the grin. She wanted to say: that sounds like you, but she didn't know if it did sound like him. It sounded like the old Larry, the Larry she'd loved – was she entitled to make such claims?

'Tea,' he said. 'If you're still no sugar and a splash of milk?'

Nancy nodded, struck by how, even though they hadn't seen each other in years, there was a sense of familiarity already. He placed down the cup of tea on the coffee table, which was strewn with broadsheet and tabloid newspapers. He sat on a chair opposite her and crossed his legs.

'It was a shock when Marcie emailed,' he said. 'I've often wondered about calling you but thought you would prefer for me to leave you alone. Otherwise you would have been in touch.'

'Marcie made this happen,' Nancy said. 'I've never been bold enough to find you. I always imagined it would be too painful after…'

Larry looked up at the wall behind him, where there was a beautiful framed black-and-white photograph of Beatrice, her arms resting on a table, her chin resting on her arms. She was wearing the cuddly mohair cardigan she'd loved so much and had the sweetest smile on her face. In the frame Larry had put a dried forget-me-not flower. The image must have been professionally shot. Perhaps by Barney.

'I don't think I ever saw that one,' Nancy said. 'It's lovely. Did Barney take it?'

Larry nodded, then pushed his fingers into his eyes, his foot moving from side to side.

'How is Barney?' asked Nancy tentatively. 'Do you ever see him?'

Larry stood up and placed his cup on the coffee table. He moved over to the window, pushed his hands into his trouser pockets and stared out at the view.

'Barney's very ill,' he said. 'He's in hospital. That's where I've been this morning. He's gotten worse.'

'Oh, I'm sorry,' said Nancy, putting down her cup. 'Are you – I mean, do you… does he…?'

'Live here with me?' said Larry. 'Yes. We travel together. I do the words, he does the photographs. He's very good. Very well respected.'

Nancy's heart turned over. She remained silent. She wondered if there would be any further discussion about their relationship, but true to the Larry she used to know, he offered nothing more.

'I should get back to the hospital before too long,' Larry said, suddenly brisk. 'I don't want to leave him for too long. He gets anxious.'

Nancy's face burned. All of the old hurt she had felt came rushing back and she swallowed at the lump in her throat. Was he going to ask anything about her life?

'Should we talk about what happened with Beatrice?' she said, clearing her throat. 'That... that... newspaper article hurt me deeply. Do you know what happened to me afterwards?'

He stared at her.

'The newspaper reporter caught me when I was feeling very, very angry,' he said. 'You'd gone off on holiday with William, without telling me, and this terrible thing happened. I couldn't understand why you'd lied to me. If you were having a relationship with the man, why couldn't you just say?'

Nancy couldn't help but laugh at that.

'Larry,' she said, 'you were the one lying to me. I was willing to keep quiet then about Barney, to save you and myself further pain. I wanted you to be true to yourself and to have a relationship with Barney if that's what you wanted. Barney told me you were too proud to tell me the truth but that you were living a lie with me. I tried to set you free, Larry, for God's sake! I went off with William, my friend and not a lover, for a holiday and didn't tell you because I knew you'd twist it. Anyway, I don't believe that was the real reason you were angry.'

Larry rubbed his chin.

'Something you said just then, about setting me free,' he said. 'I know you think you set me free but I was angry with you, because

I was forced to confront what I didn't want to confront. I had tried so hard to be married to you – and I loved you and our darling daughter – but then you were threatening to expose me, make me admit what I wanted to deny. I felt caught out. I was happy as we were. It was harder then, to be out, not like it is now. My family would never have accepted it – they were devastated when you left. So was I.'

'But, Larry,' said Nancy, half-crying now, 'how could I have stayed? You say you were happy, but you weren't really, and I didn't want to share you with Barney, and Barney didn't want to share you with me. He left me in no doubt about that.'

'Oh, Nancy,' he said, falling silent for a few moments before continuing. 'In truth I was angry with myself. If I hadn't been with Barney, if you hadn't discovered that I was having a relationship with Barney, we would have been on holiday together… and none of this would have happened. If you—'

'If I hadn't left Marcie and Beatrice on the beach,' Nancy said, 'it wouldn't have gone so tragically wrong.'

She leaned her elbows on her knees and her chin in her hands, staring at the carpet.

'You know, your dad came to see me on the day the paper came out and he punched me in the face,' Larry said. 'Had a strong right hook on him! He told me I was a weak and pathetic man. He was right. I was weak and pathetic. I blamed everyone else for what happened, but in truth, what happened to Beatrice was a tragic accident, Nancy. It was the most appalling, tragic accident that nobody could have predicted or prevented. That's all there is to it.'

Nancy's lip quivered.

'I came to the hospital once, St Anne's, but I'm sorry to say I saw you, in the garden, sowing seeds or something, and my stomach sank,' he said. 'I couldn't stand to see you so diminished and I thought you'd never recover. From that moment on, I went about life as if you and Beatrice were *both* dead. I've never allowed myself to look back.'

Nancy raised her eyebrows, astonished that he could actually do that.

'We should have had this conversation years ago,' said Larry. 'Have you… remarried? Are you okay?'

'I live on my own with five cats,' she said. 'And I work part-time in a school. Well, I did.'

A silence hung between them for a long moment, then Larry walked over to the sofa and sat beside Nancy. He gently lifted her right hand and placed it in his hands.

'I always admired how genuine you were,' he said, 'and how much you loved Beatrice. You were a brilliant mother, always putting her needs first. I know how utterly devastated you were when she died. I should never have spoken to that reporter. I wasn't thinking straight.'

For a moment, they sat there, unspeaking and unmoving, before jumping at the sound of the doorbell.

'That will be Marcie,' said Nancy faintly. 'She wants to talk to you. There's something she needs to get off her chest. I think I'll wait outside. I need some fresh air.'

They both rose from the sofa and moved to the front door. Larry buzzed in Marcie and the two women shared a small smile. Nancy walked down the stairs, her legs feeling jelly-like and her head light. Outside, she blinked in the sunshine and crossed the road to the beach, where she lay on her back on the shingle, eyes closed. Larry's words repeated in her head: *It was the most appalling, tragic accident that nobody could have predicted or prevented. That's all there is to it.*

Chapter Twenty-Nine

'Your marriage ended because Larry was having a relationship with a man?' Marcie exclaimed. 'Seriously? Were you angry with him for lying to you?'

Nancy and Marcie were back in the car, drained and exhausted by the Hastings visit, relieved it was over. Marcie drummed her fingers on the steering wheel.

'Of course I felt angry,' Nancy said. 'But when he denied it, I didn't want to corner him. I just told him it was over. There was something about Larry I felt compelled to protect.'

'Why?' Marcie said, screwing up her nose. 'When I found Gerard cheating I went absolutely ballistic and made sure he was completely aware of how much I was suffering!'

'I couldn't bear to see him squirm, or suffer, or have to confess,' Nancy said. 'I didn't want to put him through that. Or myself, really. I wanted to keep what we'd had as something I could remember with love and not with anger and resentment. It didn't exactly work out how I'd hoped.'

Marcie whistled between her teeth.

'You are something else, Nancy,' Marcie said. 'I wish I had your powers of forgiveness.'

'Actually, I'm not sure it was forgiveness,' said Nancy, folding a handkerchief in her lap, 'more a realisation that he was who he was. *Is* who he is, and was fundamentally not going to change, despite the fact he had married me. I felt sorry for him that he'd felt he had to pretend to be someone he wasn't in the first place. Also, as stupid as it might sound, I didn't want to hear him say he'd never really loved me. I wanted to believe that he had.'

Nancy took a deep breath.

'Did you talk to him about Beatrice?' she continued. 'About the day on the beach?'

'Yes,' Marcie said.

'What did he say?' Nancy said.

'He said it was an accident, that nobody could have known what would happen and that nobody should feel responsible.' Marcie sighed. 'He added that he still has nightmares about it.'

Nancy nodded. She knew the nightmares well. Sand. Darkness. Unable to breathe, as if someone was standing on her chest in heavy boots. She couldn't let herself go there. *This too shall pass.* She switched on the radio. Leaning back in her seat, she turned to Marcie.

'Can we go home now?' she said. 'I think I'll sleep for a week.'

Marcie shook her head. 'I'm afraid not,' she said. 'There's someone else I think we should see. It's an hour or so from here, but William is expecting us.'

'William?' Nancy exclaimed. 'Oh, Marcie, this is like an episode of *This Is Your Life*!'

Marcie frowned, and Nancy shook her head. 'You're too young to remember,' she explained. 'It was a programme where a guest was invited on and surprised by all the people from their past.'

'Sounds dangerous! I bet there was a thorough selection process,' Marcie replied. 'Some guests must have had awful skeletons in their closets.'

'Maybe everyone does,' Nancy said, as rain started to fall on the windscreen.

Travelling towards London, Nancy fell silent. In the city's outskirts, she felt far from home. A mass of houses, people, cars and lights crammed in together, making it difficult to tell where one person's life ended and another's started. She thought about her own neighbours and how, besides Alfie and Jonah, she barely knew the people on her street. They lived metres apart yet she barely knew their names. Nancy sighed, vowing to herself to change that. Possibly, she realised, they were not so different to her.

Seeing Larry had been a revelation. How must he feel now that Barney was dying? That he'd lost everyone? She wondered if they would ever see each other again and doubted it, somehow. He himself had admitted that he never looked back, but simply kept on moving.

'We're here,' said Marcie, turning to give Nancy a quick, reassuring smile, turning into a residential street and slowing down. 'It's that one. Number fifty-one. Looks like a spaceship!'

Nancy stared at number fifty-one. The house was huge and incredibly modern, with some of the walls made of glass so everyone on the outside could see straight inside. As if they were a living television set.

As they parked up outside, she watched in amazement as she recognised William, who was filling a jug with water in the kitchen. At the table nearby, there were two healthy-looking, tanned teenage girls with long, dark-red hair, dressed in gymnastics leotards. They must have been to a class. Yoga or Pilates. There was a woman there too with a swinging ponytail, dressed in running gear. Nancy swallowed. It looked like William had created a whole new life for himself. Perhaps it was a male thing, but both William and Larry had appeared to charge headlong into their futures – while Nancy had floated in a no-man's land in between, unable to disconnect from the past.

'You and William were partners once, weren't you?' Marcie asked, turning off the engine. 'I mean, before we went on holiday?'

'Yes, when we were teenagers,' Nancy said, remembering when William had pressed her to get engaged. She could never picture them being together in the longer term. Eventually they had split up over a dream.

'I dreamt you were kissing someone last night,' William had told her one day. 'Someone that wasn't me.'

His tone had been blaming. He was clearly annoyed that she could be unfaithful, even in dreams.

'Oh?' said Nancy. 'And what did you do when you saw me kissing him?'

'Nothing.' He shrugged. 'I just walked past.'

It had been the last straw for Nancy – the ultimate demonstration of his passivity. Even in his dreams he was passive! She had ended the relationship there and then – convinced there was more passion and energy in store for her. In fact, she already had her eye on someone. A reporter who worked at the newspaper office next to the bridal boutique… Larry.

'I ended it,' Nancy told Marcie. 'He was always more of a friend than a lover.'

How juvenile all that seemed now. What luxury it was to end a relationship based on a dream!

They waited in the car for a moment, the windows steaming up with their breath. Several people walked briskly past – everyone walked more quickly in the city.

'Come on,' Marcie said. 'Let's go in and stay for an hour, then travel home. William says he has something to give you.'

Nancy sighed, just wanting the whole thing to be over. She unclipped her safety belt and pulled down the passenger-side mirror, wiping the steam with a finger until her reflection was revealed. A person couldn't be any paler.

'I look like I need a blood transfusion,' she said. Marcie laughed, and Nancy grinned. Marcie's laugh was infectious. Nancy was glad of it.

At the door of William's home, Nancy held on to the wall to steady herself. The doorbell chimed and then came the sound of William's footsteps. She wondered, for the hundredth time, why she had agreed to come.

'Deep breaths,' Marcie whispered. Nancy held her breath as the door opened. William was there, leaning on a stick with his left hand, a smile on his face and with his right arm extended, welcoming Marcie and Nancy in.

'William,' said Nancy, taking his hand. Broken images from the last time they were together jabbed at her in sharp little stabs. Finding it difficult to make eye contact with William, she was grateful to him when he pulled her into his chest and hugged her tight. She squeezed her eyes shut, struggling not to weep.

'Come and meet my family,' he said, inviting her and Marcie into the living room. Nancy sniffed and followed him through the hallway into the kitchen, which was half made of glass. The red-headed girls and their mother, Nancy assumed, smiled kindly. William had obviously briefed them. They treated Nancy as if she was an escapee from the asylum, which she realised she was in a way. He introduced them all and everyone shook hands.

'It's wonderful to meet you,' said his wife, Anna. She searched Nancy's face, hoping for a similar response, but Nancy was not able to give it. Instead, she fiddled with the straps on her bag, unsure where to look. Wherever she placed her eyes in William's house, apart from his walking stick, there was beauty, life, success, photographs bearing huge smiles with big white teeth, framed certificates and wealth. She felt as if she'd been delivered into their home from a wholly different planet.

'You have a beautiful home,' Marcie said. Nancy was pleased that Marcie was able to say what was expected, while she stood stunned, like a rabbit in headlamps.

'I hope you'll join us for dinner?' William said. 'We're all vegan since it's supposed to help with my arthritis.'

The smells from the cooker were amazing but Nancy's stomach turned over. Sitting with William and his family for more than just a few minutes longer was impossible. The last time she had seen William was inside St Anne's.

Sensing Nancy's discomfort, Anna invited her to see the garden. Nancy followed her outside and stood, shivering, in the open French doors, looking at the well-groomed plot.

'William has always cared deeply about you,' Anna said. 'He wants you to know that, but as you probably know, isn't very good at explaining his feelings. He is very kind, in his heart.'

Nancy nodded. When she had been at her absolute lowest, he had destroyed the horrible evidence. Painted the wall and ripped up the carpet. That was an ultimate kindness. She felt her shoulders drop a little.

'You're right – he is,' Nancy said. 'Sorry, I'm not sure why I'm here, encroaching on your evening like this.'

'You're not,' Anna said. 'William has something for you. He's been wanting to give it to you for years. Please, stay for dinner.'

Nancy shook her head. Why was it that some people were so able to manage their lives? How did some people move from one part of their life to another, apparently seamlessly?

'What did William do with his house in Norfolk?' Nancy asked.

'He sold it eventually,' Anna said. 'He did it up first – and that's where I met him. I went on holiday to the village and we bonded. We came back to London, which is where I'm from, where we had children. My parents left me a house in their will and we knocked part of it down and rebuilt this place. Please, would you like a drink at least?'

Nancy thought about everything that had happened to William since Norfolk. Meeting Anna, falling in love, marrying her, having two daughters, moving to London, rebuilding a house and a life. Envy clung to her no matter how hard she tried to shake it off.

'No thank you,' she said. 'I'd like to get home, thank you.'

William was standing behind her. She spun on her heels and apologised to him, then to Anna – and to Marcie, but she wanted to go, had to get home; she'd forgotten the cats needed feeding – she really must be off. The atmosphere changed, and William's expression darkened. Anna left the room for a moment and William dug his hands into his pockets.

'I know it must be hard to see me,' he said, 'after what happened. I wish I had been able to save Beatrice. I wish that more than I wish anything. I'm sure you must blame me.'

Nancy shook her head and quickly wiped her eyes. She rushed towards William and embraced him, trying to communicate everything she felt. None of this was William's fault. 'No, I do not,' she said, 'and I never have. Please, do not ever think that.'

William held her tight, before releasing her and limping across the room to a set of drawers. He opened the top one and pulled out a small box.

'This is for you,' he said, handing it to her. 'Open it later.'

'Okay,' she said. 'I'm sorry, William, I need to get home. It's been a long day. Thank you for this. I can't—'

Nancy shrugged, not knowing what else to say. Marcie pulled on her cardigan and followed her outside. In the street, Nancy gulped in the cold air and walked quickly to the car. Feeling William and Anna's eyes on the car, staring through the glass door of their kitchen, she briefly waved and willed Marcie to hurry up and get the engine started. Neither of them said a word until they hit the motorway.

'You couldn't get out of there fast enough,' Marcie said. 'It must have been painful, but now you can stop wondering about Larry and William. You know now. I hope you'll understand why I did that, for you and for me.'

She found a smile for Marcie and patted her hand.

'Yes,' she said. 'I know. Thank you.'

Nancy was quiet on the journey home. She didn't have the energy to do anything other than watch the rain hammering down on the windscreen, the wipers hypnotically swishing left and right. She clung on to the little box in her palms.

When Marcie dropped her off, it was almost midnight. Nancy kissed her goodbye on the cheek, climbed out of the car and walked towards the house in the darkness. Unlocking the front door, she smelled paint. Jonah had painted more of the hallway and the floor was covered in dust sheets. There was a ball of Alfie's on the floor, his coat and shoes. His possessions made the house feel different, more alive. Elsie ran and greeted her, meowing and pushing her face against Nancy's legs. William came too, then Tabitha. Nancy fussed over them and, glancing through to the living room, she saw Hope, curled up and fast asleep on the sofa.

'I'll get you your milk,' she said, moving into the kitchen to put down their blue saucers, only to find the job had already been done. She smiled gratefully.

In her bedroom, Nancy pulled off her clothes and climbed into bed, all the time thinking about the little box that William had given her. Once under the duvet, she carefully opened it. There was a small parcel inside, wrapped in tissue paper. Unwrapping it, she gasped as the necklace Beatrice had worn on that day on the beach slipped through her fingers onto the cover. Gently picking it up, she looped it over her fingers and marvelled at how small it was – and how beautiful. She touched each of the alphabet beads that spelled out Beatrice's name. A hundred memories of Beatrice swept into her thoughts. Thanking William in a whisper, she folded the necklace back into the tissue paper and tucked it under her pillow to keep safe while she slept.

Chapter Thirty

On Wednesday morning, when she walked through St Joseph's gates, her heart threatening to burst out of her chest, she felt every parent's eyes glued to her, whispering mums and dads having half-disguised but perfectly obvious conversations about her.

There's that woman who lost the plot—

Did you hear what happened?

Did you know that she tried to kill herself? You'd think that the school would—

I feel sorry for her.

Apparently she threatened one of the boys in Year—

Do you know her daughter died? Can you imagine what that must—

People say she has thirty cats—

Every time she approached a group of parents, their conversations abruptly ended. Nancy felt like a walking exclamation mark. Whatever she was, she felt as if there was a giant arrow swinging down from the clouds and pointing at her. Even Alfie was keeping his distance.

'Come on, Nancy,' she whispered to herself, 'be brave.'

She knew what she had to do. Once through the reception doors, she knew she had to go straight to Mr Phillips's office, where she would tell the headmaster everything about her past, Stuart, Jonah and Alfie, and face the consequences.

Dropping her bag on her desk, she felt as if she was about to face the firing squad. Emma, the only other person already in, gave her a sympathetic look.

'I'm going to see Mr Phillips,' Nancy told her.

'Good luck,' Emma whispered.

Knocking on the headmaster's door, Nancy's knees felt incredibly weak. She loved her job in the school but knew she was probably about to lose it.

'Come in,' he summoned her, glancing up, unsmiling, as she entered. 'Please take a seat.'

Nancy cleared her throat and began her prepared speech. In her hand, she clutched Beatrice's necklace like a set of worry beads.

'Mr Phillips, I know what you're going to say,' she said. 'I know I shouldn't have threatened Stuart Loveday and no doubt you've heard all about my past, plus that I'm taking care of Alfie Payne and his dad, Jonah. I offered them somewhere to stay because they had nobody else. I know I've not done things the right way, but I've only ever wanted to help. That's only ever been my intention. I've enjoyed working in this school and hope that you know how much I regret my decision to confront Stuart, but—'

Mr Phillips put his head in his hands. She paused for breath.

'Nancy,' he said, 'please could you let me speak? When you work in a school, with children, some of them vulnerable, we need to be aware of boundaries. This isn't just to protect the child, it's also to protect you, as a member of my staff. It's a safer-working-practices issue, a code of conduct that we have appropriate boundaries in place. Of course, I can understand why you felt compelled to help, but I'm disappointed you haven't kept me informed. There needs to be clarity; things need to be documented and arrangements monitored.'

'I know,' said Nancy despondently, 'I just—'

'As I said, this is to protect you as much as anything,' he interrupted. He stood up from his seat. 'Sometimes things can happen. A family might suddenly make allegations against you that are untrue, but against which you'll struggle to defend yourself.'

'I don't think Jonah would—' Nancy started, but Mr Phillips interrupted again.

'You'd be surprised what can happen. And there are other services that can help families in trouble,' he said. 'It's not all on your shoulders. It's not all up to the school.'

Nancy cleared her throat.

'I know that I should have informed you about all of this, Mr Phillips. I did try to tell you about the bullying on the day of the fair, but you were busy,' she said. 'I should have tried harder, but I had to do something. Alfie and his dad are my *neighbours*. All that stands between my house and theirs is a garden fence that has, anyway, fallen down. I felt offering them a place to stay for a couple of nights was the right thing to do. My moral duty, friendship, being a good neighbour, whatever you want to call it. If it means that I lose my job here, then so be it.'

She took a deep breath. Mr Phillips lifted his hands in the air and dropped them back onto the desk.

'And then there's the question of the complaint from Mr Loveday,' Mr Phillips went on. 'I have to say I don't like the man and I set him straight about the Equality Act and how it's against the law to discriminate against someone who – and I'm not necessarily referring to you – may have, or have had, mental-health issues. In fact, I read in the newspaper recently that half of all teachers have been diagnosed with mental-health issues. So.'

He raised his eyebrows. Nancy gave the tiniest smile.

'You will not lose your job, Nancy,' he said curtly, 'but please consider yourself warned. You must assure me that you will keep me informed of your involvement with the Payne family. These things can blow up in your face. You're a human being, I get that… you're a good, kind-hearted human being, but please be careful. I would hate for us to lose you.'

With that, she was dismissed. Slowly, she walked back into the front office, where Emma was on the phone to a disgruntled parent and Frances was putting school-trip forms into a folder. Both women looked up with questioning expressions and, when she indicated everything was okay with a nod, Emma smiled and held her hand to her heart in relief and Frances gave her the thumbs up. Nancy exhaled in relief.

On her desk there was a thick white envelope, addressed to Nancy Jones, and written with a calligraphy pen that made 'Nancy' look incredibly elegant. Inside was an invitation to Emma's wedding, to be held in September, for Nancy and a 'plus one', and a sprinkling of tiny gold foil hearts. She spilled them out onto the desk and pushed them around with her fingertips, blinking away tears.

'I hope you can come, Nancy,' said Emma, when she had finished her phone call. 'I'd love for you to be there.'

'Thank you,' said Nancy. 'Thank you so much.'

'It's a pleasure,' Emma said, giving her a kind smile, then averting her eyes to the door. 'Uh-oh, here comes trouble.'

Nancy spun around to find George standing at the door of the office, his left cheek and the left side of his forehead badly sunburned, as if he'd fallen asleep in the sun, lying on his right side. Nancy felt her face flame a volcanic shade of red. Memories of her attempt to kiss him made her feel faint. She wished she could go back to that moment. George cleared his throat.

'I wanted to apologise for the way I spoke to you the other day, Nancy,' he said, blushing himself. 'I was out of order when we were having a cup of tea together and I said you shouldn't have spoken to Mr Loveday the way you did. Please forgive me.'

Nancy could tell that his speech was rehearsed but that he was obviously, in actual fact, forgiving her. Nancy shyly tried to communicate her thanks to him with a smile. She took his hand and briefly shook it.

'Of course,' she muttered. 'Let's forget about it, George.'

Emma then came over to Nancy's desk and started digging around in her bag. She pulled out small organza bags of wedding favours and lined them up for Nancy, Frances and George to review.

'Sugared almonds, fortune cookies, personalised lollipops and chocolate shapes,' Emma said. 'Which do you prefer? Oh, did I tell you that my dressmaker has had a heart attack? She's going to be okay, but she won't be back to work for a while and I need to find someone to finish what she started.'

Nancy stared at her hands, but George gently nudged her arm.

'Weren't you telling me that you used to make wedding gowns?' he said.

Nancy blinked and gave a small nod. Emma's mouth fell open.

'You never said!' she cried. 'Well that's sorted then. You can come over to mine next week and see the dress. I don't think it'll need much doing to it, but I'd love a matching veil. Can you do veils?'

Nancy released a small laugh. 'Yes,' she said. 'Yes, I can.'

As everyone returned to their desks, Nancy experienced the strange sensation of her past connecting with the present and taking her into the future, like a road. Not a straight road, but a road all the same.

Chapter Thirty-One

On Friday morning – fancy dress day – there was a giant owl on the roof of the dinner hall, a purpose-built building at St Joseph's. A giant owl with a human body and a face which looked very much like Alfie.

'Alfie,' gasped Nancy, frozen with fear as Alfie, dressed as Hedwig, crouched on the flat roof, while Mr Phillips, dressed as a pirate, on the ground beneath tried to coax him down.

'Stand back!' shouted George, dressed as Elvis Presley, herding the crowd of dragons and scarecrows and wizards and more Harry Potters than you could wave a wand at out of the way. Nancy, dressed as Miss Havisham in a wedding dress fashioned out of fabrics she'd found in her boxes of material, quickly squeezed through the crowd towards the building. Though George was locating a ladder, Nancy climbed from a bench onto the roof of a gazebo which was a few feet away from the roof.

'Alfie!' she called up to him. 'Alfie, look over here, it's me!'

She called until she had his attention, then gingerly walked from one side of the gazebo roof to the other.

'What's it like up there, Alfie?' she asked, hands on her hips. 'Is it a good view?'

Alfie stared at her and then slowly nodded.

'Are you going to come down?' she asked. 'I'm cold here in my wedding dress and one shoe.'

'No,' he said, wrapping his wings around him. 'Why are you wearing one shoe?'

'It's what Miss Havisham, the character I'm dressed up as, did,' said Nancy. 'Everyone thought she was nuts, but she was just sad. Are you sad, Alfie? You do know that although those wings are really good, you can't actually fly in them?'

'I heard you telling Marcie that she and Stuart can move into your house,' he said. 'You don't want me and Dad there anymore, do you? I want to go home anyway. I want my mum. It's my birthday.'

His voice cracked. Nancy's heart broke. Of course she and Jonah had made a fuss of Alfie at breakfast, with a gift and the promise of cake after school, but really, he just wanted to see his mum. She kicked off her one shoe and stepped as close to the edge of the gazebo roof as she could, to get closer to Alfie.

'Listen,' she said, 'your mum knows it's your birthday; perhaps she's got something planned. You'll have to go home after school and check whether the postman has been.'

As soon as she said the words, Nancy regretted it. Perhaps Rose had nothing planned – perhaps she'd forgotten it was Alfie's birthday.

'Why's everyone staring at me?' he said. 'What's the caretaker doing with that ladder?'

'Everyone is worried about you,' she said. 'They're all scared you'll fall. George wants you to come down the ladder.'

He shifted, to see all the people. Surprise drifted across his expression.

'All of these people are worried about me?' he asked.

'Yes, Alfie,' she said. 'Sometimes people are too busy to show it, or too preoccupied with what's going on in their own lives, but they do care about you. Why don't you come down and show all the children your wings? They're pretty amazing. Stuart will be jealous.'

Alfie looked at his wings and stroked a feather.

'Come on, Alfie,' she said, 'before we get blown down.'

From below, she heard the sudden scream of a woman yelling at the top of her lungs.

'Alfie!' she screamed. 'Get down from that roof this minute! What on earth are you playing at?'

Both Nancy and Alfie glanced down to see Alfie's mother, Rose, standing in the playground, with her hands on her hips. The twins, like two tiny birds, stood next to her legs, craning their necks and pointing up at Alfie, calling his name. Rose had a wild look about her and at her feet was a bag spilling over with wrapped gifts. Alfie shifted in his position, the edges of his mouth turning up ever so slightly.

'I think she's got something for you,' said Nancy.

Nancy registered that she was trembling, but when Alfie stood up and he wobbled precariously, she firmly raised her hand to keep him still until George got the ladder into place.

'Wait, Alfie,' she said. 'Wait for the ladder. It's coming.'

'What the bloody hell are you thinking of?' shouted Rose, shaking her head in fury. 'Get yourself down here, Alfie.'

Alfie inched forward to the edge of the roof where Nancy was standing.

'I'm coming, Mum,' he said, taking a step forward towards the roof of the gazebo. Nancy held up her hands, ready to break his fall if he slipped.

'Hang on!' called Nancy, to Alfie and to Rose. 'He might slip. Wait!'

As soon as she'd said the words, she heard the sound of Alfie's foot slipping off the edge of the roof. Quickly, Nancy threw herself towards him, extending her body and grabbing hold of the school building with one hand, managing to block Alfie's fall with her bridged body and other hand.

'Hold still, Alfie,' she said. 'I've got you.'

But she wouldn't be able to stay in that position for long. Her legs were visibly shaking. The crowd fell silent. Seagulls ducked and dived. Rose had her hands in her hair, then on her neck.

After what seemed like forever, George got the ladder in the correct position and hoisted first Alfie, then Nancy down to safety.

Back on the reassuringly concrete surface of the playground, the crowd burst into applause and Rose rushed towards Alfie, taking him in her arms and clutching him to her chest. He was still wearing his costume and when Rose lifted him up to swing him around, it caught the wind and she appeared to be holding a huge bird that was flapping his wings. George rested her hand on Nancy's shoulder and gave it a gentle squeeze.

'Good work, Miss Havisham,' he said, winking at her. 'I've always had great expectations of you.'

Nancy, trembling in her white wedding dress, winked back.

Chapter Thirty-Two

Larry arrived on the first day of the school summer holiday. When he walked through the rusted iron gate into Nancy's overgrown garden, the gate fell off its hinges. Hearing the crash, Nancy opened the front door to investigate, holding Hope, like a little white cloud with a shaved bottom, in her arms. She rushed into the garden, brushing against a lavender bush alive with bees and butterflies, stunned to find Larry with the rusty gate in his hand. Dressed in black jeans and an immaculate pale-yellow shirt, he gave an apologetic half-smile, carefully placing the gate down on the ground.

'Larry,' she said, almost keeling over. 'What are you – I mean, why are you…'

Larry rubbed his chin and sighed.

'Barney is dead,' he said, his eyes brimming with tears. 'He was only fifty-seven. The funeral was Thursday. I can't stay in the flat on my own in Hastings. The silence is killing me. I got up this morning and came straight here. I didn't know if I'd be unwelcome, but I thought I'd take the risk.'

He shrugged, his smile a wobbly line. Nancy blinked.

'Of course you're welcome…' she said, pulling herself together. 'Please, come inside.'

Inside the hallway, William immediately launched himself at Larry's shoes and pushed his face up against his ankles. Larry bent down to pat the cat's head.

'Hello, young man,' he said. 'Aren't you handsome?'

Straightening up again, Larry noticed Alfie lying on the floor in the hallway, pulling a toy mouse on a string for Batman to catch, while there was the scraping noise of Jonah filling a hole in the plaster in the dining room. An expression of surprise set on his face.

'You have people…' said Larry. 'I didn't realise you had people… You said you lived alone.'

Alfie turned to Larry and waved.

'Th-thi-this is Alfie,' stuttered Nancy. 'And his dad Jonah is in the dining room. They're my neighbours and they've been staying for a few days. Going home tomorrow, in fact. Come through to the kitchen. Please. Gosh, this is…'

Larry lifted his hand in greeting to Alfie and followed Nancy through to the kitchen. She closed the door. William collapsed down onto a chair, shoulders bunched over like a deflated balloon.

'I'm so sorry about Barney,' she said, resting her hands on her hips. 'When did he die?'

'A week ago,' Larry said, leaning on his elbows. 'I wasn't even with him! I'd gone to the dentist because I have this ache in my tooth that won't go away, and when I was there, I got a call with the news.'

Nancy, not knowing what to do, opened the window, poured water into the kettle and put it on to boil. With trembling hands, she reached into the cupboard, hoping she would find some biscuits and not a dead spider. Thankfully, she located a packet. She set them down on the table.

'He had a blood clot on his brain,' Larry said, 'which he put down to stress. He was a grumpy old fool. Always was, wasn't he? Even back then when you knew him? Cross about everything, making everyone else feel bad. He'd complain about anything: noisy fireworks that were much noisier than years ago, the Christmas produce in the supermarkets too early, Brexit, the benefits system, gloomy weather, teenagers in hoodies, the world going to pot. He was funny with it, though, you know. He had me in stitches a lot of the time. I guess that's what I loved about him.'

Nancy nodded. Larry swallowed.

'I didn't plan to fall in love with Barney,' he said quietly. 'It just happened.'

He shrugged again. Nancy shrugged too. They both let out a nervous laugh.

'He loved Beatrice,' Larry said. 'He took some beautiful photographs of her. I've brought some with me, to give to you. I should have done this years ago. After you left the flat in Hastings, I remembered I wanted to give them to you.'

Apart from the Polaroid she had rescued from Marcie's house, Nancy didn't have photographs of Beatrice up around the house. She sometimes thought people like Marcie and Jonah, who knew about Beatrice, must feel she had a cold heart not to have any up, but it wasn't that. She simply hadn't been able, but perhaps now, she would try.

Pouring tea for them both, she took a seat opposite Larry and watched him pull out a brown envelope from his bag. His hand shook as he handed them to her. She pushed on her reading glasses. With a racing heart, she carefully slid the photographs out of the envelope and placed them on the table, staring at the one on the top of the pile. It was of Beatrice playing swingball in somebody's garden. A garden she didn't recognise. It must have been during a weekend she'd spent with Larry. Larry was playing against her and the two of them were laughing, mouths open wide.

Gently, she traced her finger over Beatrice and let out a puff of air through her nose. She looked at the next – Beatrice in Larry's flat, lying on her stomach on the carpet with her ankles crossed in the air, intent on a picture she was colouring in. Beside her there was a half-eaten bowl of ice cream. Carefully, she handed it to Larry, who looked at it too and smiled. There were more, about a dozen more. In every image she was content, smiling or laughing – clearly she had also liked Barney.

'They're beautiful,' she said, struggling to find the words. 'Barney was an amazing photographer.'

'Shame he couldn't make it to our wedding, ha!' Larry said. 'There's a photograph I wanted from you. It was of the time we went camping – remember?'

'Of course I remember – the tent blew down!' Nancy said.

'Yes, but earlier that day, before we got to the campsite,' he said, 'we walked down to the sea and went in up to our knees – and Beatrice just launched herself in, remember? In all her clothes! You took a photo of her dripping wet and laughing; I remember how much I loved it. She seemed so free. I'd love to make a copy if you still have it?'

Nancy thought of the linen cupboard and the boxes inside filled with Beatrice's possessions, photographs and memories. She felt overwhelmed and ashamed that she hadn't done anything about them in all these years. It must have shown on her face.

'You haven't got rid of everything, have you?' he asked. 'I mean, I wouldn't blame you if you had…'

Nancy shook her head.

'No,' she said. 'I have kept everything of Beatrice's, but it's all in boxes, in a cupboard upstairs. I intended to go through it, but I've never got to it. I know it will be difficult. I know there will be things in there I haven't thought about in years.'

Tears pricked her eyes and she quickly blinked them away. Larry touched her hand.

'Let's do it together,' he said. 'If you have the time today, let's go through her things. I should have come years ago to do this and to talk to you. I've realised that I'm very good at not looking back, but now – now I want to look back. I wish I hadn't left it so long. Now Barney is dead, I realise how quickly time goes.'

Nancy carefully put the photographs back into the envelope but leaned one of them, of Beatrice playing swingball, up on the windowsill. The sun caught the top of it, turning it gold. Hope sat next to the photograph, also bathed in gold, purring gently and staring into the kitchen with her soft blue eyes.

'Yes,' she said. 'I'd like to go through her things with you, Larry. Maybe I've been waiting for this moment. Let's go upstairs and I'll show you the boxes.'

She opened the kitchen door, surprising Jonah who was standing there, obviously listening in. His cheeks flushed.

'Jonah, this is Larry, my ex-husband,' she said. Jonah shook Larry's hand.

'Alfie and I are going out into the garden,' Jonah said. 'To see what we can do when I'm fully operational. We'll be out from under your feet tomorrow.'

'Thanks, Jonah,' she said. 'I'm sure there's some work to do in the garden, but I like the way it feels like a jungle. I don't want to change it too much. I don't think I'm a manicured-garden type of person and the cats love it.'

'Roger that,' said Jonah. 'Come on, Alfie. Perhaps we can mend the fence then?'

'The fence can stay down too as far as I'm concerned,' said Nancy. 'Unless you want it up?'

Jonah grinned. 'No, not at all, Ms Jones,' he said. 'Not at all.'

Nancy led Larry upstairs to the linen cupboard, all the while feeling hyper-aware that he was in her house. Since meeting him again in Hastings, she'd realised that seeing him again wasn't so terrifying. He was just Larry, the man she'd loved, married – and divorced. They'd had plenty of bad times, but plenty of good ones too.

'I packed up the boxes soon after she died,' Nancy said, standing in front of the linen cupboard, 'and once I moved here from my dad's house, I stored them in this cupboard, fully intending to sort everything out.'

Feeling dizzy with anticipation, Nancy tried to pull open the door. It was stiff, and she had to yank it to open it properly.

As the doors opened she held her breath. Nothing happened. In front of her was a stack of cardboard boxes in various sizes, sealed with parcel tape, on which she'd written labels such as 'clothes', 'schoolbooks' and 'toys'. Larry stood beside her, their shoulders touching.

'Shall we start at the top,' he said, 'and work our way down?'

Nancy couldn't speak. Tears spilled down her cheeks. She wiped them quickly away, busying herself with stroking Elsie, while Larry carefully lifted out Beatrice's possessions.

'Shall I take them into your bedroom and put them on the bed?' he said. 'Is that okay?'

Nancy nodded, stuffing a tissue into her sleeve. When they were out, the two of them stared at the collection for a moment and sat down either side of them. Ripping off the parcel tape, Nancy opened the cardboard flaps of one box, which was packed with Beatrice's clothing. She lifted out the pair of needlecord dungarees that she had stitched for her daughter and held them up. It felt as though Beatrice was standing there in the room. An echo of her voice drifted into Nancy's ears; a faint aroma of her drifted into her nose. Goosebumps burst onto Nancy's skin. Larry cleared his throat and shook his head.

'Good God,' he said. 'I haven't seen them in years. She loved these, didn't she? I had no idea you'd kept them.'

All Nancy was good for was nodding. After carefully laying out Beatrice's dungarees on the bed, Elsie immediately curling up on top of them, Nancy pulled out the rest of the clothing piece by piece: school uniform, a leotard, a party dress, her first pair of shoes, a ballet skirt, shorts and pyjamas, holding the clothes to her nose as she did so, memories bursting into her head.

'A Babygro!' Larry said, openly weeping now as he unwrapped tissue paper. 'Look how tiny she was.'

'Can you remember, that's what she wore home from the hospital,' Nancy said and, digging into the bottom of the box, added, 'and here's her identification wristband.'

Nancy kissed the tiny ring of plastic which said 'Baby Jones' on it and passed it to Larry, who did the same. For a fleeting moment, Nancy could almost feel the shape and weight of baby Beatrice in her arms. Ted, sensing Nancy's emotional state, climbed onto her lap. She stroked him, grateful for his unswerving affection.

After the clothing, they went through boxes of schoolbooks, smiling in delight as they read through her Free Writing exercise books, rediscovering that she wrote imaginatively and beautifully. There was a pile of happy little drawings of animals and creatures and houses with wild gardens and a note Beatrice had written to Nancy too, saying she loved her and wanted to marry her when she grew up. Nancy's heart contracted.

'I remember her writing that,' said Larry, sitting closer to Nancy now and reading over her shoulder. 'She left it on your pillow. Such a sweet girl. She took after you.'

The next box was packed with teddy bears that she had kept on the end of her bed in a regimented line. If one was out of place, she wasn't able to get to sleep. Nancy held Tabitha, Beatrice's favourite teddy, to her chest.

'She slept with Tabitha every night,' she said.

'Can you remember when she left her on the bus?' said Larry. 'That was an horrendous day! Thanks heavens the driver didn't just bin it.'

'I know.' Nancy smiled. 'I think I kissed him when he said he had it.'

'Did I hear you call one of your cats Tabitha?' continued Larry. Ted was still in Nancy's lap but Elsie had moved to the floor beside Tabitha and the cats sat patiently to one side like helpers from the St John's Ambulance.

Nancy blushed and then thought, *What the hell, I might as well tell him.*

'Yes, I have a Bea, Ted, Elsie and William too,' she said.

'But not one named Larry?' said Larry, trying not to look hurt.

'No,' she said. 'I considered it but I couldn't work out how I felt.'

'I understand,' said Larry, 'and I apologise.'

Larry and Nancy continued to go through the boxes until late afternoon. They were thoroughly engrossed in sorting through the possessions, each item a tiny reminder of their precious daughter. Though there were tears wept – each of her things tiny treasures, prompting memories they shared – it was joyous too.

'We were so lucky to have her and know her and love her, weren't we?' said Larry, in a croaky voice. Nancy nodded.

'What's that saying?' said Larry. 'Better to have loved and lost than never to have loved at all. I really believe that.'

He was holding a shoe in his hand. It was navy-blue leather, from Clarks, with a tiny strap across the middle of it. They were the first shoes Beatrice had ever worn.

A memory, clear as day, burst into Nancy's head. Nancy had been kneeling down on the carpet and was holding out her hands to Beatrice. *Come on*, she was saying, *you can do it – trust me*. She remembered the determination and look of surprise on Beatrice's face as she took her first steps. Nancy closed her eyes, trying to hang on to the memory, before it blew away like a feather on the breeze. She looked towards the window; it was now late afternoon. They had been there for hours. A comfortable silence fell.

'If only I—' she began, but Larry rested his hand on her arm to stop her talking.

'It was just a dreadful accident,' he said. 'A dreadful, tragic accident. Nobody could ever have known that would happen. We have to appreciate the precious time we had.'

Nancy walked over to the window and opened it, letting the sea air blow into the room. She leaned on the sill and looked towards the quay. The water was flat, and seagulls sailed across the sky. In the distance, she saw Terence packing up his easel and it was as if everything fell into place. A sense of peace enveloped her like warm, loving arms.

Chapter Thirty-Three

'You know you said that we could stay in your spare room…?' Marcie said when she arrived later that evening. She held a carrier bag in one hand, stuffed with clothing, and Stuart's hand in her other. 'Don't look too closely at me; I left the house in a hurry.'

Despite her friend's plea, Nancy's eyes dropped to Marcie's checked trousers.

'Mum has her pyjamas on,' said Stuart, with no hint of humour. 'She'd gone to bed early with a headache, then Dad said she had to get up. They started arguing and Mum grabbed me and—'

'And here we are,' finished Marcie. 'And Stuart has something he wants to say to Alfie, if he's still here?'

Stuart stared at the floor.

'Yes,' said Nancy. 'He's in the living room, and of course you can stay, but, Marcie, Larry's here too. He arrived this morning. We've been going through some old memories.'

Marcie looked taken aback.

'Is he?' she said. 'In that case, you have a full house. We can go to a hotel.'

'No,' said Nancy, 'I'd very much like you to stay, Marcie. Come in. I need to get some provisions, though; I don't have anything. Only cat food!'

Nancy felt her stomach grumbling and realised she'd barely eaten a thing all day.

'I have brought wine with me,' Marcie said. 'You know me. So that's something. Larry, hello again.'

Larry had appeared by Nancy's side and greeted Marcie with a kiss on either cheek. Marcie pulled two bottles of red wine out of her bag and handed them to Larry, who took them into the kitchen and proceeded to open one – and quickly return with a collection of mugs and glasses.

'Food,' said Nancy. 'We'll need some of that. I'd better go to the shop.'

'Don't worry, Ms Jones… I mean Nancy,' said Jonah. 'I know a fantastic Chinese takeaway. I'll sort that out for you right away. I'll just get a selection of dishes, shall I?'

'Here,' said Larry, pulling his wallet from his jeans. 'Let me give you the money.'

'Thank you, both of you,' said Nancy. 'Is Alfie going to be okay?'

'I want to say I'm sorry,' said Stuart. 'Where is he?'

Nancy led Stuart into the living room, where Alfie was sitting on the end of the sofa, the arm of which had been clawed to rags by the cats, with Batman curled up on his lap. The kitten, from the look of his flickering paws, was in the middle of a dream about hunting. Alfie continued to stare at Batman and didn't look up when Stuart entered the room. His shoulders were rigid and high, as if ready for attack.

'Stuart has got something he wants to say to you,' said Marcie, poking Stuart between the shoulder blades. Stuart glared at her and went to sit on the sofa next to Alfie. Still Alfie refused to look at him. Batman lifted his head and meowed.

'I'm really sorry,' said Stuart. 'I've been so horrible to you. I've been awful. I wish I could take it all back. I'm sorry.'

Jonah came into the room, limped over to Alfie and put his hand on his son's shoulder.

'Why?' Jonah asked. 'Why have you made Alfie's life miserable?'

Stuart shrugged and his bottom lip gave way to tears.

'Crocodile tears don't wash with me,' said Jonah. 'Tell us why you've done this.'

'I… don't… don't… know,' he muttered. 'I felt angry and like I hated everyone and that I wanted to punish someone. I'm sorry. I shouldn't have done it. I know I'm a bully. I don't want to be a bully. I'm sorry.'

'"Sorry" doesn't really cut it though, does it, mate?' said Jonah crossly. 'Why should Alfie forgive you?'

Stuart continued to cry, and while the adults looked at one another, not knowing what to do next and questioning whether this was a good idea, Alfie gently lifted Batman down from his lap and placed him on the floor. Batman ran into the hallway and sat in Stuart's Nike training shoe, emptying his bladder while he was in there. Alfie tapped Stuart on the arm. Stuart looked up from his hands, his face tear-stained and as red as a tomato.

'I'm really sorry, Alfie,' he spluttered again, snot erupting from his nose. Marcie handed him a tissue. Alfie let out a laugh but quickly covered his mouth.

'Do you want to try on my wings?' Alfie said. Stuart gasped in astonishment. Jonah's chest puffed with pride and Marcie folded her arms over her chest, raising her eyebrows at Nancy.

Stuart nodded, still looking deeply ashamed.

'Come on then,' Alfie said. 'We don't have long. We're going home tomorrow. My mum is coming home!'

Nancy didn't miss the delight in Alfie's delivery of his last sentence. Stuart had previously taunted Alfie that Rose was never coming home. Now, Alfie could tell him that the opposite was true.

'Does everyone want to sit down in here when the food comes?' Nancy said. 'There's more room here than in the kitchen.'

There was general commotion about who should sit where and where the takeaway would go when it arrived. Nancy moved her sewing machine off the table and brought in some plates and cutlery from the kitchen at breakneck speed, not wanting to leave her guests unattended for too long. Embarrassingly, she didn't have enough cutlery but had saved some chip forks from the fish and chip shop, so would have those herself. The kids could use a spoon, couldn't they?

Just then the takeaway delivery boy rang the doorbell, holding down his finger on the bell for one, extremely long, burst. Nancy flung open the door.

'Never thought anyone even lived here,' he said, handing over a selection of white plastic carrier bags filled with cartons. Nancy thought it was rather like Christmas – being given all these boxes to open. She took the bags, while Jonah handed the delivery boy cash.

'I could hardly get through those hedges and the holly trees nearly knocked my head off,' he said. 'You want to cut them down, love.'

He dropped his eyes and bit his lip.

'I live here,' said Nancy. 'And the hedges and the trees are *exactly* the way I like them, *love.*'

She slammed the door shut in the delivery boy's face and took the steaming bags to the living room, where Marcie was topping up Larry's glass with wine. William and Ted, intrigued by the smell of hot Chinese food, were in hot pursuit of the carrier bags.

'It's here,' Nancy said, bustling into the front room, with the bags.

'… have travelled all over the world,' Larry was telling Marcie. 'I've been to some incredible places.'

Nancy left the room for a moment to collect a couple of big spoons from the kitchen then put them next to the cartons that Jonah was beginning to open. William was sniffing the lid of one, but nobody seemed to mind.

'… most interesting places I've ever been are some of the proper-ties I've helped do up and decorate,' said Jonah. 'You get to find out some funny things about people when you go into their homes.'

Nancy froze, hoping that he wasn't talking about her.

'You're right, Jonah, it's not necessary to travel the world to find out more about people,' said Larry, nodding and drinking his wine. 'There's much truth in that, but seeing new places keeps me interested. Barney and I used to travel together.'

'I'm so sorry about Barney,' said Marcie. 'I remember him. I remember Beatrice talking about Barney too. She liked him a lot.'

'Thank you,' said Larry, wiping his eye. 'And, Marcie, why are you here with Nancy?'

Marcie flapped her hands around in the air in front of her face, as if batting away a fly. Her eyes were suddenly glassy.

'I need a day or two away from home to try to sort a few things out,' she said. 'Namely my marriage. We're in a bit of a mess.'

'Oh I—' said Larry.

'That makes two of us!' piped up Jonah. 'Cheers to that.'

Marcie burst out laughing. 'Yes, cheers!' she said.

'What is this?' Larry said to Nancy. 'You're rescuing people as well as cats now?'

Nancy gave a little shrug and bit into a sweet and sour chicken ball, her cheeks pink with the company and the wine. She ate quietly, as the others continued to talk, and Larry regaled them with stories of his travels. As she listened, Nancy's heart filled with warmth and affection. These people, though not a conventional family, felt a little like a family she could call her own. She let herself imagine they were.

Though the children went to bed earlier, the adults stayed up until well after midnight talking and drinking wine. Marcie and Stuart stayed in the upstairs spare bedrooms, and though Larry said he could sleep in the bath, or on Nancy's bedroom floor, she told him they might as well share her double bed. When the house was quiet, Ted and Elsie had curled up at the bottom of the bed, and Tabitha had claimed Nancy's pillow, while Hope hid under the bed. Larry took off his shoes and lay down under the covers, otherwise still fully dressed. Nancy blew the cats a silent goodnight kiss and got in next to Larry. They lay together, staring up at the ceiling, blinking in the darkness. After a while, Larry cleared his throat.

'I was so ashamed,' he said. 'I couldn't admit that I was having a relationship with Barney. I couldn't admit I was gay.'

Nancy could hear her heartbeat in her ears.

'Why?' she asked. 'You've always been a brave person. Courageous.'

'I don't know,' he said into the darkness. 'At that time, in the eighties and early nineties, it was different. People forget that. It's wonderful that people can be who they really are now. Gay couples can get married and have children and it not be a big deal. But *then*, I couldn't face the reporters knowing, my parents, my brother, your father. *You.* Obviously I felt I let you and Beatrice down spectacularly. But I loved you both, Nancy – I did love you. I wanted for our marriage to work and I kept fooling myself that I was doing the right thing by trying to make it work, but you were right to force us to separate. I'm grateful to you for being brave.'

'We loved you too,' Nancy said. *Still do love you*, she thought but didn't say.

Reaching across the empty space between them, she took Larry's hand in hers and gave it a gentle squeeze. He returned the squeeze, and didn't let go.

Chapter Thirty-Four

Nancy woke late the next morning to William gently pawing her ear. Sitting up in bed, sunlight streaming through the gap between the curtains, she saw that Larry's side of the bed had been made up, and his bag was gone. Her heart dipped but then lifted again when she heard the sound of voices drifting up the stairs from the kitchen. The house was a happier place with people filling the rooms.

Wrapped in her dressing gown, she went downstairs to find that Larry had fed the cats and was stroking Hope, who was sprawled on her back with her soft pink paws in the air.

'I can see why you love cats,' he said. 'They're so affectionate. Especially this white one. What a beauty! I was waiting for you to wake up before I go. I'm heading off this morning. But maybe we can stay in touch? Make up for lost time a little. Talk about Beatrice together, you know, share our memories of her?'

Tears rushed to Nancy's eyes. She blinked them away.

'I'd like that, Larry,' she said, pushing her combs into her hair. 'Where are you going to go?'

'Back to Lyme Regis,' he said, gazing out of the window at the horizon. 'We never did climb Golden Cap, did we?'

Nancy rested her hand on Larry's arm and he turned to her, acknowledging her gesture with a smile.

'I'll walk you to the station,' she said. 'Give me a few minutes to change.'

Upstairs, Nancy dressed in a floral print skirt and top, but today she added a red necklace and left her hair loose. It suited her like that.

Leaving Marcie and the others in the house – Jonah gathering his and Alfie's belongings together preparing to return home – she walked towards the train station with Larry. It was the most beautiful day; a bold, bright blue sky and already almost twenty degrees. On the platform, where day-trippers were arriving into Christchurch, she handed Larry the photograph of Beatrice that he had requested. The image of her soaking wet on the beach, after she had jumped into the water while still dressed and laughing uproariously, captured her very essence.

'Anything else you'd like,' she said, 'please say and I can send it on to Hastings.'

Larry was mesmerised by the photograph. 'Thank you, I'll treasure this,' he said. 'Don't wait with me. I would rather we don't say a big goodbye and all that.'

They hugged one another and Nancy turned to leave. When she looked back at him, he was still gazing down at the photograph but then glanced up and raised his hand in a final farewell. He smiled, and Nancy smiled too, a sense of relief washing over her.

The sun warm on her back, Nancy walked homewards thinking about Marcie and how she could help her sort out her problems. Would therapy help? Separation? Her own place? Nancy wasn't sure, but she would give Marcie the space and time, in Nancy's own home, to do whatever she needed. It would be a pleasure, she thought secretly, to have her to stay.

With the slightest spring in her step, Nancy turned a corner into Mill Road. It was a quiet street that she didn't often walk down, with children riding bicycles and scooters up and down the pavement, a man stripped to the waist mowing his front lawn, an elderly woman inching along on her walking stick with her equally ancient sausage dog, music playing from a radio. Deep in thought, Nancy's eye was caught by a poster, which had MISSING and an image of a cat, pinned to a tree. Approaching it so she could read it clearly, Nancy's heart skipped a beat when she recognised the cat in the photograph as Hope, though, according to this poster, her real name was Violet. She read the description, which said Violet was greatly missed and if anyone had any information about the cat, which had disappeared earlier that month, could they please contact Sinead Hunter on a mobile number or email address.

With shaking hands, Nancy fumbled with her bag and pulled out her mobile phone. She immediately called the number and, with a quivering voice, explained to Sinead Hunter that she had Violet and had been looking after her since finding her injured by the quay, and that she'd advertised on social media but hadn't heard anything. Sinead, delighted, explained that Violet was her father's cat, and they arranged that Nancy would deliver Violet later that day.

Putting the phone back into her bag, Nancy felt torn. Though she was happy to reunite Violet with her owner, she felt an ache in her heart. She didn't want to lose Hope, who she'd nursed back to health and loved. Hope had become one of the family – *her* family.

Later, Nancy set off to the address Sinead had given her, to return Violet to her rightful owner. The other cats didn't seem too concerned when she broke the news that she was leaving, but Violet herself seemed restless – as if all she wanted to do now was go home.

Carrying Violet in a cat carrier, she arrived at a Victorian house which had been divided into flats and located the door to the ground-floor flat. There was no doorbell, just a piece of paper sellotaped to the glass that had 'please knock' written on it in black biro. Tentatively, she tapped on the door and, hearing footsteps approaching, her heart thumped. The door opened and Nancy's jaw dropped when she recognised Terence English, the painter from the quay. He erupted into laugher, clapped his hands together and shook his head.

'It's you!' he exclaimed. 'Nancy… And Violet, my beautiful Violet. What on earth happened to you, Violet?'

Framed by the door, Terence himself could have been a painting, with his mop of curly hair and eyebrows like the bristles of his paintbrushes, his eyes bright. At the sound of his voice, Violet released a loud, heartsick meow.

'Come in!' he said, taking the cage gently from Nancy and standing aside so she could enter. Nancy walked into the hallway and couldn't help staring. Around a centralised, huge gilt sunburst mirror, the walls were covered with photographs and paintings, some clearly done by his own hand. Her eyes travelled to the doorway leading through to the living room, where she glimpsed big red sofas peppered with cushions, and vases containing cut flowers, and shelves and shelves of books. Next to a grandfather clock, there were shoes nailed to the walls.

'People that have stayed here,' he explained, when he saw her staring at them. 'We used to have lodgers – all sorts of people – and when they left I asked them for an old shoe to remember them by. Don't judge a person until you've walked a mile in their shoes and all that. Those shoes remind me of that in my daily life.'

Nancy smiled and nodded enthusiastically, accidentally knocking into a hatstand displaying various old-fashioned hats.

'My father's,' he said. 'He was a milliner. This place is rammed full of memories. I should probably have a clear out.'

Placing the cat carrier down on the floor, Terence opened the door. Violet stepped out of the cage and immediately tried to get onto his lap. He lifted her up gently as if she was a newborn baby and pushed his face up against hers. Violet, purring loudly, seemed to smile.

'Poor thing has had a funny haircut!' he said with a laugh. 'Thank you for rescuing her, Nancy – thank you so much. I love this cat. People think I should have called her Snowy, but Violet was my late wife's name. Makes me feel better to speak her name aloud every day. People think I'm crazy, no doubt. Would you like to stay for a bit? We could sit in the garden and have coffee. I've made a pot for two. Force of habit.'

Nancy nodded, too stunned to speak. *Makes me feel better to speak her name aloud.*

'It's through here,' he said, carrying Violet out into a small walled garden and gently setting her down on the grass, stroking her head and ruff. 'If I'd known it was you that was coming I would have smartened myself up a bit. You always look so elegant.'

'I do not!' she exclaimed, blushing and laughing. Self-consciously she fiddled with her red beads.

He gave her a delightful grin. Nancy hesitated, sensing that although joining him for coffee was a step into the unknown, there was a certain inevitability to it. It was a step forward.

From the relative darkness of the kitchen, she watched him for a moment in the sunlit garden, setting out the cups, Violet at his feet. She took a deep breath. Nothing would ever change what had happened in her life, but perhaps it was time for her to unlock her heart a little.

'Are you coming outside, Nancy?' Terence asked.

She nodded. 'Yes – yes please,' she said, stepping out into the sunshine.

The garden was a slightly dishevelled stretch of lawn with an apple tree in the centre and riotous borders of wildflowers. It was warm, the sunlight golden, the aroma of coffee delicious.

'Please have a seat,' said Terence, pulling out a chair for her.

And there they sat, two strangers and a beautiful white cat, weaving a figure of eight between their legs like a skater on an ice rink, binding two souls together with invisible thread.

A Letter from Amy

Dear Reader

I want to say a huge thank you for choosing to read *They Call Me the Cat Lady*. If you did enjoy it, and want to keep up to date with all my latest releases, just sign up at the following link. Your email address will never be shared and you can unsubscribe at any time.

www.bookouture.com/amy-miller

Inspiration for this book came from various places. When I walk my daughter to school I pass a rather neglected house with a wild overgrown garden. The curtains are always pulled, but there are usually a couple of cats camped in the garden, so it started me wondering about who lives inside… This train of thought then led me to think about my late father. In the last years of his life he had severe mental illness, spent several years in and out of psychiatric wards and let his flat go to rack and ruin. He completely changed as a result of his illness, which was brought on by various tragic incidents in his life, and by the end of his life was barely recognisable as the person he once was. The people he met in the latter part of his life might have pitied him or avoided him completely.

It started me thinking about how people are perceived and judged and that those people who seem different, or outside of the norm in some way, are often that way for a reason. Perhaps they carry sadness in their hearts. Perhaps one tragic day their life changed irrevocably. My character Nancy is not a social outcast, but she's secretive and lonely, trapped by her past and convinced that she will always be that way. She has a yearning to help other people, to rescue animals and children – despite the boundaries that society insists on putting up. I wanted to write a story where people would treat Nancy with kindness and reach out to her, so she could finally accept her difficult past and move into the future with peace in her heart.

And that's where the cats – and my mother-in-law – come in. My mother-in-law is a fantastically kind woman and has had to cope with various major bereavements in her life. Her parents both died, suddenly, when she was a child, and as an adult she named her two cats after them. Ted and Elsie. You might recognise them from the story! I thought it was a really lovely idea and wondered if other people might do the same thing… As for cats themselves, I have always been a big fan and firmly believe they sense how you are feeling and try to comfort you with their warmth and affection.

Finally, I've set this story in Christchurch because it's where I live. Though various locations do exist, such as the quay, for example, I've changed names and street names.

I hope you loved *They Call Me the Cat Lady* and if you did I would be very grateful if you could write a review. I'd love to hear what you think, and it makes such a difference helping new readers to discover one of my books for the first time.

I love hearing from my readers – you can get in touch on my Facebook page, through Twitter, Goodreads or my website.

Thanks,
Amy Miller

AmyMillerBooks

@AmyBratley1

Acknowledgements

My thanks go to the amazing team at Bookouture, including Jenny Geras and Kim Nash, as well as my agent Veronique Baxter. I'm hugely thankful to the people I talked to who helped me get parts of this story factually correct, such as my friend and veterinary consultant, Roanne Dow, members of staff at a local junior school, friends and relatives who are teachers, and another who is a paramedic, as well as my mum, Anne Cook, for sharing memories of her life and experiences. In terms of reference material, I found the TV documentary *Cat Ladies* (2009) insightful and the book *The Nine Emotional Lives of Cats* by Jeffrey Masson an interesting read. I'm eternally grateful to my family, husband Jimmy and my children, Sonny and Audrey, for putting up with me tapping away at the computer – and finally, to Willow, our family cat, for sitting on my keyboard and keeping me company while I write.

Printed in Great Britain
by Amazon